"Marry me, Tess."

"Wh-what?" She sat up, leaning against him.

"Before we go any further, I am asking you to marry me. I believe we will suit very nicely. You won't need to worry about the bracelet and money anymore. I will settle up with Stedman. We can even work on my cases together."

"Oh." She looked dumbfounded and doubtful. "You mean it? You want to marry me? It's not because you feel you must? Because of this..." She waved vaguely at their surroundings.

"It will solve all our problems. I need a wife. You don't want to go to Yorkshire. And we can do this whenever we want."

"I really wasn't planning on getting married at all."

He stilled. "I see."

"You don't see. Every man in my life has let me down. Father. Grey. I should have been able to rely on them. By marrying, I put myself in yet another man's hands."

So that was why she was so independent. He should have guessed. "You can rely on me. I swear it."

Author Note

Jaimie has threaded through several books over the past few years. He kept popping up in the Gilvry stories and played a pivotal role in Michael and Alice's story, *Captured for the Captain's Pleasure*. It seemed he was not going to go away until he had a happy ending of his own. I hope you enjoy reading it as much as I enjoyed writing it.

If you want to know more about me and my writing, please visit my website, annlethbridge.com, where you will find all my social media links. If you would like to write to me directly, you can do so at ann@annlethbridge.com.

ANN LETHBRIDGE

—

Rescued by
the Earl's Vows

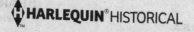

HARLEQUIN®HISTORICAL

Recycling programs for this product may not exist in your area.

ISBN-13: 978-1-335-52263-4

Rescued by the Earl's Vows

www.Harlequin.com

Printed in U.S.A.

In her youth, award-winning author **Ann Lethbridge** reimagined the Regency romances she read—and now she loves writing her own. Now living in Canada, Ann visits Britain every year, where family members understand—or so they say—her need to poke around every antiquity within a hundred miles. Learn more about Ann or contact her at annlethbridge.com. She loves hearing from readers.

Books by Ann Lethbridge

Harlequin Historical
and Harlequin Historical *Undone!* ebooks

Rescued by the Earl's Vows

The Society of Wicked Gentlemen

An Innocent Maid for the Duke

Rakes in Disgrace

The Gamekeeper's Lady
More Than a Mistress
Deliciously Debauched by the Rake (Undone!)
More Than a Lover

The Gilvrys of Dunross

Captured for the Captain's Pleasure
The Laird's Forbidden Lady
Her Highland Protector
Falling for the Highland Rogue
Return of the Prodigal Gilvry
One Night with the Highlander (Undone!)

Linked by Character

Wicked Rake, Defiant Mistress
One Night as a Courtesan (Undone!)
Secrets of the Marriage Bed

Visit the Author Profile page
at Harlequin.com for more titles.

This book is dedicated to two amazing young women, my daughters. Their support and their friendship are the most valuable things in my life. I wish them every happiness wherever life's trails take them in the future.

Chapter One

Jaimie, Earl of Sandford, reread the report he'd received from the Home Office on yet another burglary in Mayfair. The fourth in a month. In the words of Mr Robert Peel, the Home Secretary, the *ton*'s uproar of indignation demanded immediate action.

Strangely, in most instances nothing of any real value had been taken. Rather, the perpetrators committed acts of mischief, tossing papers around or spilling ink on valuable carpets, before they left. In every case, the occupants had been fast asleep in their beds above stairs. All were badly unnerved.

Were these robberies committed by the same individual or individuals? Or was this rise in criminal activity simply coincidental with regard to timing and modes of entry?

Experience had taught Jaimie not to believe in coincidences.

'And I told *you*, miss. He won't see you.' Growler's deep rasp permeated his door and Jaimie raised his gaze from the document at the unusual occurrence.

Growler's throat had been ruined by smoke from the chimneys he'd been forced up as a small child. The man rarely raised his voice above a murmur.

Do not let yourself be distracted, my boy, not in matters of importance. His father's words echoed comfortably in his mind, invoking a vague memory of his five-year-old self trying to master the complications of the letter *f.* How right Father had been. He again perused the sentence describing the latest robbery.

'You *has* to leave, miss.' Louder this time. Very loud for Growler.

Jaimie cursed as he again lost his place. Never once had he heard the fearsome-looking Growler raise his voice to a woman, whose sex he revered to the point of ridiculousness. And now he was shouting at one?

The woman's reply, if she made one, did not penetrate the solid oak door.

The knock a moment later brought him to his feet and around from behind his desk. Anyone brave enough to stand up to Growler was worth taking a look at, no matter how important the report.

The door inched open.

'Yes, Growler?'

The crack widened to half-open, revealing the burly figure of his second in command. The ex-bruiser's face creased into worry. 'There's a lady wanting to see you, me lord. I told her you was busy, but she's insisting...'

No *lady* would be visiting him in the suite of offices Jaimie rented in Lincoln's Inn. 'Tell her—'

At that moment, a short, veiled female figure draped from head to toe in mourning black strode past Growler as if he wasn't there. No mean feat, given the man's size and threatening posture.

'You may tell me yourself, Lord Sandford.' She angled her head towards Growler. 'That will be all, thank you.'

Jaimie bristled. 'Growler—'

'Right you are, miss.' Clearly relieved, Growler made good his escape.

Astonished and amused against his better judgement, Jaimie turned to the woman. 'I beg your pardon, madam, but—'

'I require your services to locate a missing person, my lord.' She spoke as if he hadn't said a word.

Amusement changed to annoyance. Damn and blast the article *The Times* had written about his miraculous recovery of a child stolen by a nursemaid. Now every female in London of marriageable age wanted him to find something they had lost. Usually a handkerchief or a puppy, because having forgotten about him for years, they now realised he remained one of the most eligible single gentlemen on the marriage mart, even if he was a widower. His stomach slid away.

The thought of having to find a second wife always made him feel slightly nauseous, though find one he must. Eventually. It was his duty to his title as his cousin, the heir presumptive, reminded him regularly.

He folded his arms across his chest and gave his visitor a hard stare.

'Well?' she countered in response to his silence. The veil shifted with her exhale.

The urge to peek beneath it and see if the face

matched the clear, cool tones of her beautifully modulated voice took him by surprise. As did the realisation that Growler had been correct in describing her as a lady. Though exactly what sort of lady she might be remained in question.

He certainly wasn't going to give her the satisfaction of asking for her name.

'If you are missing a person,' he said, keeping his voice level and far more pleasant than he felt she deserved, 'I suggest you return home and request the assistance of your closest male relative. If you don't have one, I recommend you seek the aid of your footman'

A toe tapped somewhere beneath the stiff, expensive silk of her skirts. 'I have it on good authority that you are the best person for this particular task.'

There it was again. A voice full of calm matter-of-factness, but with a surprising musicality. A richness— He cut off his wandering thoughts. 'Madam, I thank you for your confidence in my abilities, however, I regret I do not have time for any new projects at this moment. I am fully engaged and likely to be for some time. Good day to you.'

'I can pay you.' Clutched between thumb and forefinger she held out a pearl ring.

Annoyance rose in his gorge. Did she think he wasn't a gentleman? That his refusal was based on monetary concerns? He forced the feeling down. It was a dangerous emotion when dealing with women, especially one who was clearly distraught despite her carefully calm voice. He did not hide his displeasure. 'A hundred pounds' deposit. Cash. Before I will so much as consider the project.' The ring was clearly worth nowhere near that much.

She gasped, her fingers trembling around the ring, the little puff of air again lifting the veil, but still giving no clue as to her age or state of health. Or her looks.

Her shoulders slumped.

He felt...irritated instead of pleased at her defeat. Without a word he waved her towards the door, shepherding her in that direction with an outstretched arm. Now close enough to inhale a light waft of lavender. A floral statement of serenity, grace and calm, but... He frowned. Primarily, the flower symbolised distrust.

She probably did not understand that last. For what cause would this privileged and probably spoiled young woman have for distrusting anyone? Again, he had the urge to peek beneath her heavy veil and see her face. Something about her called strongly to his curiosity.

He shooed her towards the door through which she had arrived.

Thankfully, she did not resist. Or argue. Or try to flatter him. She left, leaving him feeling somehow guilty, perhaps even that he'd been unkind to ask for such an outrageous sum to find her missing person, when he'd done it purely to put her off.

He closed the door firmly behind her and leaned one shoulder against it, listening to Growler's low sympathetic rumble, though the actual words were now indistinct. In short order, silence descended in the adjoining antechamber.

Jaimie strolled to the window and watched his visitor make for the hackney carriage waiting at the curb. Discreet, then, this woman. Most of them flaunted their identities in the hopes of attracting his attention. She entered into negotiations with the driver. Finally, the jarvey nodded agreement. Suddenly, he had to know who she was.

Jaimie strode across the room and snatched open the door. 'Have someone follow that woman, Growler. I want to know whom she has lost.'

Growler's jaw slackened, then he was on his feet and dashing for the door. 'Yes, me lord.' A moment later, he was thundering along the hallway outside the office.

Another glance into the street showed a small lad he did not recognise running hell for leather after the hackney and leaping easily on to the back runner. Not something Jaimie would have encouraged, but hitching a ride on hackney carriages was common practice among the street urchins and unlikely to attract attention.

He sighed and repressed his unease. Why was he even bothering? No doubt, despite the lady's obvious distress, her supposed quest would turn out to be nothing but a hum. Blast it, he had far more important matters on his mind than the vagaries of a strange female. He fought to recapture the memory of his father's voice, but all he could hear were those cool, clear tones. *I require your services to locate a missing person.*

The cheek of it. She hadn't even done him the courtesy of showing her face. But that voice… Blast it, he would not let the woman ruin his day.

He picked up the report. *A ring.* She'd offered to pay him with a ring. She must indeed be desperate.

* * *

Tess ignored the butler's frowning look as he took in her outer raiment. Thank goodness she'd remembered to remove the swathe of crepe she had used as a veil before she arrived home, though she had been glad of its concealment during her interview with Lord Sandford. It had certainly hidden her blushes both then and in the jewellers where she had sold the ring his lordship had so disdainfully rejected. While the ring hadn't been worth a great deal, she could at least pay someone to make some preliminary enquiries on her behalf.

She mounted the stairs heading for her third-floor chamber, thinking back on her meeting with Lord Sandford. He was nothing like what she had expected. A peer of the realm engaged in solving crimes and disappearances? She'd expected some elderly scholarly sort of chap, one of those eccentrics one heard about, not a noble young man in the prime of life who looked like a Greek statue.

How was it possible that so handsome an exterior hid so arrogant a man? My word, he was shockingly handsome. Just thinking about him had her heart beating faster. She'd had trouble even uttering a word when she'd first entered his office. Tall and lean and stylish was her first impression. Handsome as sin in the manner of fair-haired Englishmen, though his eyes had been a velvety brown rather than a bright blue.

On the other hand, his arrogant lack of curiosity had been dreadfully irritating. Talk to her closest male relative, indeed. Ask a footman! Clearly, he'd thought her problem too trivial for his lofty attention. Not that she had intended to provide him with too many details, apart from the name of the person she wanted to find. She wasn't stupid enough to trust in a man's ability to do things right.

Take Father. He couldn't even manage to leave his affairs in proper order. Even though his sudden death had happened more than a year ago, she continued to have trouble believing he had taken his own life without making proper provision for his children. And yet, it was typical of the way the man had lived his life. He'd preferred to gamble on something turning up, rather than setting to and putting time and effort into the land his family had occupied for centuries. She'd done her best to make up for his lackadaisical ways, but each time she thought they were making progress, he'd taken what little bit of money she had managed to save and gambled it on a horse or the turn of a dice in the hopes of doubling his money. Hopeless. No, if she wanted to find her half-brother Grey, she needed to take charge of the search. Yet the pittance she had received for the sale of her ring would not take her very far at all.

Her maid, Mims, looked up from her folding as Tess entered. 'There you are, my lady. Her ladyship is looking for you. I told her you had stepped out for a breath of air, like you said. You are to go to her drawing room the moment you return.'

Tess nodded. 'Thank you, Mims. Help me change.'

In short order, Mims had her out of the blacks she'd worn after her father died and into a sprig-muslin morning gown, ready to present herself to Wilhelmina, Lady

Rowan, wife of Tess's cousin Phineas, who had inherited her father's title, his debts and, as the new head of the household, Tess's upkeep. The latter they both wished to be rid of as soon as possible.

She took a deep breath, calmed her turmoil and entered the drawing room where Lady Rowan, a faded blonde, reclined on the daybed idly flicking the pages of a copy of *La Belle Assemblée*. She looked up with a frown. 'Tess, your maid said you went out?'

'I needed to return a book to Hatchard's.'

Wilhelmina's nose seemed to twitch. 'If you had told me you were going, I would have asked you to pick up a book for me. You would think after all we do for you...' She sighed. 'Never mind, I will ask Carver to release one of the footmen from his duties.'

Tess forced a conciliatory smile. 'My apologies. I did ask at Hatchard's if they had anything for you, Cousin. They said they had not.'

Wilhelmina waved a dismissive hand as if she wasn't the one who had just accused Tess of being thoughtless. She frowned. 'Do sit down. You are making my neck ache.'

Of course, had she sat down without an invitation, her cousin's wife wouldn't have said anything, but a look of annoyance would have crossed her face and left Tess feeling off balance. She took the chair at right angles to the *chaise*. 'Mims said you wanted to see me.'

'Our plans for this evening have changed. Rowan has an important dinner at his club. We will go on ahead and he will meet us later at the Petershams'.'

Good news. Phineas's false jocularity always put her

on edge. She put his odd manner down to his discomfort at being around a woman who was his equal and who didn't fawn over him the way his wife did. They had conversed about her supposed intractability more than once. No wonder he could not wait to marry her off.

At first the idea had appealed. However, none of the suitors to whom he had given his approval were men with whom she could envisage spending the rest of her life. Indeed, it was his most recent suggestion that had sent her hot-footed to see Sandford. Alas, to no avail.

'Are we leaving home at ten as previously agreed?' Tess asked. Another of Wilhelmina's delightful little habits was to impart only part of the information one needed and then give one a look of irritation or even a scolding when one arrived too early or too late or was found to be waiting for something that had been cancelled. A habit that niggled.

'Yes. Ten. It is a costume ball with masks. I am going as Good Queen Bess.'

Thankfully, that she did know. She had managed to sneak a peek at the invitation. Wilhelmina always went to costume balls as Queen Elizabeth, whereas Tess loved dressing up as something different each time. 'I am going as Artemis.'

Wilhelmina's brow wrinkled as she clearly tried to recall the Greek goddess. 'Nothing risqué, Tess. You don't want to give Mr Stedman a distaste for you.' Wilhelmina's vague expression sharpened. 'Definitely no trousers this time or you really will end up in Yorkshire with Tante Marie. Rowan is at the end of his patience.'

The usual threat to send her north to live with an

embittered ageing relative made its appearance each time she showed a morsel of spirit. They would do it, too. Look how they'd tossed Greydon, her illegitimate half-brother, out on his ear without a shilling to his name. She'd been horrified to come home and find him gone.

Poor Grey. It had been so unfair. But she hadn't heard from him in all this time. He must know she would worry about him. Especially since he had taken with him the only piece of property of any value that she owned. Her diamond bracelet. If Cousin Phineas ever discovered the loss, things would go hard for Grey. Not to mention that she needed it back if she was to avoid marriage to the unpleasant Mr Stedman.

She certainly understood why Grey did not visit, but at the very least, he should have written. Explained his actions. Her stomach dipped. Surely Phineas wouldn't intercept his letters? That she would not believe. Far more likely was that Grey had forgotten all about her in his new life. Another man who had failed her badly. They were a wholly unreliable lot. She would certainly take him to task when she found him.

She bowed her head to hide her frustration. 'Nothing risqué, Cousin. I promise.' Though the idea of giving the narrow-minded, moralistic Mr Stedman a distaste for marriage to her appealed mightily. And she might have to behave very badly, if she could not locate Grey. Although the thought of being banished to Yorkshire sent a shiver down her back.

'Would you like me to ring for tea, Cousin?' she asked.

Somehow she would find Grey before Stedman made his offer. Unfortunately, she wasn't sure how much longer she could hold him off.

Jaimie tied on his mask and left the carriage around the corner from the Petershams' town house. There was no point in wearing a disguising costume if one was going to waltz up to the front door in a lozenged coach. He adjusted the folds of his black cloak and pulled up the cowl. Costume balls were generally not his idea of a good time, but dressing as Death had appealed to his macabre sense of humour. After all, he'd been responsible for more than his fair share. It would also prevent anyone from guessing his identity and allow him to move around without exciting any interest. A useful advantage for tonight's endeavour.

He handed over his invitation to the footman at the door and strode up the stairs to the first-floor ballroom behind a couple in the guises of Pan and a shepherdess. The man's large backside stretched his tights to the limit in a most unsettling way and the lady kept dropping her lamb, requiring her escort to bend over to retrieve it. Jaimie averted his gaze. Finally, they made it to the top and Jaimie eased his way through the crowd of masked and colourfully clothed guests, many of whom were sweating profusely in their heavy costumes and the sweltering room.

Those costumes ranged from angels to gladiators and most took one look at him and either moved aside or peered into the cowl, trying to make out his features only to discover it useless because of his mask.

He scanned the room for his objective. Artemis, according to Growler's information.

An interesting choice. A goddess who protected young women. Artemis was also known as Diana the huntress to the Romans. Should he read anything into her choice?

It had taken Growler and his team little effort to learn about Jaimie's morning visitor. An unremarkable daughter of a deceased earl who had been placed under the protection of the new title holder. She was now in her second Season on the marriage mart. The question of whom she might be seeking remained unknown. Not his concern. Something else entirely had brought him here this evening.

And...there she was: Artemis, standing among a group of costumed ladies and gentlemen, watching the dancing. The lushness of her figure took his breath away. The expression on her round pretty face was one of complete innocence, despite the wanton tumble of chestnut locks falling down her back to her waist. If her costume had not been described to him in intricate detail, he would never have recognised her as the dumpy female who had stood toe to toe with Growler's menacing presence earlier in the day.

This morning, he had thought her short and a little squat in her enveloping black carriage dress. The funereal clothing she'd worn had hidden every one of her charms. Apart from her voice. And her scent. Tonight, the artfully draped, white Greek robe arranged to leave one creamy dimpled shoulder bare also revealed a gloriously curvaceous figure in perfect proportion for her diminutive size. The bow and quiver slung diagonally across her body divided her breasts in a most mouth-watering fashion.

While her mask obscured the top half of her face, her lips were lush and full, and beneath them her chin came to an obstinate jut. At his approach, her gaze wandered over him for a brief second and came back, her eyes widening, not in recognition but in shock.

He sprang the trap.

'I didn't think you would recognise me, my lady.' He kept his voice to a low whisper.

'I do not,' she said, turning that delicious shoulder to exactly the right angle for discouragement. 'Have we been introduced?'

'Sadly, no.' At their meeting she had known his name, but he had not known hers. Now he took delight at putting her at the same disadvantage. She glanced at him again, clearly trying to see into the shadows of his hood.

'Would you care to dance, my lady?'

Beside her, Lady Rowan eyed him up and down. 'Lady Rowan,' he murmured. 'How regal you look to-night as Queen Elizabeth. Might you give your permission? I promise I will bring the Lady Theresa back to you safe and sound.'

The older woman relaxed at his polite tone and clear knowledge of who they were. 'Certainly, sir. One set only, mind, Theresa.'

A tiny pursing of the Lady Theresa's lips was the only sign of irritation at the admonition. He admired her forbearance. It must be galling for such an independent lady to be treated like a child.

'Who are you?' she asked with laughter in her voice as he led her into a set. 'I didn't think I knew you at all, but the way you bamboozled my cousin...' She shook her head. 'You must be an acquaintance to know she loves that costume.'

'I admit I have seen it before.'

They moved up the set and the figures of the dance did not allow for conversation until they were standing out, waiting to join the neighbouring couples when the round of steps were complete.

'I give up,' she said. 'You are going to have to tell me your name.'

'The Grim Reaper.'

She raised her brows. 'Very well, keep your identity hidden. It matters not to me.'

There was more than a little defiance in the declaration. For a moment, Jaimie considered revealing his identity. But that did not suit him at all. Not yet, at least. Having seen her, he now wanted to discover the reason this young lady had risked her reputation so precipitously by seeking him out. Perhaps her heart had been stolen away and it was the thief she was seeking?

Something he would not encourage.

'Is not the whole idea of a masked ball to be someone else for an hour or two?' he murmured in teasing tones.

'Death?' She made a scoffing sound. 'Is that not a strange choice? Most men like to play some sort of heroic figure. You prefer to remind us of something unpleasant, yet something we must all face at some future time. I wonder what that says about you as a person?'

Her light clear voice held amusement and her brown

eyes twinkled gold. She released his hand and moved into the next figure of the dance.

What *did* his choice of costume say about him? He pushed the thought aside. It was a disguise, that was all. A way of remaining anonymous. Of ensuring no tongues would start wagging about his first appearance at a ball in years, or his invitation to her to dance.

He found himself wishing it was a waltz he'd secured rather than a country dance. Only because it would have afforded more opportunity for conversation, not because he wanted that lovely, lithe, deliciously curved body floating along beside his and responding to his touch.

'Am I to understand you dislike masquerades?' he asked as he walked her down the set. 'That you find them beneath you, perhaps?'

The fulminating look she gave him took him by surprise. 'Masquerades are very well in their way. It is—'

'It is?'

Another glance came his way. This one puzzled. Then she smiled and he felt as if something had struck him behind the ribs. 'I think if one could attend under the right circumstances, it might be fun. If one could really do as one wished for once.' She glanced over to where her cousin stood chatting and fanning her face. 'One cannot have everything one wishes, can one?'

'One cannot,' he agreed.

Instinct told him that, despite her calm demeanour, there was an underlying worry behind the light words. The anxiety he'd sensed in his office seemed to have increased.

He'd deliberately led her into a set with an uneven number of couples and when once more they were standing out, he bowed. 'It is uncommonly hot in here, my lady, may I offer you some refreshment before I return you to Queen Elizabeth's side?'

'As long as you don't suggest we go bag a rabbit or two in the garden, I would like that.'

He laughed. Couldn't help it. 'Really? That was the best one of your swains could do?'

'I should have known better than to have explained my costume to him or to have expected him to behave like anything but a fool.'

Startled by her vehemence, he led her out of the set.

'A gentleman you know, I presume?' he enquired.

'Indeed. He thought he was being amusing. He actually suggested that the costume would serve me better without the bow. Fat lot he knows about Artemis,' she muttered.

Jaimie took two glasses of the non-alcoholic punch which he knew without a doubt would be horrible. While the champagne would have been more fun, self-defence prevented him from being the cause of anything untoward. *It is a gentleman's duty to protect a lady*, his father's voice reminded. On that occasion, he had guided his mother around a puddle. Sort of. Only a little bit of her hem had trailed through it. It was one of the few mental images he had of his parents.

He guided Lady Tess towards the French doors. 'Let us avail ourselves of the terrace. There are tables out there and waiters.'

For a moment he thought she might baulk. Again,

she glanced over at her cousin, who was not looking their way. 'We can ask her permission,' he suggested. He was after all a wolf in sheep's clothing and seeking permission was what a sheep would do.

She squared her shoulders. 'No. I was out there once already. My cousin did not object.'

Her voice sounded grim. Who was the idiot who had annoyed her? Whoever he was, Jaimie could only thank him for sparking her spirit.

He ushered her to one of the tables on the terrace, seating her where the light from the nearby lantern would fall on her face while leaving him in shadow. He set her drink in front of her before sitting down.

'Warm enough?'

'Yes, thank you.'

Too bad. He'd had a notion to put his cape around her shoulders and let it absorb some of her perfume. The scent of lavender had lingered in his office all day. Serenity, grace and calmness in the language of flowers, along with that disturbing underlying meaning of distrust. All but the last seemed too milk and water for this spirited lady, though she had certainly shown calmness when she visited his office. Dianthus, for boldness, would suit her better. Though she had been veiled, so perhaps lemon flowers should be in the mix... His mother had made a great study of the language of flowers and her notes were one of the few items he treasured.

She sipped at the punch and made a face.

'Terrible as usual?' he asked, amused.

'Awful.' A smile curved those full lush lips. 'It is all right at first and then...' She gave a little shudder.

The movement did something to his blood. Made it run faster. Hotter. Not something he wanted in regard to this particular female. He forced himself to focus on the task at hand. Putting her at her ease so he could extract the information he wanted.

'How are you enjoying the Season?' A safe topic when it came to young ladies on the town. He sat back and waited to hear about all her conquests and gowns.

'It is as bad as the previous one,' she said with a small laugh.

How devastatingly honest. The hairs on his nape stood up. It was the same feeling he got when he started to get close to a criminal he was chasing. A sense of anticipation. It didn't make any sense that he should feel it now, with her. 'Why is that?'

'I beg your pardon. You will think I am an ungrateful wretch after my cousin's kindness in giving me this opportunity.'

'Speaking the truth is not always a bad thing.'

She chuckled, a small rather painful sound. 'It is if you are seeking a husband. Men expect a woman to be biddable and modest and not speak out of turn.'

'I see.'

She twisted the stem of her glass, gazing down into the liquid. 'My father encouraged me to offer my opinion, but to some I am ill-schooled.' She pursed her lips thoughtfully and he experienced an urgent need to see if they tasted as exotic as they looked. 'And here I am doing it again. If I'm not careful I'll find myself packed off to Yorkshire.'

'Why Yorkshire?'

'My cousin has an aunt who lives there. She's a—'
She stopped and leaned back in her chair with a sigh.
'Why on earth am I telling you this?'

'Because I'm a good listener? She is a...?'

'She is an unhappy elderly lady who has already
worked three companions into the ground.'

She had modified what she intended to say, but the
meaning was clear. 'You see yourself as number four.'

'I will be if—'

He waited in silence. She would either tell him or
she would not. For some strange reason, he really hoped
she would.

The notion of hoping anything in regard to this forward young woman took him aback. Her worries were
nothing to him. He was here for quite another purpose.
The sooner he remembered that the better.

She glanced up at his face briefly, or at least into the
darkness of his hood, yet somehow he sensed that she
could see him when logic said she could not. Finally she
dropped her gaze, staring down at her gloved hands.
'This Season is my last chance to oblige my family.'

Was it not every well-bred girl's duty to oblige her
family? And yet she sounded so weary, so defeated, his
skin tightened with the urge to rush to her defence. As
infuriating as she had been at his office, this hopeless-
ness was far worse.

Really? What nonsense. He didn't know what he
was thinking. He sipped at his drink and almost gagged
when it hit the back of his throat. 'Why so?'

She put her glass down with a little click. 'It is not
something I should be discussing with a stranger or

anyone else for that matter.' There was a forlorn note to her voice, though she tried to hide it with a smile.

'Is there no one in whom you can confide?' Now why had he asked that question? Of course, he knew why. He knew how alone he had felt growing up without his family. With only servants for company and a gruff guardian who came once a month to check on his progress. A surprising and unwanted flash of memory recalled a cousin who would now be around this young woman's age, were she alive. Had she survived, she also would have been alone growing up. Because of him.

A pang squeezed the breath from his lungs. Regret for what might have been. For the loss. He forced it back where it belonged. Nothing could be gained by such maudlin thoughts. The cases were not at all similar. This girl clearly had a caring family who gave her everything she could possibly need. Young women loved their drama. It was likely all a storm in a teacup.

She shook her head. 'There was someone,' she said, with a small sad smile. 'Not any more. He—'

He? A twinge of something unpleasant tightened his gut. Interesting. He would never have imagined feeling anything that hinted of jealousy. He waited. And waited. Would she say more? Reveal her innermost dreams and wishes. God, he hoped not. And yet clearly she had aroused his curiosity.

'A...a childhood friend I haven't seen for quite some time.'

A friend. The relief was out of all proportion to the information imparted. 'What happened to him?'

'He went away.' She waved vaguely into the dark.

Why the hell did he have the feeling there was a great deal more to the story? Was this the person she'd wanted him to find?

Chapter Two

Why *was* she telling him all this, Tess wondered. Was it his anonymity causing her to drop her guard? If so, it was bound to be a mistake. Tess glanced over her shoulder. No sign of her cousin. No hope of rescue there. And indeed, it was perfectly acceptable for a man to escort her outside where other couples and groups were sitting at tables surrounded by servants. It was hardly secluded, yet it somehow felt intimate. As if they were completely alone and confidences would be in order.

How did he do that? Give her the feeling he was trustworthy, when experience had taught her never to trust any man?

Why, she didn't even know his name and yet she felt drawn to him. Was it the timbre of his voice? His aura of youth and health, despite the horrible costume?

Oh heavens, *why* had she worn the bow and quiver in the mode of a huntress? It was making breathing quite difficult. She slipped one arm out of the strap.

He was on his feet in a second. 'Allow me.'

As he leaned close to ease the confounded thing over her head without disturbing her coiffure, she inhaled a deep breath of his cologne. The scent of sandalwood with another undertone...bergamot, perhaps. It seemed...familiar.

He placed the bow and quiver on the table between them and resumed his seat.

She stared into the depths of his hood, but even his eyes were shadowed. 'Are you sure we haven't met before?'

He placed a gloved hand above his heart. 'I assure you, my lady, we have never been introduced before today.'

Surely his voice had a familiar ring to it...

'You didn't tell me what made you choose Artemis?' The smile in his voice made her imagine a flash of white teeth in a handsome face. Oh, really? He was probably ancient, with a horrid moustache and a bald spot.

She sipped the nasty drink. Something hot and wicked coursed through her veins, the desire to shock him out of his nonchalance. Shatter the ease with which he lounged in his chair in complete anonymity. 'She shoots men.'

Aha! It wasn't much of a reaction, a slight shift in his posture, but it was something.

A ghostly laugh reached her ears. He wasn't in the least discomposed. He was amused.

Something to admire about him at least. She grinned. 'Rakehells beware. My arrow tips are sharp.' He could take the warning however he pleased.

He reached for the arrows as if to test her words,

then for some reason thought better of it. She frowned at the gloved hand resting on the table, curled inward, the little finger out of alignment.

'Why did you choose Death?' she asked.

'It is easy to accomplish. A black cloak. A mask. A sickle I left at the door.'

His answer seemed evasive. Most irritating. She did not play such stupid games. 'Shall we go back inside?'

'As you wish.'

Lack of interest coloured his voice. Recognition dawned in a flash. The scent. The little finger. If not the low voice, then its mocking boredom. Oh! Such a cleverly worded denial about not having been intro-duced before today...

She leaped up, the chair falling backwards, clattering on the flagstones. 'You!'

He was on his feet almost as quickly. 'Lady Tess.' His hand grabbed her arm as she staggered, unbalanced. 'Take care.'

She wrenched her arm away. 'What game are you playing, Lord Sandford?'

'My lady. You are mistaken—'

'No. I am not. How did you find me? And more to the point, why bother after you turned down my request?' Oh, heaven help her, he was going to expose her to her cousin. The wretch.

'I thought to return this.' He retrieved a small item from the folds of his cloak. The pearl ring she'd sold. 'A lady should never sell her jewels using her own name if she wants to keep their disappearance a secret.'

She snatched it out of his hand and forced it on over

her glove. 'A gentleman doesn't go sneaking around following a lady.' Oh, no! Now people at the other tables were looking at them. 'I suppose you plan to tell my guardian?'

He took her arm. 'Don't make a scene, young lady. Think of your reputation.'

'Bah. No one knows who we are and no one cares. It is a masquerade.'

'By morning gossip will abound. Your costume fools no one.'

'Whereas yours is the perfect disguise.' How like a man to avoid taking any responsibility.

He held out an arm. 'Come, let us take a turn about the shrubbery as if that was our intention for getting up all along. I am told it is quite beautiful at night.'

'It is dark. We won't be able to see a thing.'

'Even better.'

She swallowed the urge to laugh at his scorn of the poor shrubbery. Tried to hang on to her anger.

'Very well, but I expect an explanation of your behaviour.' She snatched up her bow and slung it over one shoulder. 'And don't even think about trying anything untoward. I did not lie when I said my arrows were sharp.'

'Last thing I need is an arrow in my backside,' he muttered low in her ear. Not quite the voice she'd heard this morning—this time there was laughter in it. How surprising. And attractive. And intriguing.

Dash it all, the man was a menace.

Also surprising were the lanterns all along the garden path. Soon they were out of earshot of the couples on the terrace, but not in the dark and not out of sight if anyone had cared to look for them.

'Well?' she asked peremptorily.

'Well what?'

She started to turn back. 'I see you are still playing games.'

He held her fast by the crook of her elbow, his hand firm but not painful in its restraint.

'Let me go.'

'It is no *game* when a respectable young lady comes alone to the chambers of a bachelor.'

The emphasis on the word game sounded bitter. 'What are you suggesting, sir?'

'That you took a risk with my reputation as well as your own. I have no intention of being forced into marriage.'

She gasped. Blood ran hot through her veins. Tension had her shaking. 'You think I would marry you? I don't like you, sir. Not one bit. I gave you my reason for coming to see you this morning. You gave me your answer. We have no need for further communication.'

'How can you say you don't like me? You don't even know me.' Again he sounded amused. He was like a cat playing with a mouse. A very large self-satisfied cat.

'You will return me to my cousin at once,' she said with all the dignity she could muster.

'But what about this person you need found?'

'Do not trouble yourself, my lord. I have made other plans.'

'It would be no trouble to me. Others, however, might

take weeks to find your answer. I had the impression your matter was urgent.'

Oooh, he was so very annoying! Even if he did have the right to boast. 'I have changed my mind.'

He turned her to face him, bending to peer into her face as if he could read her expression behind the mask. 'I don't believe you.'

While she could not see his face, his intensity made her breathing quicken and her heart flutter strangely.

He tipped her chin with a finger, staring into her eyes. Mesmerised, she could not move. 'Let me take you driving tomorrow and you can tell me all about it.'

At the graze of his breath across her cheek, her insides tightened. He dropped his hand as if burned. Had he sensed her reaction? Oh goodness, she hoped not.

Panicked by her untoward response to his touch, she opened her mouth to refuse. Closed it again as her brain overtook her emotions. This was what she had wanted, was it not? His help. 'Very well. I will, of course, return the money you paid for my ring.'

'I don't want your *money*.'

There was a seductive note in his voice. Her body trembled. Shocked, she gazed up into the void where his face should be, a face she could see in her mind's eye. She had no trouble recalling the mocking smile on his lips. 'What *do* you want?'

She had meant to sound impatient. Dismissive. Instead she sounded scared. Weak.

'I will inform you when we meet tomorrow.'

She wanted to argue, but she also wanted to find

Grey. Seething, she walked at his side, trying to think of suitably cutting words.

He turned them back towards the terrace, strolling as if there were no undercurrents rippling beneath the surface of their silence.

At the French doors, she dipped a curtsy. 'Thank you for a pleasant dance and conversation.'

'Pleasant?' he murmured.

Really, the man was impossible. On legs that felt stiff and awkward, with a heart pounding loudly in her ears, she marched in the direction she had last seen Wilhelmina. When she glanced back, he was gone.

Oh heavens, what would he want? And how far was she prepared to go with this man? Her stomach gave an odd little pulse.

Dash it, she would insist on gentlemanly behaviour, no matter what.

Jaimie had spent the half the morning expecting a note from Lady Tess politely refusing their engagement to drive. And the other half being annoyed by his lack of concentration on his work.

He wasn't certain whether he was pleased or sorry when no such note made an appearance. Of course there was a good possibility that he would arrive at the Rowan front door and be informed that her ladyship was out.

And that would be that.

Whatever had possessed him to invite her to go driving, anyway? It wasn't as if she was the sort of woman whose company he enjoyed. She was prickly and combative. A less subtle female he couldn't imagine. She didn't even know how to flirt. They might have traded all kinds of barbs about those arrows in her quiver.

Yet surprisingly, he'd enjoyed her directness and her willingness to confront him. He'd always thought debutantes an insipid, simpering lot. What he did not like, however, was that she had occupied too much of his thoughts these past few hours. He kept wondering how she had recognised him beneath his costume. Something had given him away. Perhaps she'd tell him what it was at their meeting. He certainly would not ask. He intended to keep their relationship strictly business.

He pulled his phaeton up outside the town house and his liveried tiger jumped down and held the horses' heads while he knocked on the front door.

'I'll let her ladyship know you are here, my lord. Will you come in?' the butler said.

'I'll wait out here. My tiger has the horses, but they're a mite fresh.'

'Very good, my lord.' The butler closed the door.

Not instant rejection then. He returned to his phaeton.

A few moments later Lady Tess tripped down the steps followed by an elderly maid. Last night she'd looked like a tasty morsel in her figure-hugging Greek robe. Today she almost looked like any other young lady of the nobility. Her pale green-and-white-striped carriage dress came up high at the throat, with several tiers of ruffles up to her chin. The gown fell to the ground with a festoon of flounces around the hem. A leghorn bonnet decorated with flowers and ribbons the colour of the dress perched on her head—but a few chestnut curls framed her astonishingly lovely face, perfect in shape and proportion, except perhaps for that stubborn little chin.

It would be easy to dismiss her as an empty-headed beauty if one did not see the underlying determination in her expression and the intelligence in those amber eyes. Had she arrived at his chambers without her veil, he might have dismissed her as a pretty little schemer out for his title. Had it been cleverness on her part, or a lack of artifice?

She raised an eyebrow and he realised he'd been staring. He came forward to escort her to the carriage.

She tutted. 'How are we to fit three people?'

'One at the back and two on the seat.'

He grinned at the horror on the maid's face.

'He means his tiger, Mims,' Lady Tess said, frowning. 'It is an open carriage. You are not needed.'

The maid curtsied and scurried back indoors. Lady Tess, meanwhile, wandered a little way along the path.

'Changed your mind?' he drawled. He certainly didn't care if she drove with him or not. Well, not much at least.

'Not at all. I was admiring your horses. It is not often one sees a pair so perfectly matched, although the off-side one is a little heavier in build, I believe.'

His jaw dropped. No one but his own very expert groom had noted the slight discrepancy in the horses' bone structure. 'Got an eye for a bit of blood and bone, have you, my lady?' Damn it, that was not the smoothest thing he could have said.

'I like to see a nicely matched pair. My father had a

pair of beautiful steppers. I would love to drive them.'
She leaned towards them, stretching out a hand as if to
pat Romulus. The brute showed the whites of his eyes.

Jaimie started forward. 'Be careful.'

She stopped before she got too close. 'Testy, is he?'

'Always. And, no, you may not drive them.' Never
again would any woman drive his horses.

The expected pout did not make an appearance. Instead, she cast him an expressive look. 'We'll leave that
discussion for later.'

That discussion was closed. He assisted her up on to
the phaeton and, on the way around to climb into the
driver's seat, he spoke to his tiger in a low voice. 'When
we reach the park you can take yourself off. I'll pick
you up at the gate for the drive back.'

The lad touched his cap. 'Yes, me lord. But stir yer
stumps, would ya? His fussiness would like to be orf.'

Jaimie stroked 'his fussiness' along his neck and
down his wither and the horse settled before he sprang
into the carriage and took up the reins. The boy leaped
up behind.

The animals weren't quite as energetic as they had
been on the drive over, but they were still feeling their
bits. He urged them into a spanking trot, feathering
between a couple of slower carriages and into a break
in the traffic. Lady Tess sat calmly with her hands in
her lap, clearly trusting him not to tip her into the road.

Most normal ladies were notoriously nervous about
anything that looked the least bit hazardous. Then there
were the reckless ones, like his first wife, who took ridiculous risks. Clearly, Lady Tess fell into the latter

camp. And he was a twice-born fool to get involved with her nonsense.

'We are fortunate the weather is clear today,' he said as they turned the corner at the end of the street. Weather being the safest topic of conversation.

'After the rain of the past few days, we are fortunate indeed,' she replied coolly.

As they entered Hyde Park, many heads turned in their direction. Open mouths and wide eyes abounded. News of his driving Lady Tess would be all around town by the end of the evening. His teeth gritted at the thought, but it couldn't be helped. There were only so many respectable ways to talk to a lady in relative private and this was one of them.

The gossips would be jumping to all kinds of conclusions. Did she know that? The horses slowed to a funereal pace as they joined the traffic mincing down Rotten Row.

His tiger jumped down and hared off.

Lady Tess frowned.

He was getting quite a few frowns today. 'I told him to go, because I do not want our conversation overheard.'

The frown cleared. 'Where better to be alone than in plain view of the world.' She chuckled. 'I can see why you are good at what you do.'

'What I do?' He quirked a brow.

'Finding people. Investigating things.'

Damn that article, though few knew the real depth of his 'investigations' as she had called them. And it was as good a time as any to get to the point of this drive, even if he was enjoying her company more than he would have imagined. 'Who is it you want me to find?'

She hesitated. 'May I have your assurance you will keep my confidence, no matter what?'

He probably ought to be insulted by her question. Indeed, on one level he was insulted. On another, the fact that she was even considering giving him her trust felt like an incredible compliment. Why would that be?

'Why are you smiling in that mocking way?' she asked. 'Did I say something you find foolish?'

Prickly little thing. 'I didn't realise I was smiling.' But if he was mocking anyone, it was himself. At the way she kept surprising him. 'And, yes, you can be assured that anything you tell me will remain confidential.'

She drew in a deep breath, drawing his attention to the snug fit of her carriage dress. To the way it moulded to the soft curves and hollows of her petite form. He turned his eyes resolutely to his horses. He was not here to flirt with the woman. He was here because she needed his help, despite that she irritated him beyond endurance.

'I am trying to locate my father's bailiff, Mr Freeps. He left for another position shortly after my father died.'

Not what he had expected at all. He had been waiting for something along the lines of the boy she had spoken of, or another sold or pawned item she wanted back.

'Surely your cousin's man of business would have this information?'

'Yes, and he would immediately report my request to my cousin.'

'I see.'

'What do you see?'

The defiance in her voice, her wariness of his motives, struck him on the raw.

He gave her an impatient glance. 'I see why you do not wish to go to your cousin's man of business. Why exactly do you wish to find this man Freeps?'

'Why is that any of your concern?'

'And when I find him, what then?'

'*If* you find him, you will provide me with his address. That is all.' She pressed her lips together.

'Lady Tess, I realise you and I are not well acquainted and I am sure I have no interest in your secrets, but I do not work for anyone unless I know the full story. For example, should you wish to accuse this servant of theft, I would need to know this, so he is not forewarned.'

She stiffened at the word theft. He pretended not to notice.

'If, however, it is simply your intention to reassure yourself of this person's wellbeing, I can include that sort of information in my report.'

Her hands clenched in her lap.

'It isn't either of those things, is it?'

'No.' Her voice was low and being held under tight control. 'I need to ask him something. In person.'

He frowned. 'Something of a private nature, then?'

'Yes.'

Damn the woman. What on earth was she hiding?

* * *

Lord Sandford was the most annoying creature Tess had ever met. Why couldn't he simply do as she asked? 'There is no reason for you to know anything apart from the name of the person I would like found and their last-known address. I would have known this had I not been absent from home at the time of his departure.'

She had been prostrate after her father had died and Cousin Phin had packed her off to an aunt in Bath to *recover* her wits.

'Are you implying there is some sort of injustice you hope to redress?'

The surprise in his voice irritated her beyond rational thought. 'Is that so impossible to believe?' Unfortunately, it was far more selfish than that. She ignored a pang of guilt. After all, he might be more likely to help her if he thought her reason altruistic rather than self-serving.

A sudden urge to tell him the whole truth, to tell him about Greydon, took her aback. She couldn't. What if he told Rowan? She dared not take the chance.

His voice dropped to a low seductive murmur. 'You have not yet heard my price for undertaking this service.'

Her stomach gave a little hop. She risked a glance at his face to find him looking at her with a small smile on his lips as if he was once more amused.

She swallowed. It was the one thing that had kept her awake all night. What on earth would he demand as payment? He had said at the masquerade that he didn't want money. Heat scalded her cheeks. 'Tell me.'

'Before I impart this person's whereabouts to you,

you will tell me the real reason you wish to find him. The full truth. I will have your word on that.'

'You would trust my word?'

'Why would I not? I trust until a person proves unworthy.'

'And if they do prove untrustworthy?'

'Then I seek retribution.'

A shiver passed over her skin at the hint of menace in his words. She glanced over at him, trying to read his expression, but he seemed completely focused on guiding the horses out through the gate and there was no way of guessing what might be on his mind.

'Well?' he asked when they had moved into the traffic on Park Lane.

'I accept.' She would simply have to tell him a truth that did not lead to Grey and if he didn't like it, too bad. She handed him a piece of paper with Freeps's full name on it and some other bits of information about his family she had remembered that might come in useful. 'This should help you find him.'

He tucked the note into his waistcoat pocket without even so much as a glance. No doubt he'd be handing it off to one of his minions since it was likely he had far more important clients requiring his services.

Resentment tightened her chest. She took a deep breath. She could not afford resentment. His offer was what she had wanted all along.

Life was becoming exceedingly complex. What with Cousin Rowan and now Lord Sandford, she felt as if she was walking through a meadow full of cows. One misstep would cause no end of mess.

A new topic of conversation was needed. 'Where is the Sandford estate?'

He stiffened. 'Why do you want to know?'

Hah! What an interesting reaction. 'No reason. I am simply making polite conversation. It is something I can easily look up in Debrett's should I be interested enough. Which I really am not.'

He made an odd sound, like a laugh being turned into a cough. '*Touché*, Lady Tess.'

'We are not engaged in a battle, Lord Sandford.'

'Merely a war of words.' Again that disdainfully amused tone in his voice.

They neared the corner of Piccadilly. He slowed just enough to let his tiger leap up behind them. She glanced over her shoulder. 'Isn't that a little dangerous?'

'Na, miss. I does it all the time. Saves getting the horses all of a bother.'

She blinked, surprised the tiger had answered her directly. The Earl said nothing when she had expected him to issue an admonition to the lad for impertinence. She was surprised yet glad when he did not.

'Sandford is in Derbyshire.'

So he had decided to be civil after all. 'I have never been there. I grew up in Kent.' She gave a little shiver. 'I hear it is cold and rainy in the north.'

'It can be rather bleak in winter, can it not, Remmy?'

'Yes, me lord. Proper chilly.'

'But it has a stark beauty that grows on one.' He sounded almost wistful.

The north must have some redeeming qualities, she supposed. 'Do you go there in the summer?'

'I never go there if I can help it.' The words were spoken in a flat tone of voice.

She bit her tongue to stop herself from asking why. Theirs was a business relationship, nothing more. He didn't seem to be the sort of man who would take kindly to someone prying into his personal life.

'I would miss not visiting my home.' Her chest squeezed painfully. Unless she could get her bracelet back, it was likely she would never see it again.

Lord Sandford cast her a sideways glance. 'Is something wrong?'

She realised she was gripping the side of the carriage for all she was worth. She dropped her hand into her lap. 'Not a thing.'

His eyes narrowed. 'Come now, Lady Tess, your expression was one of pure horror.'

'I should be more careful with my thoughts, should I not?' Particularly around him. He noticed too much.

He frowned. 'Is there something you are not telling me? Something with which I can help?'

Hope lifted her heart. No. What was she thinking? He would never understand a woman desiring to make her own life choices rather than be dependent on a man, be that a husband or a cousin. She took a deep breath, forcing herself to think clearly. She gave him a tight smile. 'I think it would be unwise to accept any offer of assistance from you, Lord Sandford. Who knows what sort of price you would set?'

The tiger gave a little snigger.

'Round two also to you, Lady Tess.'

He pulled up at her cousin's front door. 'It has been a pleasure.'

'When will I hear from you?'

'When I have something to report.'

She wanted to press him, but did not dare in case he changed his mind. Men were such obstinate, fickle creatures.

He jumped down and escorted her to the door where he bowed over her hand. 'I will let you know when I have news.'

The butler opened the door to his knock.

Sandford touched his hat. 'Good day, Lady Tess. Thank you for a pleasant afternoon.' He sauntered back to his carriage.

Blasted man. He really was the most annoying individual she had ever met. He thought he could get away with anything just because he was rich and handsome.

So very handsome. If any man could be described as an Adonis, it was he. And he drove to an inch, handling the ribbons with expert ease. It had been impossible not to notice all the ladies casting admiring glances his way.

Pah. What did that have to do with anything?

Chapter Three

Two days had passed since Tess had given Lord Sandford the information about Freeps and there was still no word. All morning she had been sitting in the drawing room with her needlework in hand, listening for the arrival of the mail.

And when it came, she had received nothing.

She was being foolish. Too anxious. A single gentleman did not write notes to a single lady who was not a relative or an intended. She certainly had no wish to set alarm bells ringing in Wilhelmina's feather brain. If they thought Lord Sandford was trifling with her, they'd have her sent north in the blink of an eye. Or they would if Mr Stedman wasn't still showing a marked interest in her.

Wilhelmina drifted in wearing her Phineas-has-issued-an-edict face. Edicts had been issued more and more frequently of late. Tess tensed.

'Good morning, Theresa,' Wilhelmina said with a vague smile. 'I missed you at breakfast and couldn't find you anywhere afterwards.'

Worse and worse. Tess let her needlework fall into her lap and forced a cheerful smile. 'I went for my usual early morning walk.' The walk her cousin did not approve of.

Wilhelmina's glance sharpened. 'With your maid, I assume.'

Poor old Mims was far too old to be trotting along at the pace Tess preferred. 'I took one of the footmen.'

'Carver gave his approval?'

Tess gritted her teeth. 'He did.'

A vaguely disgruntled expression flitted across her cousin's face. 'That is good then. He always complains to me when his schedule for the day is altered without his knowledge.'

That wasn't it at all. Wilhelmina loved her role of Countess and she loved catching Tess out in one mistake or another. Tess had quickly learned how to avoid her traps. Not that Wilhelmina realised Tess was on to her. She was far too self-absorbed.

Her cousin took the chaise longue and reclined along its length. 'Ring for tea, there's a dear.'

She could have rung for tea before she sat down, but it amused her to treat Tess like a servant. Tess put her embroidery aside and got up to tug on the bell pull beside the hearth.

'How is your work coming along?' Wilhelmina asked the moment she sat down.

'Very well. I have it half done.' She was embroidering a cushion cover for her trousseau at Wilhelmina's suggestion.

'May I see?'

Wilhelmina accounted herself an expert needle-woman, though she rarely set a stitch herself. Tess thought it might be because she was becoming short-sighted and didn't want to wear spectacles.

She took the piece over. Her cousin sat up and made a space for her on the chaise.

Oh, yes, she definitely had some instruction to impart from dearest Phin. Tess sank down beside her. 'I only have one bird left to finish.'

Wilhelmina held the fabric up to the light. 'I think you need a couple more French knots here. See, there's a space. What do you think?'

Dash it, the woman was right. The French knots had taken her for ever to complete and had made her fingers sore. She had known a few more were needed, but didn't think anyone would notice. 'Thank you for pointing it out, Cousin. I'll be sure to fill in the gaps.'

With a self-satisfied smile, Wilhelmina handed the work back. 'I did tell you we are attending the Halli-wells' ball on Friday, did I not?'

'You did, indeed.'

'Which gown will you wear?'

Tess mentally ran through her meagre wardrobe. She had already decided which gown to wear, but if she named it, Wilhelmina was sure to prefer a different one. 'The pale green, I think. I like something with a bit of colour.'

True to form, Wilhelmina frowned. 'Not for the Halli-wells. All the younger ladies will be wearing white.'

'Hmm. There is the white-and-silver tissue, I suppose.'

'You have worn that one at least four times. People

will start to talk. No. Wear the one with the roses festooned at the hem and neckline.'

Tess bowed her head in compliance and to hide her smile. It was the dress she had planned to wear all along.

How much nicer this would have all been if she could have been friends with her cousin's wife. They could have enjoyed this Season together as. Instead it was a battle of wits and Wilhelmina had so few of them it was becoming quite boring.

'Why not wear your mother's diamonds? They will look perfect with that gown. Phineas reminded me only this morning that you have never worn them.'

The breath rushed from her lungs. She swallowed the lump in her throat. 'I...umm... I am not sure where her bracelet is.' She winced at how feeble she sounded. 'I put it away somewhere. The clasp was broken.'

'You don't know where you put a diamond bracelet? Well, I must say, that is careless in the extreme. Have that maid of yours look for it and we will send it to Rundell & Bridge for repair.'

'I hate to put Phin to the expense,' Tess managed. 'Who knows how much it might cost?'

Wilhelmina frowned. 'I shall have to ask him what he thinks. In the meantime, please find it.'

Tess nodded. 'Yes, Cousin. I will do so.' The reprieve would give her time to think up some more plausible excuse as to where the bracelet had gone. Right now her brain seemed to have frozen solid. She began to relax.

'Oh, and by the way, Theresa...'

Tess tensed again. 'By the way' *always* heralded Phin's less pleasant admonitions and instructions.

'As you know, my dearest Phineas has your best interests in mind and he has agreed to meet with Mr Stedman to discuss,' her voice rose to an excited squeak, 'the settlements.' She clasped her hands together. 'Isn't it exciting?'

Tess stared at her cousin's wife. 'Mr Stedman hasn't yet asked for my permission to approach Phin. I thought...'

Her voice tailed off at Wilhelmina's annoyed expression.

'Phin said I might have a little more time,' she continued valiantly. 'I hardly know the man.'

'It is a preliminary discussion only,' Wilhelmina said, but her expression was just a little too smug. 'You know, if you wish to get to know a gentleman, you must make an effort to spend more time in his company. Phin is concerned that Mr Stedman might ask for repayment of your father's debts at any moment, particularly if he is made to wait too long for your answer.' She shook her head sadly. 'If only your father hadn't left the estate in such a mess, we wouldn't be in this position. You do understand, do you not?'

A pang of guilt twisted in Tess's chest. Until after his death, she'd had no idea Papa had borrowed a large sum money from Mr Stedman. Perhaps she could have helped him avoid such a thing if only she had known. Perhaps he would have avoided the accident with his gun.

Her blood ran cold. 'Yes, Wilhelmina. I do understand.'

A sly look crossed the other woman's face. 'Who was that gentlemen dressed as the grim reaper at the masquerade the other night? You never did say. You wasted a good deal of the evening in *his* company.'

Her stomach sank. 'I have no idea. I thought you knew him. He left before the unmasking. And it was only one dance.'

'You did go outside with him.'

'I also went outside with Mr Stedman.'

Wilhelmina pressed her lips tightly together for a moment. 'Well, I am glad we have had this little talk. I am sure you will do your utmost to assist your family. I will see you at dinner.'

Accepting her dismissal, Tess tidied up her needlework and traipsed up to her chamber. Now she was really in trouble. How was it Phin had recalled her mother's bracelet when he had not mentioned it once in the past year? If she was going to avoid marriage to Stedman, she needed to find Grey quickly.

'There is a person to see you, my lord.'

'A person?' Jaimie looked up from his paperwork and recoiled at the odd look on Rider's face. One of shocked indignation.

He frowned. Some of the men he employed at the agency were of the rough-and-ready sort, but none of them would come here to visit him. They would go to Growler by way of the back door. Growler was ostensibly his secretary and lived in. The butler no longer took any notice of Growler's comings and goings, much as he disapproved of the erstwhile bruiser.

'Did he give his name, Rider?'

'It is not a *he*, my lord.'

Jaimie pushed to his feet. 'A woman?'

Rider sniffed. 'A female, my lord, who refuses to state her business either to Growler or to me and refuses to leave without seeing you.' He coughed behind his hand. 'Growler thinks you will want to see her, but I can have a footman—'

'Growler thought...' It must be an informant. Jaimie raised a hand. 'I had best see her. Bring tea, would you, Rider?' He might as well take a proper break from what he was doing, now he had been interrupted, rather than continue to sit staring into space. 'Make sure you put biscuits on the tray.' Nothing like one of cook's biscuits to loosen an unwilling tongue.

'Very well, my lord.' He stepped back.

An oddly rotund figure in an old black woollen cloak, its hood drawn low so as to hide the wearer's face, sidled around the butler and into the room.

'Hey, you!' Rider said. 'I told you to wait.'

Jaimie let out a shocked laugh. 'It's all right, Rider. Fetch the tea, please.'

With a huff of annoyance, Rider departed, his whole demeanour imparting the silent news that if this sort of thing continued, a man of his dignity would be handing in his notice.

She pushed the hood back to reveal a floppy mob-cap. The only thing that looked the least bit like her was her face.

'Who are you supposed to be now, Lady Tess? I must say, I prefer Artemis.'

'Hah,' she said, but there was a smile in her eyes he had never seen before. A naughty smile that hit him low and tightened his body in places a gentleman was required to ignore in the presence of a lady.

She threw off the cloak and untied the sash holding two pillows, one at her front and the other in the small of her back. 'It's not funny. I am dashed hot.'

He tamped down the urge to smile. Fought the allure of her lush body. His first wife had been tall, elegant and slender, while Lady Tess was all soft curves and tempting dimples. But it seemed in temperament, the ladies were much the same. The last thing he wanted was to be drawn into Lady Tess's orbit.

He retreated into studied indifference. 'This really is beyond the pale, you know,' he said in bored tones.

'It was the only way to escape the house unnoticed.'

He frowned. 'That is not what I meant and you know it. No lady should visit a gentleman's abode in the middle of the night.' He glanced at the clock. 'Good heavens, girl, it's gone one in the morning.'

'I had to wait until everyone was asleep.' She grinned and he had to stop himself from grinning back. 'Also I thought I might be more likely to catch you at home after midnight.'

Naive child. In his wilder days, he'd rarely come home before three in the morning, and if he was home, she might have caught him at home with a houseful of guests enjoying themselves in ways no respectable lady should be aware of. These days, he preferred to spend his time in the conservatory, with his plants. He narrowed his eyes. 'Do you do this sort of thing often?'

'Not any more. When I was at school in Bath, I and

some of the other girls used to sneak out to get decent food, like cake and ice cream.'

'Good Lord! What a hoyden you are.'

She waved a dismissive hand. 'That is not important. Have you found Freeps?'

'As promised, I sent a man to Kent the moment I came back from our drive.'

'When do you expect his return?'

'Tomorrow or the day after. I had some other errands for him to perform while he was there.'

She shook her head and paced to his desk, picking up the silver letter opener and putting it down again. 'He will be too late.'

'What is the urgency?'

She stared at him. For a moment he thought she might tell him the whole story. She shook her head. 'Circumstances beyond my control.'

The worry in her eyes gave him pause. She wasn't the sort to worry. She was the sort to solve a problem. Case in point, her visiting him at his office and her arrival at his house tonight. A most irritating sort of a woman. The managing kind. Yet for some reason her expression of anxiety still troubled him. Hester, his first wife, had done things she wasn't supposed to just because someone told her she couldn't. Lady Tess, however, seemed to have a purpose behind her mad starts. For some reason far beyond rational thought, he wanted to uncover that purpose.

Rider brought in the tea tray. His eyebrows climbed to his hairline when he saw this new version of Jaimie's guest. He put the tray down with a decided bang. Cups and saucers rattled ominously.

Jaimie glared at his butler, but the man was right. This situation was completely improper and had to stop. And it would as soon as he'd solved the problem that had brought her to his door. 'Sit down. Have a cup of tea.'

'I can't stay long. Someone might go into my room and find Mims there instead of me.' But she did sit.

To his surprise, he liked the sight of her sitting in front of his teapot.

She gave him a startled look when he sat next to her rather than opposite. Dammit, she really was an innocent. If she had gone to any other man's house at such a late hour she might have discovered herself in serious difficulty.

He waited until she had poured the tea, had drunk it and eaten a biscuit. 'Perhaps you would like to tell me exactly what circumstances have changed?'

She put down her cup. 'Things are moving more quickly than I anticipated. Freeps may be able to put me in touch with someone I need to speak to. Urgently.'

'Then why not say so before? My messenger could have asked him for this other person's directions. Why are you being so dashed secretive?'

'Some secrets are not mine to tell.'

He stilled, instinct honing in not on the words, but the softening of her voice and the sadness in her expression.

'A man?' he asked, his voice icy. He should have seen this coming. This was just the sort of romantic idiocy Hester would have engaged in.

She swallowed, looking torn. He didn't care what came out of her mouth, a man was involved. And she was dragging him into the mess. Hester had played him for a fool more than once, and in the end it had caused her death. But he had learned his lesson far too well.

He stood up and carried the tea tray to his desk. 'I'm sorry, there is nothing more I can do. I will pass along the information regarding Freeps when my messenger returns and that will be an end to it. It is time for you to leave.'

When he turned back, she had risen. The look of betrayal in her remarkable brown eyes stopped him short. Against his better judgement, he gentled his tone. 'I cannot assist you in some sort of clandestine relationship, Lady Tess.'

Her gaze slid away. 'It is no such thing, I swear it! I cannot imagine why would you think so.'

He prowled towards her. 'Can you not?' Then he must make her understand. Give her a lecture of the avuncular sort. Point out the error of her ways, and the possible consequences…

But as he gazed into her lovely face, the words he sought escaped him.

She lifted her chin, gazing up at him with a tiny frown on her brow. Without another thought, he leaned closer and brushed his lips across the silk of her luscious mouth. Tasted the lush plump curve that had been a temptation from first sight.

Her lips parted on a gasp of shock, but she did not draw back. If anything, she leaned a little closer.

He firmed the kiss, lingering over the soft sweet

pressure of her mouth on his, feeling her body soften, hesitant and trembling, but eager. She made a small sound low in her throat, half moan, half something he couldn't name. He stroked a finger down her cheek, tasted her sigh.

He flicked his tongue along her bottom lip, a tiny little sip of innocence that was only a beginning.

Innocent.

He broke away, stifling a curse. What the devil was he thinking? The woman was far too alluring for her own good was what he was thinking.

She gazed at him wide-eyed. Her tongue touched her bottom lip in a brief exploration, as if she, too, could not quite believe what had occurred.

Should *not* have occurred.

'That is why you should not come to a gentleman's lodgings in the middle of the night. It could lead to something…untoward.' He kept his tone cool, but damn it all, his blood was running hot. And his breathing was nowhere as steady as it should have been. 'When my messenger returns I will give you the information you asked me to acquire. At that point I wash my hands of the whole business.'

With seeming difficulty, she regained control of her breathing. Good. He hoped she was suffering from the same sort of discomfort he was. Embarrassment, mostly.

Her shoulders straightened. 'I expected better behaviour from a gentleman.'

Typical. Now she was blaming him, as if he had invited her here. He glared at her. 'You should not go to any man's house without a chaperon if you place a smidgeon of value on your reputation.'

She turned her face away from him. 'Well I certainly won't do it again, will I?'

Dear God, was she going to cry? Guilt assailed him. Dammit, she was the one in the wrong, not him. But grudgingly, he found himself saying, 'Tell me who it is you actually seek, and I will decide whether or not to assist you further.' What the hell was he getting involved in?

She paused in picking up her cloak and threw him a glance of dislike. He gritted his teeth against the desire to apologise for his brusqueness.

'The friend from my childhood I spoke of at the masquerade.' Fury sparked in her eyes when he curled his lip. 'He is a friend. Nothing more.' Her hands clasped together at her waist, her knuckles showing white. 'He is in a position to assist me with a small problem.'

Hell and damnation. His horrified gaze went straight to her waist. 'What problem?'

She flushed. 'You are horrible, you know that? And it is none of your business. I simply need to find him.'

If she wasn't being so mysterious, he wouldn't be jumping to conclusions. He frowned. Perhaps she feared some sort of blackmail? A letter written to a lover? Something given away that did not belong to her?

Keeping such secrets always ended in disaster. 'You should ask for help from your cousin.'

'I cannot.'

This friend obviously meant a great deal to her if she was prepared to take such risks. Perhaps it was a friendship as she said, or perhaps it was more. He suspected the latter despite her denials. Clearly, though, she was not going to tell him anything more unless he could find a chink in her armour. 'What is the worst your cousin is likely to do, if you tell him? Send you to his aunt in Yorkshire?'

Her spine stiffened. 'Did you have to mention her?'

Trying to make her see sense was getting him nowhere. He couldn't think why he was bothering. 'I will send you a note the moment I have the information you seek.'

'No. My cousin will wonder...'

Now she cared about the proprieties. He smiled a grim smile. 'And now you know the reason your family tries to protect you.'

She coloured, no doubt recalling their kiss.

'Well then, what engagement do you have tomorrow night?' he asked.

She looked startled.

'I am invited to all the best places, you know.' He swallowed the urge to chuckle at her look of chagrin. 'I promise you, I will be discreet.'

'We are to attend Lady Bloomfield's musicale tomorrow evening.'

'Very good. I will see you there. In the meantime, let me get you back into your disguise and send you home in my carriage. You should not be wandering the streets at this time of the morning.'

She gasped. 'I couldn't possibly arrive in your carriage. Someone might see it.'

This time he laughed. 'Do you think I am not up to

snuff when it comes to intrigue? My dear Lady Tess, the carriage will be unmarked and it will drop you around the corner from your cousin's house, but my driver will ensure you go inside before he leaves.' He'd make sure Growler drove her home. He would find the location of this Freeps and that would be an end of the imbroglio. He had enough going on in his life, without adding the problem of a woman who didn't trust him an inch.

Thank goodness when he decided to take a wife again, it would be a nice, quiet girl who would be happy embroidering handkerchiefs, producing his heirs and behaving herself with decorum. He wished he'd married a woman like that the first time. A woman more like his mother. A faint bedtime memory of a sweet voice singing drifted across his mind. He tried to recall her face, but it drifted away like smoke on a breeze.

Bitterness filled him. He had so few memories of his parents and they were getting more and more elusive. Forcing his mind back to the present, he picked up the sash and one of the pillows. 'Come on, then. Let's get you ready.'

The sooner she left, the sooner he could get back to what was important.

And yet as he tied the sash around her now bulky form his unruly body expressed a strong desire to take her out of her clothes, not bundle her up.

Dammit.

Chapter Four

The Bloomfield music room was full to bursting. Seated in a row near the front, only by sheer willpower did Tess squash the urge to look over her shoulder to see where Sandford was seated.

'Sit still, Theresa,' Wilhelmina hissed. She glanced worriedly at the man on Tess's other side, the man whom Phin wanted her to marry. Somewhere in his late thirties, Mr Stedman wasn't much taller than Tess, and his pale complexion and portly figure spoke of a sedentary life. Fortunately, at the moment he seemed oblivious to everything but the young lady playing the harp. A most uninspired performance in Tess's estimation, but perhaps she was not in the mood for music. She nibbled her bottom lip. Would Sandford keep his promise? And if so, how would he manage to speak to her without attracting attention?

The piece finally concluded to polite applause.

'Brava!' Stedman called out. Several people turned to stare, but he seemed oblivious to that, too. He half-turned in his seat. 'A fine example of the young lady's talent, Lady Theresa. When might I have the pleasure of hearing you play or sing?'

When the sun ceases rising above the horizon?

'Theresa has a lovely voice,' Wilhelmina hastened to say. 'Perhaps when you have dinner with us next week she will oblige us.'

Tess gritted her teeth at their insistence on using her full name. Could she really stand listening to her name spoken in that precise way for the rest of her life? She might not have a choice if Grey couldn't be found. And even he was located he might be unable or unwilling to assist… She forced the doubt aside. Grey would not let her down again. He must only have meant to borrow the bracelet, perhaps to pawn? Surely he would have intended to redeem it as soon as possible and return it to her?

'Refreshments are served in the Egyptian drawing room,' their hostess announced from the front of the room.

Mr Stedman offered his arm and, along with the rest of the guests, they shuffled along their respective row and were herded out of the gilt music-room doors. The invitation had spoken of a select gathering, but to Tess it looked as if every member of the *ton* were present. All except Sandford. Dratted man.

Mr Stedman hissed out a breath. 'Lady Theresa. My arm. Your grip.'

She loosened her hold. 'I beg your pardon.'

He patted her hand where it now rested lightly on his sleeve. 'Do not fear, I shall protect you.'

He couldn't protect a rabbit. A baby one. She smiled

absently, scanning the faces around her, but given her lack of inches she could not see beyond those standing closest.

The drawing room proved to be a nightmare of overcrowded heavily carved furniture representing all manner of strange beasts, such as crocodiles and ibis. One had to be careful not to bark one's shins on sharp claws or beaks while manoeuvring around the people crammed inside.

'I must congratulate Lady Bloomfield on her daughter's performance,' Wilhelmina said. She swanned off in a rustle of royal-blue silk.

'I shall get us some tea,' Mr Stedman announced. 'Wait right here.'

Was she to pretend to be a statue? Tess inched out of the centre of the room to stand beside a low table by a window.

Finally, she could breathe. And have a proper look about her.

'Lady Tess.'

She nearly jumped out of her skin at the sound of Sandford's voice so close to her ear and the light graze of his breath across the top of her shoulder.

'Lord Sandford! You startled me.'

'You were expecting me, were you not?'

'Yes, but—' She glanced up into his haughty expression. 'Do you have to creep up on a person?'

Her heart sped up. Because he had startled her—nothing else. And if the recollection of his kiss had flashed into her mind, it was only to remind her to be extremely careful around this man.

He gave a soft laugh. 'One would be hard pressed to sneak about in here.'

That low laugh made butterflies take wing in her lower abdomen. So annoying. She glanced towards the teacart. Mr Stedman was on his way back with two teacups in one hand and a plate of biscuits in the other.

'Do you have news for me, my lord?' She kept her voice low in case anyone was listening, but could not keep the urgency out of her tone.

His eyes were sympathetic. He had no reason for sympathy, unless… Her stomach dipped.

'Excuse me.' Mr Stedman thrust a teacup and saucer at Tess. 'Lady Theresa, your tea. I put plenty of sugar in it.'

Of course he would. She usually only took cream, but he'd made her tea the way he liked his.

And how had he moved so quickly through the crowded room? She ground her teeth in frustration. 'Mr Stedman, may I introduce you to Lord Sandford?'

Her swain visibly brightened. He set the plate down on a nearby table, and with an overly friendly expression reached out to shake Sandford's hand, pumping as if it would cause nobility to spill forth and anoint him. 'Please to meet you, my lord. Very pleased.'

Tess sipped at her tea, naughtily wondering how the stiff nobleman would handle such an effusive greeting.

Sandford raised an eyebrow. 'Stedman.' An awkward pause ensued.

Stedman swallowed down a sip of tea. 'What about this business of Ireland, then, my lord? Damn lot of Catholics wanting the same rights as Protestants.

Divisive, I call it. Taking positions that belong to good Christian men.'

'Truly, sir?' Sandford looked down his nose. 'Personally, some of my best friends are of the Catholic persuasion and are all able men and certainly Christian.' Sandford's gaze shifted to her. 'What is your opinion on the issue, Lady Tess?'

Tess tried to hide her surprise. He wanted her opinion? But the mocking curve to his lips gave him away. No doubt he wanted to make her say something she would regret.

Stedman's face darkened. He put up a hand to forestall her answer. 'Lady Theresa thinks as her cousin thinks, I should suppose.'

Rebellion rose inside her. 'I think people should be judged by what they do rather than because of their religious leanings.'

Mr Stedman looked so affronted that she wished she had held her tongue. And then she didn't. Now she really was getting to know him better, the idea of being married to this man was becoming more and more distasteful. 'Lord Sandford?' she enquired sweetly.

'I agree wholeheartedly, Lady Tess.'

'*Theresa,*' Mr Stedman muttered. 'Lady Theresa.' He glared at Sandford.

Tess took a sip of tea to hide her smile of triumph, poor victory though it might have been.

A bored expression passed across Sandford's face. He bowed. 'If you will excuse me, my lady, I see an acquaintance.' He wandered off and the next moment was deeply engrossed in conversation with Lord Canning, a known supporter of Catholic emancipation.

Tess swallowed a laugh at the look of fury on Mr Stedman's face. Oh dear, she really was beginning to dislike him very much indeed. How very awkward.

'You may smile, Lady Theresa,' he said stiffly, 'but one expects a man in his position to set an example, not go about inciting unrest. Next thing he'll be supporting the idea that women should have a say in Parliament. I would have thought better of a friend of the King's. And as for you supporting such reactionary views, well, I am shocked. Mother would be most dismayed.'

She opened her mouth to issue a set-down, then closed it again, with the greatest difficulty. One could hardly cause a scene, like refusing a proposal as yet to be made, in such a public place, but, oh, she hoped Sandford had good news. A feeling of dread in her stomach promised something else.

A servant near the door rang a bell.

'Time to return to our seats,' she said.

'Yes, indeed. Come along, Lady Theresa. We don't want to lose our places.'

She wanted to lose *him* with all her heart.

As they moved towards the music room, she glimpsed Sandford paying close attention to the words of a most elegant female. Tall and willowy and blonde, she was exactly the sort of woman men preferred. Her heart seemed to dip and that was ridiculous. She was disappointed that they hadn't had a chance to talk, that was all.

The only reason to even notice Sandford existed, she told herself, was that she needed to find Grey.

The evils of her situation suddenly felt unbearable. With her father's death her life had turned upside down and her expectations had changed dramatically. If only things could go back to the way they were before that day, life would once again be perfect.

A childish wish for things that could never be. She had to find her own solutions now.

She glanced at Stedman and repressed a little shudder.

While he listened to Lady Caroline with half an ear, Jaimie watched Lady Tess walk out of the drawing room on Stedman's arm. Why on earth would a woman as lively and intelligent as she put up with such an idiot? The way the man put a hand in the small of her back as he ushered her out of the room exhibited a possessiveness Jaimie found distasteful in the extreme. Devil take it. Lady Tess was none of his business. And once he delivered his news, his obligation was at an end.

If only she had not looked quite so trapped when Stedman had handed her that cup of tea, he might have been able to ignore his instinctive urge to remove her from the man's presence. He knew what it was like to be trapped by physical weakness. He'd wanted to applaud her spirit when she had stood up to the man and to plant Stedman a facer when his rebuke caused her to shrink. To make matters worse, he had yet to deliver his bad news to her. He should have blurted out the information and left it at that. Case closed. But the dread in her eyes as he began to speak made him think she had already guessed the news was not good. He hadn't thought he was that transparent.

He certainly wasn't going to give her bad news in front of Stedman.

Dammit, why did he care? She was nothing to him. Right now he should be in his office interviewing victims of crimes, or following up with fraudulent lawyers, not standing around in a drawing room. *A lady deserves protection*, whispered the familiar voice in his ear.

Dash it. Lady Tess needed protection from herself and it should be performed by a member of her own family. She'd already distracted him for two days and he still didn't know why she needed to find this childhood friend so desperately. He hated unanswered questions. It was what made him good at what he did; the need to ferret out answers when others did not realise there was even a question. Until he found the answer to the mystery of Lady Tess, her problem would continue to force its way into his mind at inconvenient moments. Once he had the answer he would go back to matters of real importance. Like the robberies in Mayfair.

He smiled at whatever Lady Caroline had said. She made a sound of annoyance and turned her head as if to see who had caught his attention. He deliberately shifted his focus to another young lady.

'Sandford,' Lady Caroline said. 'You are hopeless.' She shook her head and walked away.

Clearly she thought he was some sort of lothario. A complete misapprehension, but he grabbed the opportunity to jot a note on his calling card before making his way through the press of people returning to the music room, where he saw, with satisfaction, that Lady

Rowan was deep in conversation with her hostess and moving only slowly towards her seat.

Jaimie slipped into the seat beside Lady Tess. When she realised it was he, she gave a little start and shot him a glance full of annoyance.

He smiled back. 'Lady Tess.'

Her escort frowned. 'That is Lady Rowan's seat.'

'I'll be sure to give it up should she arrive, but I believe she has chosen to sit with our hostess.' He pulled his programme from his pocket. 'I see we are to have the pleasure of listening to the Severn sisters sing a duet. Do you sing, Lady Tess?'

Her escort cleared his throat. 'I am assured Lady Theresa has a lovely voice.'

A cool draught wafted through the room. Some kind soul had opened a window.

Lady Tess, in her filmy off-the-shoulder gown, gave a little shiver.

'Where is your wrap, Lady Theresa?' Stedman asked in a disapproving voice.

Lady Tess gave him a strained smile. 'I did not bring one.'

He puffed up his chest. 'You should always bring a shawl, Lady Theresa. One never knows when it might be needed. Mama says a lady should never be without her shawl.' He eyed her gown disapprovingly.

For a moment Jaimie thought the pompous ass might also make some disparaging remark about her gown's deliciously revealing design. His shoulders tensed. He really would like to plant Stedman a facer.

'Your mother sounds very wise,' Lady Tess said

calmly. 'I look forward to meeting her. Is she always so perceptive?'

'She is indeed,' Stedman agreed, clearly diverted. He chuntered on about the wisdom of his mother while Jaimie exchange a glance of…of something, possibly amusement, with Lady Tess.

'I am sure she will be able to provide you with instruction when we are wed,' Stedman smugly finished up his discourse.

A cold hand fisted in Jaimie's gut. So that was how things stood. No wonder she was tolerating the man's inanity. He should have realised.

He became aware of the tension radiating through the woman beside him. Of the clenching of her jaw. Clearly, she was not happy about Stedman's declaration. Indeed, now he thought about it, the words seemed to be issued as something of threat and he grimly recalled her telling him at the masquerade that this Season was her last chance to *oblige* her family.

'Am I to offer my congratulations, Lady Tess?' he asked, raising an eyebrow.

'Nothing has yet been finalised, my lord,' she said stiffly.

'But it will be,' Stedman added with a possessive note in his voice and a smug gleam in his eye.

Instead of feeling relief that with the acquisition of a fiancé he would soon be able to forget all about Lady Tess and her problems, he was startled to realise the determination to get to the bottom of exactly why she had sought his help in the first place had only strengthened.

At the front of the room, the Severn girls sang the

chorus for the second time and Jaimie sat back in his chair, shifting slightly, folding his arms across his chest. He poked Tess's upper arm with the edge of his card.

She gasped and glanced down.

He wiggled the card, held in his fingertips.

Understanding flashed across her face and a moment later she snagged the card and was sliding it into her reticule. She didn't even give it so much as a glance. Clever girl.

The young ladies at the front of the room continued to enchant their audience. Now he recalled why he rarely attended this sort of entertainment. It was a painful reminder of similar events when his mother was alive. Times when he'd listened from out in the hallway because he was too young to enter into polite company.

His mother had known he was there and always left the door slightly ajar. He found himself smiling at the recollection of her conspiratorial act, though in the end it had been her undoing. The presence of the young lady at his side made it difficult to focus on the past. The way the neck of her gown skimmed the luscious swells of her creamy skin above her neckline battled for his attention.

Damn it all. Why were those precious memories fading so rapidly?

A disturbance at the end of the row heralded the arrival of Lady Rowan. 'It appears your cousin has returned,' he murmured into Lady Tess's ear, inhaling a last lungful of her lovely lavender scent.

She shivered.

Ah. So she was not quite so indifferent towards him as she made out. He felt a surge of satisfaction and rose to his feet, turning a genial smile on Lady Rowan. 'I beg your pardon, my lady, is this your seat?'

'It is,' the woman said, clearly refusing to be charmed.

He edged out of the row to allow her to sit down and walked out of the music room.

Once she had a chance to read his note, the next move was up to Lady Tess.

And why did he hope that she would take him up on his offer?

Dash it, this was so unnecessary. Tess had finished dressing slightly earlier than usual this morning, knowing the servants were fully occupied with their chores below stairs. At a time when she knew Carver would be most put out if she asked for an escort.

If Sandford had been unable to locate Freeps, why had he not simply said so? Why the mysterious note that he would meet her on her usual morning walk? And how did he know she walked every morning?

Against her better judgement, she slipped silently down the stairs and out of the front door. The rain from last night glistened on the flagstones, but there were big patches of blue overhead, allowing the sun's rays to steal into the streets and gild brass door knockers and puddles alike. Marching towards Green Park, she squinted against the glare and enjoyed the breeze along with the false sense of freedom.

When she'd first awoken, she'd half-hoped she could

use the rain as an excuse not to meet Sandford. The man made her feel too…unlike herself. It was the only way to describe it. If she wasn't feeling hot, then she felt cold when he looked at her or came close to her, or frowned at her. It was all the fault of that brief, shocking kiss. Too brief, if her desire to do it again was anything to go by.

How could one trust a man whose kisses made her feel so…so wanton? She flushed hot just thinking about those sensations.

Blast, that was not what she should be thinking about. More to the point, what if he told Phin what she'd been up to? To an outsider, her cousin had been more than fair, given that Father had left her nothing in his will. Her cousin had footed the bill for her come-out and all the clothes and fripperies that went with it. As much as she hated it, he was even trying to find her a husband willing to accept her without a dowry. If Phin found out, he'd be furious at her lack of gratitude and pack her straight off to Yorkshire.

Her best hope was that Grey had used the bracelet as collateral to get him started in some venture and not followed in her father's footsteps and just gambled it away. He knew she had been hiding it from Papa as a means of staving off the bailiffs should it become necessary. He could not have been so mean as to intend to steal it outright. She hoped.

Once she had it back, Phin would be able to use it to pay off the last of her father's debts and all would be well. No more need for her to marry anyone in haste. Perhaps there would even be enough left over to give her a small competence of her own. Maybe she could even go and live with Grey and keep his house...?

But if he had sold the bracelet? Then she would never forgive him. It would be the ultimate betrayal.

She entered the Park through the gate near the Queen's Walk and strolled towards the pond. Her usual route. Where on earth was Sandford? Finally she spotted a tall, lithe figure sauntering towards her and breathed a sigh of relief.

He removed his hat and bowed when their paths crossed as if by accident. He glanced about with a frown. 'Where is your maid?'

Startled, she stared at him. 'Really? You think an assignation would be less scandalous if I brought my maid along?'

His lips tightened. 'My dear girl, this is not an assignation, merely a chance meeting. Now you leave me no choice but to escort you home.'

'Really, there is no need. As you say, it is a chance meeting. We will simply part when we reach the street.'

He looked thoroughly annoyed.

'I often walk on my own. No one will think anything of it.'

'Well, they should,' he said, his tone frosty. He held out his arm. 'Please, Lady Tess, we are drawing unwanted attention. Let us walk.'

The only people here were a couple of goose girls and a few cows. She sighed and took his arm. They walked in silence for a moment.

'My man was unable to speak to Mr Freeps.'

Her stomach sank. 'I see.'

'Well?' he said.

'Well, what?'

An elegant eyebrow shot up. 'You were to tell me the full story before I imparted the information I have gathered. One way or another I will get to the bottom of it, so you might as well tell me now.'

'I suppose you will go to my guardian if I do not.'

Silence greeted her words. When she glanced at his face, she beheld a grim expression. He pressed his lips together as if he would not answer, then shook his head slightly. 'Lady Tess, I am no tattletale. I will merely employ the resources at my disposal to discover that which you refuse to reveal.'

As if he could. But, oh, it would be so nice to talk to someone apart from Mims, who merely listened, nodded and said nothing helpful apart from *it will all be all right, you will see, my lady.*

She inhaled a deep breath. Took the plunge. 'I wanted to ask Freeps if he had any idea where I might find my... my cousin, Greydon Hammond. I need his help with a personal matter.'

His gaze searched her face as if he could see into her mind. 'My informant tells me Hammond left your home shortly after your father died. Under some sort of cloud. What help could he provide that your cousin Rowan cannot?'

She froze. Stopped stock still. Fear and anger warring in her chest. 'Your informant? You have been poking around in my family business?' She gripped her parasol tighter. 'I suppose that is how you knew about my morning walks.' Anger running hot in her veins at his intrusion, she turned and marched back the way she had come.

His long legs easily kept pace. 'I am an investigator, Lady Tess. It is what I do. Why you came to me. My people are trained to do the same.'

Heaven help her, the man was a menace. Going to him had been a terrible mistake. She quelled the urge to hit him over the head with her parasol. 'Well, you are not very good at what you do, or you would have found my father's old bailiff, Freeps.'

'I beg your pardon? The man died months ago. How is that a failure on my part?'

Freeps was *dead*? The breath rushed from her lungs. Guilt ached in her chest. She should have sought Grey out sooner. Now she would never find him and the sense of loss had nothing to do with a stupid diamond bracelet. She took a deep steadying breath and forced calm into her voice. 'I am sorry to hear that he died, though he was very old, I know. It is a good thing my reason for seeking him out is of no great importance.' The last thing she wanted was a terrible hue and cry, with the Runners chasing after Grey for taking her bracelet.

He shot her a clearly disbelieving look. 'It mattered a great deal, if it brought you to my house in the dead of night.'

She longed to tell him the truth. Yearned to do so. Keeping all her worries locked inside left her exhausted, unable to sleep. Her worry about Grey. Her father's debts passed along to Rowan. Yet how could she reveal such scandalous family secrets to a stranger?

If she was honest, there never really was any hope

of escaping marriage to Mr Stedman. Yet still she was loath to give up and do nothing to try to save herself from such a fate.

How much information did she dare impart? It would have to be enough to satisfy Sandford's curiosity or he would never leave her in peace. 'Grey has something of mine he promised to return. Unfortunately, he and I lost touch.' The latter hurt far worse than anything. Grey had been such a large part of her life growing up. In the end, Father had treated him very badly, indeed. Still, even if he no longer had the bracelet, he could at least have written and let her know how he did. He was the only real family she had left that she actually cared about.

'I see.'

'What do you see?'

'That this young man must have taken advantage of you in some way.'

Why did he have to think the worst of everyone and look at her in that cynical way, as if she was some sort of gullible fool? It was most annoying. 'You are wrong. I loaned him something of my own free will.' She would have, had he asked.

He said nothing for a moment or two. 'And you would like its return?'

'It would be nice, but it is not important.'

'Perhaps if I knew what this item was, I could be of some assistance.'

'Why do you insist on wanting to help me now, when you wanted nothing to do with me before?'

He looked a little puzzled at her question. 'It is a gentleman's duty to offer a lady his assistance.'

'And if the lady does not want to be helped?'

He gazed down at her. 'Lady Tess, it is obvious to me you are in some sort of difficulty when you go sneaking around without your family's knowledge.'

'I do not go sneaking around.'

He raised a brow.

Her face heated. Dash it, she had been a little underhanded. And the last thing she wanted was him going to Phin. While Sandford had promised to keep her confidence, he was a man and they had their own stupid code which did not stretch to keeping their promises to females. He might see it as his duty, his manly honour, to bring the matter to her cousin's attention when it was nobody's business what she did with her own property. 'I believe my cousin intends the item to be included in my marriage settlements. It will be awkward if I do not have it.'

His face remained impassive, but she sensed a tension in his shoulders that had not been there before. 'It must be an extremely valuable item then.'

She sighed. She was going to have to tell him. 'It is a diamond bracelet.'

He frowned. 'Well, if you need to locate someone, the best place to start is where they were seen last.'

Her jaw dropped. 'You really will help me?'

He hesitated and she held her breath. 'A man should always pay his debts.' Though he sounded utterly bored, an accusation ran through his words.

'Grey would never intentionally let me down.'

His lips tightened in disapproval. She tried to ignore it. 'The last place I saw him was at my father's estate,

Ingram Manor. I left there a few weeks after my father died. The new Earl prefers his own house in Sussex.' She sighed. She missed the old place. 'I cannot blame him. The estate is in a sad state of disrepair.' Her father having gambled away every scrap of income... 'I thought Grey might have made contact with Freeps. They were friends of a sort.' The bailiff had been kind to Grey, taken him under his wing during Papa's frequent absences.

'And this bracelet,' Sandford went on, 'is it your personal property? Not part of the estate?'

She glared at him. 'Do you think I am some sort of thief?'

'Lady Tess,' he said gently. 'I assume nothing. I am merely gathering all the facts.'

'The bracelet was my mother's and was left to me.'

'Very well. I will visit Kent tomorrow, to see what I can discover about your...friend.'

His offer seemed too good to be true. Did he have some sort of ulterior motive? And would he impart the information he discovered to her or to Phin? 'I will meet you there.'

His jaw dropped.

She steeled herself for an argument.

Chapter Five

What the devil was he doing? He'd met the lady to give her what news he had and then wash his hand of the whole business and here he was offering to help her further out of some sort of misplaced sympathy. Who would not feel sympathy for a woman required to marry the social-climbing Stedman?

The idea that she would arrange yet another assignation with him however was unacceptable. 'My dear Lady Tess, I assure you, that will not be necessary.'

'I am not your dear,' she snapped.

He recoiled at her waspish tone. Lord knew she wasn't his dear and never could be. He couldn't imagine how such an endearment had slipped out. 'I beg your pardon. Merely a figure of speech, you understand, however the answer remains the same.'

'Without me you are unlikely to garner any information. Country people never talk to strangers.'

She had something there, but he had no intention of being alone with her again. He found her just too tempting. 'I have my methods, Lady Tess. I am no neophyte at the business of eliciting information from people. Besides, your cousin is hardly likely to agree to our meeting at so remote a location.'

She waved a dismissive hand. 'Oh, I don't plan to tell him about meeting you. I have quite another reason for travelling to Kent. I need to collect some items left behind.'

'Surely Rowan would send a servant on such an errand.'

'They are personal items. I will bring my maid, so you have no need for concern. We can meet quite by chance.'

He didn't like it.

She lifted her chin. 'I am going first thing tomorrow morning whether you agree or not.'

He could go today and spike her guns, but, dammit, she was right, her presence might well make it easier to gather information. As long as she had her maid with her and had her cousin's permission to be there...and there would be a coachman and a footman, too... 'Very well, Lady Tess. We will meet in Farningham, which I understand is the nearest village to Ingram Manor. You will offer to show me your home, but we will not be alone for a single moment.'

'Perfect.' A smile broke out on her face.

She went from irritated to lovely in a heartbeat and an odd sort of softening sensation happened in his chest. A feeling he couldn't recall ever having felt before, not even for Hester. She'd always left him feeling worried, yet intrigued, ready for some new adventure.

This sensation left him with nothing to say, as if his brain had turned to porridge.

And while he fumbled around for yet another reason she should not go, she waved an airy hand. 'I will see you tomorrow, Lord Sandford.' With that, she set off down the path.

He contemplated hurrying after her, arguing and offering his escort, but to be seen chasing after her would only attract more attention and that he did not want. He meandered slowly towards Horse Guards Parade instead. What on earth would his papa have advised in such a situation? He racked his brain. Unfortunately, not only could he not recall any advice from his father that would fit this particular situation, but thoughts of Lady Tess's distress, which she had tried to so hard to hide, kept pushing his father into the background.

There was something about this Grey Hammond that did not ring true. Perhaps Growler could shed a little more light on the chap.

His thoughts went back to the intensity of her relief when he had offered his help. Her relief and her beautiful smile. Surely he wasn't falling for her female wiles? He didn't even like her. Well, it wasn't that he disliked her, it was simply that he didn't approve of the things she did.

But he did feel a sneaking sense of admiration for her.

Not a good thing at all.

He picked up his pace, striding swiftly through the streets until he reached his Lincoln's Inn chambers, where he found Growler reading *The Times*. Something he did every morning before he started his day.

'Growler, a word,' Jaimie said, hanging up his hat.

'Yes, me lord.' He lumbered into Jaimie's office a few moments later. After a quick glance at Jaimie's face, he closed the door.

Jaimie smiled. Growler was one of those few people who could tell with a glance what was required. 'Sit down.'

Growler perched his bulk on the edge of the chair where Tess had sat only a few days before.

'Tell me about Greydon Hammond.'

Growler scratched at his chin with a surprisingly well-manicured though misshapen finger. 'Grew up as part of the old Earl's household. A cousin of a cousin. Bit of a rackety lad when he got older according to the landlord. The new Earl threw him out. Told him he could work in the stables and earn his bread.'

Hmmm, a little harsh to treat a blood relative like that. He wondered what had really caused Rowan to throw out the boy.

'He and Lady Tess?'

'Thick as thieves up to the old lord's passing. The old man treated him like a son, it was said. He left a few days before she came home from Bath from a visit to a relative. They say she was nigh on prostrate after her father died.'

'He was definitely some sort of cousin, you say?'

'Landlord at the Flying Frog said that was what he had heard, but he hasn't been there long. Bought out the old landlord.'

'Anything else?'

'No, me lord. When I tried talking to some of the

customers they got proper quiet like.' He shook his head. 'Most unfriendly, even after I bought them a pint. Seemed to be hiding something.'

Damnation, everyone seemed to be hiding something. Including Tess.

'I'm going down there tomorrow. To visit the house.'

'Won't find much there, except an old deaf caretaker. All the servants were turned off not long after Lady Tess moved into her cousin's household.'

'I see.'

The trouble was, so far he saw absolutely nothing.

The village of Farningham was just as Tess remembered. Her life had changed so much over the past year or so, happiness welled inside her chest at the old sights and sounds of the beloved village with its river running through the centre and the houses crowded along its edge. Thank heavens some things never changed. She sniffed and surreptitiously wiped away a tear.

'You might well weep, missy,' Mims said from her corner. 'Your pa must be turning over in his grave.'

Mims, who labelled herself a Maid of Kent, had been her mother's maid and, if the elderly lady was to be believed, her grandmother's before that. Old and crotchety and very dear, she could scarce see to thread a needle now, but she was Tess's last link to this place and to her beloved family.

'If Papa hadn't gambled…'

'Your pa was never the same after your mother died.' The woman pressed her wrinkled lips together. They had had this conversation before, but in Tess's eyes nothing could excuse her father's behaviour.

The coach pulled up at the Flying Frog and the footman let down the steps and helped Tess down.

She looked about her for Sandford. Dratted man was nowhere to be seen. No doubt he'd thought better of his offer. And she was glad of it, too. A night of reflection had her thinking that telling him anything had been a mistake. The excuse to come and collect her bracelet because she needed it for her marriage settlements had been inspired. What need did she have for Lord Sandford when she could do her own questioning, likely with better results?

'Mims, please go in and order lunch for Coachy as well as Rob and yourself. I am going to take a little walk.'

'You'll be needing to eat, too, my lady,' Mims said with a stern frown.

'Oh, indeed, yes. Order for me, too. I won't be long. I need to stretch my legs.'

'Going up to the house, are you? I ought to be a-going with you.' Mims hobbled a few steps. The poor dear had terrible trouble with her feet.

'No, Mims. I am not in need of a chaperon here. Papa never insisted upon it.'

Mims winced, but nodded. 'Your Pa was a sensible man.' Her hazel eyes twinkled. 'Up to a point. Off you go then, but be more than an hour and I'll be sending a searching party.'

'Oh, I shan't be gone so long, I promise.'

Mims turned about and hobbled into the inn. Tess

began the mile walk to Ingram Manor. As she strode along the road, several people dipped curtsies or lifted their hats, bidding her good day with real pleasure.

Her heart beat faster in anticipation and worry at the thought of seeing her old home. Might this be the last time she would ever set eyes on it? Certainly Cousin Phin had no use for the place and intended to sell it when the entailment expired. The thought of her home passing out of the family hurt. For all his faults, Papa would have hated the idea.

A gentleman leaning against the bridge's parapet straightened and walked towards her. A handsome, tall, rakish-looking gentleman. Lord Sandford! He had kept his word after all. Her heart gave an erratic little hop. Surely she wasn't that glad to see him? But she was. Her whole self had lit up with pleasure. Nor could she contain her smile as he sauntered towards her in his usual loose-limbed graceful manner.

'Lady Tess.' He doffed his hat and bowed.

'Lord Sandford, what a surprise.'

His expression was not in the least pleased. Indeed, it was most disapproving. 'Where is your maid?'

Oh, that. What a fusspot he was about the proprieties. 'She is in the inn, ordering lunch. I thought I would take a stroll. You have no need to worry for my safety. I am well known here.'

'Indeed.' If anything, his frown seemed to deepen.

'Shall we go up to the house?' she said before he could start another of his lectures. 'Grey might have left a message with one of the servants.'

Sandford shook his head. 'There is only a caretaker up there, according to Growler.'

'Growler?'

'My associate. You met him at my chambers.'

'Oh, him. What an odd name to be sure. While I can quite see why he might be called that, with that roughened voice of his, I do not believe it can be his real name.'

'It is the name he goes by.'

'Oh, like a *nom de plume.*' She frowned. 'There must be other servants at the house. I know it is closed, but there must be a maid or two. The gardener.'

'Growler said not.'

Could things have really got so bad? She picked up her pace. If no one was caring for the house...

They entered the gate beyond the village and walked down the drive between the line of elms. Such pretty trees. But the long grass on the lawn and the weeds growing amid the gravel was not a good sign. And then, there it was. Ingram Manor, a Tudor house with a moat running all the way around the outside of the crenellated walls.

The formal garden was also full of weeds and the house had a forlorn air of abandonment. She glanced up at Sandford, expecting to see an I-told-you-so expression on his face, but he looked unhappy, too.

'I don't understand why my cousin would let it go to rack and ruin like this,' she said sadly.

'It is a shame. It is an extraordinary place.'

They crossed the drawbridge, which was really just part of the drive, the old mechanism having been done away with more than a hundred years before, and entered the courtyard. The house seemed to fold its arms around her as it always had when she was a child, making her feel safe and protected. The tension in her shoulders fell away and she beamed up at the mullioned windows. Home. It still felt like home.

Sandford strode to the front door and rapped on it with the head of his cane.

'Oh,' she said. 'There is a bell.' She turned the handle. By way of a series of pulleys that worked the string attached to the handle, it rang a bell in the kitchen.

A few moments later the sound of shuffling feet grew closer and the door swung back.

A bent elderly man with wisps of hair clinging to his bald pate peered out at them. 'There ain't no one home and, no, you can't look round the house neither.'

'Excuse me, this is my house.' She could not keep the indignation from her voice.

'No 'tain't. Belongs to Lord Rowan and you ain't him,' the man said, narrowing his eyes on Sandford.

'This,' Lord Sandford said loftily, 'is Lady Tess Ingram. She was born in this house, fellow. And I am Lord Sandford. Stand aside and let her in.'

Tess wanted to kiss him. If he hadn't looked quite so haughty at that moment, she might have done so, too.

The fellow stepped back, if not exactly welcoming them inside, then at least letting them pass.

'What is your name?' Sandford asked.

'Leggat, my lord. I been here for nigh on a year. Caretaker.'

'Leggat? Husband to Mrs Leggat the housekeeper?' Tess asked.

The man peered at her again. 'Jenny's my daughter, my lady. When the new Earl said there was no work for her here, she convinced him to hire me to look after the place while she went off to work at the vicarage. Much in demand was my Jenny. Not that there's much I can do here except scare off the village children when they come around. And keep the nosey parkers outside. So you're Lady Tess. Jenny told me about you. Said you'd come back sooner or later. Are you going to buy the old place? Fix it up?'

She gasped. 'It is for sale already? What about the entail…?'

'Sale or rent, though there's been no interest as far as I know. A buyer would have to wait a bit for the entail to end, I suppose.'

Tess's head spun. She had known this might happen, but deep in her heart she hoped it would not. And for it to be happening so soon… 'Ingram Manor has been in our family for more than two hundred years.'

'And you're the last of them.'

She sank on to the nearest chair, the hard wooden one used by the porter in the old days.

'There used to be a young gentleman living here, a Mr Hammond, Leggat,' Sandford said. 'Did you ever hear tell of him?'

Leggat scratched an ear, then his nose. 'I heard my daughter talk of him. A distant relative. Randy young gentleman always after the maids.'

Tess winced. 'It was just a phase. Papa said all young men go through it. He never…' Oh, this was not something she should be speaking of and it was a phase that had not lasted long after Papa took Grey to task over it. The unfortunate part of it being that Tess had seen him in a corner with a maid and had asked Papa what they could possibly have been doing together.

Sandford had wandered farther along the black-and-white-diamond-patterned tiled floor of the great hall, and stopped to look up at the arching hammer beams holding up the roof.

'Have you or your daughter heard from my cousin, Grey, at all?' Tess asked Leggat quietly.

'Not a word,' Leggat said. 'Jenny was surprised. She'd taken the lad to her heart... Felt sorry for the little bastard.' He coughed and shuffled his feet. 'Beggin' your pardon, my lady,' he mumbled.

Sandford had moved on to the fireplace. He gave them a sharp look and strode back, 'What is wrong?'

The old fellow shrugged. 'Servants' gossip, my lord. Should not have repeated it.'

Tess sighed. 'What is the point of pretending any more? I know Grey was likely my father's illegitimate son and not my cousin.'

'Aah,' old Leggat said, wagging a gnarled and bent finger. 'My Jenny always said you were as bright as you could stare. No secret safe around you.'

True. She had overheard Grey and Papa arguing one day, because she had wondered why Grey had asked to speak with Papa privately. When Grey accused Papa of being his father, she had been shocked and then thrilled when Papa yelled right back that it was possibly true. Then shocked again when Papa said he didn't know for sure, given that Grey's mother was a damned whore.

She'd had to look the meaning of the word up in the dictionary.

It had come as quite a surprise. She'd loved the idea of a brother, though he was never acknowledged as anything but a distant cousin. But she and Grey had talked it over and from that day on had referred to each other as brother and sister. They had always assumed Papa would make things right for Grey. It had come as a horrid shock when there was no provision for either of them in his will.

She ran her finger over the oak trestle table running the length of the hall. Made of one long plank from a very old, very large tree, it sat fifty people and had done so when the labourers would come to celebrate the harvest or a wedding in the old traditional way.

She recalled one specific day when Grey was around thirteen. He'd refused to attend the harvest home, though he'd worked in the fields as hard as any of the other men. When he did not show up for the celebration, Freeps had admitted that out in the fields the men had teased him about his lack of a name. She had gone in search of Grey and found his note in their secret place up in the long gallery. He had always been getting into scrapes and running off, but he always told her where he had gone by leaving a note.

That time, he'd been in the loft in the stables and she'd eventually convinced him to attend the feast. As she'd suspected, none of the workers had dared tease him in her father's presence.

Frowning, she glanced at Sandford. 'If he did ever come back here, he would have left me a note.'

'Where?'

'In our secret place.' Though, of course, once Grey got to about fifteen, he was far too dignified to play such childish games. But perhaps now… 'You must have done something similar as a child?'

Sandford's expression shuttered. 'I did not.'

'Really?' Had he always been above having a bit of fun? How strange. She shrugged off the thought. 'I think we should look. Come on, up to the long gallery.'

'Lady Tess,' Sandford protested, 'the house is locked up. How could he possibly have left a note?'

She could not prevent a chuckle. 'Grey could get in and out of anywhere should he so desire.'

'Sounds like a havey-cavey sort of a chap to me.'

She turned and frowned at his expression of distaste. 'Grey was like any other boy of his age. Phin was the same, his mother said. You must have led a very sheltered sort of life as a boy if you never got into any mischief at all.'

She did not intend for it to sound like an accusation, but the pain in his eyes said she had hurt him.

An apology sprang to her lips. 'I—'

'Let us look for this note,' he said stiffly. 'Please lead the way.'

Well, at least he now knew for certain this Hammond fellow was not her sweetheart. He could certainly understand wanting to find a brother. It was with a sense of relief that Jaimie followed her up the winding staircase to the medieval long gallery that took up one side of the square courtyard around which the house was built. The Ingrams had certainly been wealthy in their time. The patterned brickwork in the courtyard would have cost a fortune, as would the display of loyalty by way of plaster likenesses of all the Tudor Kings and Queens peering down from under the eaves.

All this talk of hiding notes and creeping in and out of the house by Hammond made him feel...not superior, as he might have expected, but as if something was lacking in his life.

Envy. It was an unpleasant feeling and gave him a dislike for the Hammond fellow, despite the fact that he, Jaimie, had deserved his childhood of misery. Long hours of no company but his own had been justly deserved. He had not intentionally set light to his cousin's house, but that one action had caused the deaths of everyone in his family except his cousin Michael. Jaimie himself had been left bedridden and weighed down by guilt for years for having dropped a candle whilst hiding behind the curtains to watch the party.

Perhaps that was why, when he'd first met Hester, he'd been fascinated by her lack of guilt at the wild things she did. Wild and free. Her wilful disregard for anyone but herself was one of the reasons he'd married her. At first. Later he'd come to realise she'd been completely spoiled by her doting parents. He certainly hadn't expected her to disregard his wishes with respect to his half-broken carriage horses, though in hindsight he *should* have known forbidding her to drive them was a mistake. The word 'no' to Hester was like the call of the huntsman's horn to a pack of dogs—and it seemed that Lady Tess was of a similar bent. The sooner he washed his hands of her, the better.

They reached the landing and he followed Tess into a long chamber. All the windows looked into the central courtyard, as was the fashion in Tudor times. A large fireplace loomed in the centre of one wall and it was to this magnificent structure, with carved plaster decorations, Tess hurried. She knelt and pulled free one of the fire bricks, feeling inside with her fingertips. Shoulders slumped, she sat back on her heels. 'Nothing.'

Clearly disappointed, she rose. 'I don't understand. I felt so sure—' She bit off the words and shook her head and closed her eyes briefly. 'I certainly understand why he would not have contacted me through Cousin Phin. There was a great deal of bad blood between them. But to completely cut me out of his life like this...'

Something painful squeezed the air from his lungs. He wanted to offer comfort, or better yet, find a solution to her troubles.

'Your cousin probably thinks it would not do your reputation any good to associate with a chap like Hammond.'

She glared at him. 'Because he's a bastard, you mean? How unfair. While the father escaped the consequences of his peccadillo, Grey must carry the burden for the rest of his life?'

'I am not saying I agree with it, but it is just the way the world is.' He spoke gently. In truth he agreed with Tess. The sins of the father should not be visited on the children. Lord knew he did not want his sins visited upon any child he might have in the future.

Tess's drooping shoulders and hurt expression made him want to hold her and tell her he would make things right, but he couldn't. She still hadn't told him what was so important about her need to find this fellow. He could feel that there was something else going on, but she didn't trust him with the full truth. And why should she? He'd already proved he was not to be trusted by kissing her. Something he wanted to do again, dammit.

What Jaimie wanted wasn't important. It was the disappointment in Lady Tess's eyes that he wanted to erase. He remembered only too well how he'd felt when he'd lost his whole family in one fell swoop. He also recalled the joy when Michael had reappeared in his life after long miserable years of regret. Joy and guilt. Michael had forgiven him and was a happy man, leading the life he had been intended for, with no recriminations for Jaimie.

Jaimie had done his best to forgive himself, too, although what happened with Hester had not helped with that one bit. Perhaps the fates were giving him this opportunity to help Lady Tess, to assuage some of his guilt. For clearly, despite all of his faults, this Hammond chap was dear to her.

'Is there anywhere else he might have left a note?' he asked.

She shook her head, then hesitated. 'My old bedroom?' She grimaced. 'I wouldn't have thought so, but I always left the window open for him. It was how he came and went so easily. She smiled at the recollection. 'I never heard a thing. He was always as quiet as a cat.'

Not unlike the burglars who were entering houses all over Mayfair. The passing thought surprised him. Shocked him. Intuition played a large part in his successes. Flashes of understanding that came from nowhere. The connecting of unrelated things often happened without his understanding.

In this case it was impossible. No doubt caused by his worry that he wasn't making any progress on the burglaries because Lady Tess had him haring around the countryside on a wild goose chase for a reason she would not trust him enough to fully explain.

'I suppose we should look, just in case,' she said, her expression filling with cautious hope.

'I suppose we should.' He couldn't keep the irony from his voice.

Good heavens, what would his father have thought of all this? He tried to recall that worthy gentleman's face, a word of wisdom to fit the situation, but nothing came to him. Nothing, because he was too busy watching the sway of Lady Tess's lovely rear end as she strode to the other end of the gallery. A sight as enticing as any he'd ever seen.

What was it about this young lady that called so strongly to his baser instincts? She was a lady, for heaven's sake. A noblewoman who should be treated with the utmost respect. Not lusted after. One did not lust after ladies of the *ton*. It simply wasn't done. Especially if they were single. That led in only one direction. To the altar.

At the door, she glanced back impatiently. 'Are you coming?'

He'd like to be— Damnation.

He sauntered after her instead of breaking into the panting gallop his body demanded.

Her chamber was not far from the gallery, but up another flight of stairs. While the main window looked out over the courtyard, the attached dressing room had a narrow window that looked down on to the kitchen garden and an ancient quince tree close enough to act as a convenient ladder. Yes, he could certainly see a young, fit boy making the climb without difficulty.

Tess, meanwhile, was opening drawers and the clothes press, tossing the contents aside in her haste. Finally, she let go a sigh and plonked down on the edge of the steps to the bed. 'Nothing.'

The first place she had looked was the small trinket box on the dressing table, turning over its contents, while anyone could see there was no piece of paper inside.

Fingers pressed to her temples she shook her head. 'I hoped he might have returned the bracelet, hidden it amongst some of these things...'

She continued to search while Jaimie inspected the window in the dressing room and saw the latch was not locked. He clicked it into place without thinking.

When he returned to the bedchamber Lady Tess was on her knees in front of a trunk. She was tossing things on the floor at a feverish rate. One look at the tension of her shoulders told him she was angry. Not simply angry. Furious.

'Lady Tess.'

She glanced up, then went back to heaving items on to the floor, shoes, scarves, garters all spilling on to the rug around her knees.

He crouched beside her. 'Tess, calm down. I fear the bracelet is not here.'

She gazed at him, her eyes full of anger and betrayal. 'He promised to always be here for me. In the end neither he nor Father kept their word. Grey *knew* what that bracelet meant to me.'

'Because it was your mother's?' Jaimie hazarded, wondering if offering to buy her another would help. Hester had accumulated gewgaws in the way of a jackdaw.

'According to my cousin, Mr Stedman bought up my father's debts as a favour to him in exchange for my hand in marriage.' She swallowed. 'I hoped to use the diamonds to pay him off.'

This was her reason for needing the bracelet so badly? 'Stedman will forgive Rowan the debt in exchange for your hand?'

'I gather so. I thought I could settle the debt another way.'

He frowned. 'This debt you speak of is not yours to pay. Rowan inherited the title and the wherewithal to pay it off, so it is his responsibility, not yours.'

'Rowan has his own debts. He asked for my help.'

'And threatened to send you off to Yorkshire if you did not do so.'

'Yes,' she said softly. 'I thought marriage would be a far better fate. Now I am not so sure. But I gave my word.'

The man was a damned mushroom. 'You are more than a match for a man like Stedman. You'll have him eating out of your hand in no time.' He tried to inject humour into his voice, hoping to forestall what looked like tears glinting in her velvety-brown eyes. Hester had never wept. She had stormed and argued and made everyone miserable until she got her own way. 'Please. Don't cry.' He fumbled for a handkerchief.

She waved it away. 'I'm not crying. I'm angry.' She leapt to her feet and strode jerkily across the room. In one sweeping movement she dashed all the trinkets she had so carefully sorted through, the box, the hairbrush and mirror to the floor. Glass shattered. Oblivious to the broken glass, she pulled open a drawer and dumped that out too.

Unable to bear her anguish any longer, he took her gently but firmly by her upper arms. 'Stop!'

She glared back in defiance, but beneath the temper was such an agony of spirit, he lost the power to breathe. 'Tess.' Carefully he released her arms and lifted his hands to cradle her face. 'Tess. We'll find your brother.'

She blinked furiously. 'How?'

'Trust me.'

The doubt in her gaze challenged him to the bottom of his soul. And no matter whether she believed him or not, he was suddenly determined she would not marry Stedman, even if he had to take the man out to a field of honour and do away with him.

Tess gazed into his face for what felt like forever. An expectant silence filled the air. Reason told him to step back, but instinct overrode thought and when her eyelids fluttered, her chin lifted a fraction and she leaned into him, he brushed her mouth with his lips, a comforting little kiss that lingered when her arms stole around his neck and her soft curves melded into his body. Such a tiny little thing, but so full of spirit he'd forgotten how petite she was, how vulnerable to his greater strength.

He closed his eyes and savoured the sensation of her soft luscious body flush with his.

Step back, his brain warned. Yet, with a clarity born of instinct, he *knew* Stedman would never ever hold her like this, never comfort her, never give her her due. Her marriage to such a man would be a terrible waste…

Not his concern.

Gently, he eased her back and lifted her so she sat on the edge of the bed, then forced himself to step back.

Bewildered, Tess gazed at him. Her lips were rosy from his kiss, her breathing unsteady, her gaze oddly uncertain. She glanced at the devastation she had wrought and gave an unsteady laugh. 'I cannot think what came over me.'

He knew only too well that anger and frustration at feeling helpless. He hadn't merely broken things, he had become self-destructive, too.

He took Tess's hand in his, realising she had removed her gloves while searching. Her naked skin was soft and pale and warm. Her hand was trembling. He stroked the back of it. 'On the contrary, I find you remarkably restrained under the circumstances.'

'No, it really was a disgraceful display of temper. And then…' She coloured, a pretty wash of pink rising up her cheeks, before she averted her face. 'Then to throw myself at you like that? I do beg your pardon.'

Puzzled, he gazed at her profile. 'I think it is I who should beg your pardon. My attraction to you overcame my good sense.'

'What a bouncer,' she scoffed.

He stiffened. 'What reason would I have to lie?'

'I know full well I am not the sort of woman men lose their heads over. You are merely being kind.'

Then she didn't know men very well at all. He'd been lusting after her since the moment he saw her dressed as Artemis. 'Kindness is not my forte.'

She turned her head and searched his face with her gaze. 'I am not some green girl, you know. I see the way men turn their noses up when a hostess suggests they dance with me. Even Stedman tells me I need improvement. He advises me to go on a diet.'

'What a dolt.'

'He is the only man willing to make me an offer of marriage and that's purely because he wants an alliance with the nobility and we're desperate enough to consider him. Be honest with me, Sandford. The only reason you kissed me just now was to distract me. To call a halt to my tantrum. It had nothing to do with attraction.'

He hated that she had been made to feel so unworthy by the idiot men of the *ton*. And Stedman, a man who wanted to become her *husband*, was the worst of all.

'I...' No man of honour admitted to lusting after a lady.

'You see!' She made as if to slide off the bed.

He put out a restraining hand. 'I can assure you, I find you exceedingly alluring, Lady Tess.'

He gazed at her full lips, still rosy from his kisses, and his body hardened. 'Kind is the last thing you should think me. You make me forget I am a gentleman.'

And to prove it, he gently pressed her back into the pillows until he could gaze into her face. He traced a finger along the soft smooth skin of her jaw, over her lips, and smoothed back the chestnut curls from around her face. 'You are lovely.'

She made a face, though her cheeks flushed. 'I am ordinary.'

'Not at all. If you were, I would not be here...' He sealed his words with a kiss that started with a tender brushing of lips, a slow exploration of tongues in hot dark places, and ignited to unquenchable fire in his loins.

She shifted, turning towards him, pressing her gorgeous breasts against his chest. He pulled her closer, finding the swell of her breast with his palm, resting it there, until with a moan of pleasure she wriggled against him, seeking more. Gently, he caressed her delicious form while the blunt head of his shaft pushed hard against her hip, seeking its own pleasure. He forced his hips to still, though he did not forgo the torturous sensation of that luscious thigh against his groin—he simply held it in check while his tongue explored the hot wet recesses of her mouth.

Did she know that the heat of anger was a hair's breadth from sensual passion? And if there was one thing he had learned as a lonely boy with a heart full of loss and rage—the passion of sensual pleasure could numb the pain. For a time.

He broke their kiss slowly with a series of little licks and nibbles until he could lift his head and look down at her face. Her eyes were half-closed, her lips parted and rosy, her face dreamy. A vision of a sensual woman, delicious and enchanting...

And totally out of bounds. If he didn't watch out he'd be forced to marry the chit and, for all that he found her utterly tempting, she was not the sort of woman Jaimie wanted for his second wife.

He began to move away, to put an end to what could only be called folly, but Tess twined her arm around his neck and stroked his face.

'That was lovely.' She swallowed. 'I feel hot all over and strangely tense. I suppose to you this is nothing. A mere bagatelle.' Her eyes were hazy, her lips moist and lush, and the appeal for reassurance in her voice simply too hard to resist.

'I am filled with desire, my sweet. For you.'

A pleased smile curved her lips. 'You are?'

And having said such a thing, how could he simply get up and leave, as he had intended? The little confidence she had gained would be shredded in an instant.

She needed to feel desirable. To feel wanted.

Was he thinking with his rational mind, or was this just what he wanted to believe?

Tess tightened her arms around his neck and pressed her lips to his, this time taking the initiative by touching her tongue to his. A tentative little flick that arrowed all the way to his bollocks. And then he wasn't thinking any more—he was kissing her back and revelling in the feel of her along his length as they stretched out on the covers.

Why should she not know how much pleasure she could give and receive? He doubted Stedman would ever revere her in this way.

While he gave himself to the sensation of her kiss, Jaimie gently worked free the first button of her spencer, revealing her delicate collarbone. Breaking away from her lips and ignoring her little noise of protest, he pressed his lips to the hollow it formed and she sighed with pleasure. Another button gave way to his fingers, and a third. He spread the jacket apart, revealing the low neckline of her gown and the rise of her beautiful breasts. Saints be praised, the light summer gown was one of those that fastened with a ribbon at the front, though he'd have to get her out of her spencer to get her stays undone, if he wanted to fully enjoy the bounty of her magnificent breasts...

He kissed the shadow in the valley between them and the hand resting on his shoulder moved to his nape, Tess's fingers winnowing through his hair, sending shivers of pleasure across his scalp. He inhaled, filling his lungs with her scent: lavender and something darker. His lips found the bow and he used his teeth to tug at one of the tails. It unravelled. The fabric loosened and he pulled it down, revealing stays and shift. Front-closing stays.

Hallelujah.

He raised up on one elbow, seeking her reaction. Her eyes were open now, her gaze alert, though her fingers continued to play in his hair, sending little tingles of pleasure down his spine.

He swallowed a groan and quelled the urge to open his falls and drive deep into her heat. She was a lady, for heaven's sake, and for all her boldness, as naive as the day was long. He cursed. This was not what he should be doing. He started to pull away once more. Her hand tightened in his hair, holding him in place. With his greater strength it would be easy to break free, yet his willpower wasn't so strong.

And besides, he wasn't going to ravage her, just give her a little pleasure; let her see what she really deserved as a woman.

To his surprise, with her gaze fixed on his, she unfastened the knot at the bottom of her stays, pulling the tapes free and, with well-practised swiftness, parting them to reveal the bounty of her beautiful, heavy breasts. The peaks were hard, the aureoles the colour of soft doeskin, beneath the filmy fabric of her shift. Without thinking he licked one of the tight little buds, feeling her shiver and her moan of pleasure. She rolled towards him, giving Jaimie better access, and he took the weight of that gorgeous soft flesh in his hand and drew the nipple into his mouth again, suckling until she cried out.

While she shuddered with pleasure he pulled her skirt up over her hips, and eased his knee between her thighs. She let her legs fall open in welcome. A niggling doubt about her innocence entered his mind, but his body no longer cared what his mind thought.

His fingers traced the tops of the stockings, caressed the silky skin above in little strokes and circles. When they found the heat between her legs and combed through the little patch of curls already damp with desire, she froze.

'It's all right,' he murmured against her lips. 'I'll do nothing to hurt you.' Nothing to ruin her, though the urge to plunge his shaft deep into her heat was primal and demanding.

He caught her knee in the crook of his elbow and, sitting back on his heels, gazed at the view she presented. Damp chestnut curls, delicate rosy folds, a channel that beckoned him to drive home. 'So lovely,' he breathed. He stroked his fingers through the tight curls, seeking her centre with his thumb: the little nub that would send her flying apart, hidden deep. When he found it and circled his thumb, Tess jumped. She was so aroused already, it seemed it was impossibly sensitive. He pressed down with the heel of his palm and her moan of pleasure was fuel to the fire building inside him.

When he lightened his touch, her hips rose seeking more. A woman who knew what she wanted, even if she did not know the exact details. He could give her this knowledge, so she would know what to require from a husband.

Chapter Six

Heat rushed through every vein in Tess's body at the look on Jaimie's face as he looked at her down there. It was if he'd found some marvellous treasure. A storm of sensation rioted along her veins from the place his hand applied pressure. Heat, tingles, pulses of exquisite pleasure sent her soaring. Her limbs became liquid, moving with boneless slowness.

She draped her arms over his shoulders, amazed at their breadth and strength beneath his dandified clothes. Beneath the air of languid elegance resided a powerful masculinity.

His touch was bliss. Heaven on earth. Yet deep inside her mind clamoured a warning. Danger. Even she knew better than to trust a man in the heat of passion.

Yet her mind was sluggish, her emotions swooping and soaring with the touch of his tongue to hers, with the feel of his hand heavy on her breast and the tantalising pressure between her legs.

She raised her hips, pressing into that tormenting hand, her vision filled with darkness, her mind turned inward to that one point of pleasure. Wholly wanton. And delicious.

Even so, there was something else, a hardness against her hip, nudging at her as if seeking her attention.

His male parts. His twig and berries, Mims had called it when issuing one of her warnings about lust-filled men—something to be feared, by all accounts.

And yet… Tess let her hand stroke over the broad expanse of Jaimie's chest, over the narrow firm hip, to the place where his body pressed into hers.

He stilled, raised his head, and gazed into her face.

'No, sweetheart,' he said softly, his hand pressing down against her mons Veneris, making her squirm and moan. His mouth returned to hers, his tongue teasing at her lips, begging for entry.

She angled her face away. 'I want to touch you, too.' It was only fair.

Sandford choked and she wondered if he was laughing. Finding her amusing. She shifted so she could see his expression and he indeed had laughter in his eyes, but not the mocking smile he so often wore.

He lightly patted her curls at the apex to her thighs. A strange tingle took her breath away and tightened her insides. She gasped.

He took her wandering hand and guided it to his groin, pressing her palm against the hard ridge of flesh, curling her fingers along its length.

'It is bigger than I expected,' she said, carefully outlining the shape.

'You honour me, sweet,' he said and again he sounded amused and pleased, too. He rocked into her hand and hissed a breath through his teeth, his expression full of strain and pleasure.

Far more than handsome, perfectly beautiful.

She glanced down where his hand covered hers and the heat of his maleness permeated through his clothing into her palm. A pulse of pleasure tightened her insides.

'Can I see?'

'Saints, you are killing me.'

A flick of anger tightened her skin. She glanced down where her skirts were bunched at her waist. 'So it is all right for you to look, but not me?'

Again that choked back laugh. He released her hand. 'Have at it, my lady, but know you, there is peril in that naughty lad.'

'I'm not afraid.'

Yet the rapid beating of her heart, her sudden breathlessness, said she just might be. Pah. She wasn't completely an innocent, she'd grown up in the country—she'd seen horses in the midst of procreation. Swallowing the sudden dryness in her throat, she watched him unbutton his falls and tug free the tails of his shirt. What emerged from the white linen was nothing like a stallion at all. It was lovely. Smooth, dark with blood and gnarled with blue-coloured veins; the blunt purplish tip had the look of fine satin. She grazed it gently with the pad of her thumb.

He hissed in a breath.

She glanced up at his face. 'It is tender?'

'Very.' He once more took her hand in his and curled her fingers around the shaft. He pushed into her fist with a groan. 'Tighter, Tess. Yes. Like that.' He rocked into her, his movement steady and rhythmic, the skin beneath her palm silky, sliding along the hardness beneath. His hand left hers, leaving her in control, and she watched in amazement as a glistening pearl of moisture appeared at the tip.

His hand returned to her mons, his thumb easing deeper into her folds, and—

She gasped as the amazing sensation once more tingled along every nerve in her body.

'There you are,' he said, sounding softly triumphant, and his touch became more intense and faster—his hips moved faster, too.

He kissed her deeply.

Her body clenched, every muscle tightening deep inside. It was unbearable.

She groaned and sought to break the tension.

He broke the kiss and put his mouth over her breast. Despite her shift, the heat and wet was lovely. He suckled. A delicious shock seared her. Her breasts tightened. A streak like lightning, hot and sharp, shot from her nipple to low in her belly.

She cried out. 'Sandford!'

He groaned. 'Let go, Tess. I've got you. I will not let you fall.'

Yes. That was what was happening. She was ascending the heights. Going higher, further away.

'Hold on, Tess,' he said, his voice rough, his breathing ragged.

Her mind wouldn't work, but something knew and

she gripped him harder and then the sensation of his touches became too much, too overwhelming.

Fear gripped her.

'Let go, Tess.' Demanding. 'Let go. I will catch you.' An order.

In this he was her master. Only this. And then he altered the rhythm against that supremely sensitive flesh at her core, harder, faster. The change caught her off guard and she finally let go and flew apart.

A scream rang in her ears.

A moment later, shattered and mindless, she floated on languid heat and shocking bliss.

Aware of him once more, his hand holding hers tight around his hot length. Still moving, his male flesh hard like hot steel. He groaned a deep and feral growl. His hand brushing hers away as he buried himself in the folds of his shirttails and rolled on to his back. He groaned and shuddered.

Unable to move, she lay looking at his lovely face, all hard angles, a lean jaw, a jutting aristocratic nose, a faint haze of dark stubble on his chin and an expression of such gentleness, it pulled at something in her chest. A yearning.

Heaven help her, what had she done?

He cracked an eye open and pulled her close to rest her head upon his shoulder.

'It is all right, Tess. I promise.'

She wasn't sure if anything would be all right again.

No wonder Mims had issued such dire warnings. Because, despite the amazing experience they'd just shared, it wasn't enough. She sensed there was even more pleasure to be had, but he had kept his promise and ensured things didn't go too far. Heaven help her, was that disappointment she felt? She could not let this happen again.

Jaimie came awake with a start. The insistent prodding at his shoulder intensified. 'Lord Sandford.'

He forced his eyelids open and gazed up into the face of an anxious-looking Tess. He yawned and stretched with a feeling of well-being. 'Surely after our recent intimacies you might stoop to calling me Jaimie. All my friends do.'

Not that he had that many friends. He preferred his own company as a general rule. But to his surprise he did count Tess as a friend—of a sort. For a brief moment, he thought she would refuse as there was such an annoyed expression on her face.

'Very well. Jaimie.'

He smiled at her and she blinked and looked away. 'The caretaker is going to be coming to check on us if we do not go downstairs soon.'

His sluggish brain processed the words. 'I doubt the old fellow could make it up here.' He gave another yawn and pushed up on one elbow, taking in the fact that she was on her feet and once more encased in full armour, or at least spencer and bonnet. Her hair was also neatly ordered. She had been busy while he'd momentarily drifted off, curse it.

She moved away from the bed and turned to look out of the window. 'You should dress.'

He glanced down. Fortunately his shirt covered him.

He had no wish to shock her any more than he already had. An image of her face as she shattered in ecstasy popped into his mind and his body warmed. His body began to stir once more. Hell. That would not do.

He swung his legs of the edge of the bed furthest from her and began setting himself to rights.

How was it possible that it was be happening again so soon? Now was not the right time. But he did want it to happen again, damn him for a fool. He glanced in the mirror, ran his fingers though his hair, until it looked carefully disordered instead of simply untidy. 'Right. Shall we go down?'

She turned and gave him a raking glance from his head to his heels. Thankfully she seemed satisfied, because she nodded and took his proffered arm.

She took a step towards the door.

He halted her with a touch to her hand. When she looked up at him, he smiled at her, then brushed her lips with his. 'Thank you, my dear sweet Tess.'

A look of discomfort crossed her face, but then she chuckled, a low throaty sound that put his blood on alert. 'Thank you. Oh, how awkward it is. How does one respond after such...' she waved a hand at the bed '...occurrences?'

He swallowed a laugh. 'It is difficult, I admit. I often wonder how married couples can accomplish it day after day.'

She stiffened.

Damn, that had been the wrong thing to say. He grimaced. Why was it that around her his normal astuteness seemed to flee? 'I am sorry we will not get to travel back to town together, I must say.'

'You are?'

'Well, I must concentrate on how to find your Mr Hammond.'

The stiffness left her shoulders. A look of defeat crossed her face. 'I think Ingram Manor was my absolute last hope, quite honestly.' She glanced at the now-reordered dressing table. 'I have decided not to look any further. If Grey had wanted me to find him, he would have surely contacted me before now.'

She sounded so weary he wanted to take Hammond by his shirt fronts and give him a good shake.

Unfortunately, he agreed with her. 'I think we should speak with your erstwhile housekeeper before we depart Farningham, don't you?'

Her lips tightened. 'I suppose it would be wise. There is very little chance he would have contacted her, however.'

'No stone left unturned, Lady Tess.'

She nodded. 'And then we will simply leave it at that, Lord Sandford.'

The emphasis on the lord part made it quite clear that she intended not to have any more dealings with him either. 'I think it would be best.' At least, it would be best that she did not continue to seek this wayward brother of hers. As for the rest of it, well…

A regretful smile curved her lips. 'Thank you for not offering me false hope. I do not like to be thought a fool.'

At the top of the stairs he stepped back so she could

go ahead and once again enjoyed watching her diminutive figure. He understood that her sadness was not only about their failure to find Hammond. It was about her impending nuptials.

Naturally, she had already forgotten he had made her a promise to find her brother. She did not know him well enough to realise he always kept his word.

The caretaker, sitting on a chair in the hallway at the bottom of the steps, eyed them curiously, but if he had any suspicions about what had taken them so long he did not give them voice.

'Leggat, you said your daughter works at the vicarage,' Tess said.

The old man creaked to his feet. 'She do, my lady. Unfortunately, she is absent at the moment, seeing as how me other daughter needed her help at her lying in.'

Tess made a sound of annoyance, then laughed somewhat wryly. 'Of course she is away.'

The old man looked puzzled.

'Perhaps you might leave a note, to be delivered to her on her return,' Jaimie suggested, wishing he could magic the blasted woman out of thin air and cheer Tess up. He gave the old fellow an encouraging smile. 'When is she expected back?'

'Next week, I should think.'

'She has journeyed far?'

'To Eynsford.'

'The next village over?' A scant two miles away.

The old fellow nodded grudgingly.

'Lady Tess, since you are expected back in town, why don't I deliver your note?'

Tess nodded, but there was little enthusiasm in her expression as the old man saw them out of the door.

'You don't have to bother, you know,' she said on their stroll down the drive. 'Chasing after Mrs Leggat, I mean. There really is no point. I don't believe my plan was a very good one after all.'

It had been a dashed strange one, to be sure, and unlikely to succeed, but the misery she was trying to hide did not sit well in his gut.

'Let us try this last thing, before we give up entirely.'

Her look said she thought he was flailing at windmills.

It wasn't long before he had her safely delivered to the inn and the care of her maid. He went to the stables and called for his phaeton. He would keep his word and visit the housekeeper, but wasn't holding out much hope from that quarter. Not when Greydon Hammond clearly did not want to be found. If so, how the hell would Jaimie deliver on his exceedingly rash promise? He needed more time.

Wilhelmina bustled into the drawing room where Tess was supposedly plying her needle, but was in fact staring out of the window, lost in her thoughts. Illicit wonderful thoughts that made her blush.

'Oh, my dear,' her cousin's wife wailed. 'Such terrible news.'

Tess froze. 'What are you talking about?'

'Mr Stedman sent round a note.' Her lips pursed as if she had tasted a lemon. 'He is returning to Yorkshire, post-haste. Something to do with his mills.' She flopped on to the chaise longue. 'Oh, it really is too bad. Dear Phin was sure he would come up to scratch this week.'

Relief flooded through Tess. It was like a man facing the gallows receiving a reprieve. 'He has gone?'

'Did I not just say so? Dratted mercenary beast. A nobleman wouldn't be dashing off to attend to business matters in the middle of the Season.'

Which was why so many of them ended up in debt. 'He is expected back, though?' Tess held her breath. Had he perhaps decided against making her his wife? If so, should she be pleased or worried? After all, he still held her father's promissory notes. Would he sell them on?

She had heard of such things. The next man to buy them up could be far worse. Yorkshire was beginning to look inviting after all.

'The note said he would return,' Wilhelmina said petulantly. 'But he should have stuck to the plan. Dearest Phin is most put out.'

All right, so while it seemed Mr Stedman would return, it meant she had a few more days for some miracle to occur, like Grey showing up in the nick of time. Oh, yes, that would indeed be a miracle.

Tess slumped back in the chair. Hope was such a fickle creature. Had she not hoped for an offer of marriage, seeing it as a means to get away from Phin and Wilhelmina? *Be careful what you wish for.* A salutary lesson indeed.

For her family's sake, the best she could hope for was that if Mr Stedman finally came up to scratch, Phin could drive a hard bargain to clear all of her father's debts and Mr Stedman did not hold it against her after they were married. She sighed.

Wilhelmina shot her a sharp glance. 'Why so Friday-faced? It is not every day a penniless woman gets such a flattering offer. Do buck up, Theresa. You could not do any better than Mr Stedman. He is such a fine figure of a man.'

If one liked portly, slightly balding men. She forced herself not to grimace. It was so hard not to compare Mr Stedman to the elegant and masculine Lord Sandford. She must not. What had happened the day before must be wiped from her memory.

Her face heated, her memory not having any sort of shame.

Flattering wasn't quite the word Tess would have used for Mr Stedman's offer. She took a deep breath and pinned a smile to her lips, determined to make the best of it. 'I—'

'Oh, by the way, the bracelet. Did you find it?'

Tess's mind raced to catch up. Dash it all, she had forgotten what she had told Wilhelmina about the bracelet. 'I, um… Yes. The clasp is definitely broken. Mims took it to Rundell & Bridge for repair.'

Wilhelmina frowned. 'I wish you had spoken to me first. Dearest Phin is quite sure it is part of the estate since it is not mentioned in your papa's will.' Wilhelmina's eyes glistened with avarice, though she was clearly trying to sound sympathetic.

Tess sat bolt upright. 'It was part of my mother's settlements. All jewellery was to go to any daughter of the marriage. Father told me so.'

Her cousin's frown deepened. 'But since there is no copy of the settlements among your father's papers, how can we know that for certain?'

'I do not understand why it was not there. Perhaps Phin could look again.' She had pulled out the miniature portrait of her mother painted before her marriage earlier that morning. The bracelet was clearly visible. She had wondered whether a skilled jeweller could make a duplicate, then had decided it would be far too expensive. Now it seemed she was going to have to admit that it was lost. Not that she would ever tell them she thought Grey had taken it. Never would she betray him as he had betrayed her.

Wilhelmina pursed her lips. 'Several things went missing when that scoundrel Hammond left. Might he have stolen the documents as well?'

A cold chill walked across the skin of her neck. 'Nonsense. What would he want with my father's papers?'

'Phin said——'

The door swung inwards. Wilhelmina closed her mouth with an audible snap.

Phineas walked in with a smug look on his face, carefully closing the door behind him. 'Well, Theresa, you are a dark horse.'

What on earth was he talking about?

'I understand Mr Stedman has left town for a while,' Tess said.

Phineas shot her a hard look. 'He has, but that is not why I am here. You have a gentleman caller. I want you to accord him every civility.' He rubbed his hands together. 'Who knows, perhaps if you play your cards right, you will do far better than Stedman for a husband.'

'I haven't a clue what you are talking about, Cousin.'

'I am talking about Lord Sandford. He has asked for permission to call on you.'

Calling being the forerunner to expressing a serious interest in a lady. What was Sandford about? 'I…I barely know the man. Why would he be calling on me?'

Phin glowered. 'I no more know the answer to that than you do. But he has, so let us make the best of it.'

A man like Sandford would be a catch indeed and not just for her. Phin would bask in the glory, too.

'It is your duty to make the best match you can, after all we have done for you,' Wilhelmina said. 'Though what on earth *he* would see in Theresa I cannot imagine.'

The underlying threat of banishment was not lost on Tess. She stiffened. 'I will do my duty, Cousin.' It was her duty. As Phin was her legal guardian, he had the power to ensure she married where he chose, regardless of how she felt about the man.

Phin ran a glance over her and gave a nod of approval. 'Are you ready?'

She would have been if she had any clue as to was Sandford was up to. She nodded and lowered her gaze, marshalling every ounce of steel in her spine.

He opened the door. 'My cousin will see you now, my lord. You know my wife, Lady Rowan.'

Sandford had never looked more elegant. He bowed

with an inborn elegance few men could accomplish. 'Good morning, ladies.'

'Lord Sandford, I hope you will excuse myself and my lady, we have a prior engagement. Come along, my dear.'

Phin escorted his wife out.

Leaving her alone with Jaimie. How very odd.

Tess took in Sandford's aloof expression and felt a moment of panic, until she saw the gleam of amusement in his eyes.

She narrowed her eyes on that smug expression. 'First we hear that Mr Stedman is called back to his home in Yorkshire. Then you ask leave to call on me, like a man thinking he might become a suitor. A very odd set of coincidences indeed.'

He laughed. 'I might have known you would see through my ploy. I hasten to assure you I do not see myself as a suitor, although your cousin might have hopes in that direction.'

A little pang squeezed her heart. How foolish. She had no wish for him to become a suitor. Not in the least. 'I do not understand your intentions.'

With studied deliberation, he picked a piece of lint from his sleeve and flicked it away. 'I promised we would find your half-brother, Lady Tess, but if we are to do so before you receive a proposal from Stedman, which seemed to be the point of the exercise, I need a bit more time. So I arranged for him to have a few issues at his factory. People departing for better places of employment and such rot, necessitating that he be required to go up there himself.'

Mouth agape, she stared at him. 'How is it possible?'

'I have my methods.'

She collapsed back against the chair cushion. 'It would seem so.' With Stedman gone then there just might be a smidgeon of hope. 'Then I must thank you. How much time do we have, do you think?'

'A few days at most.'

A final opportunity.

Chapter Seven

Jaimie hadn't had quite so much fun in a long time, though it would need careful managing. He didn't actually want to end up engaged to the girl. She was too much like Hester for comfort and he would not make the same mistake twice.

Well, she was not *really* the same as Hester, who had been flighty and selfish in the extreme. Tess was practical and loyal, though a little too determined for his liking. She'd also been extremely passionate—

He cut the thought off. He intended to use his brain in all his future dealings with the lady, and to ignore the lust he felt.

'What is your plan?' she asked.

'My plan is to scour London and its environs using the resources at my disposal.'

'I see.'

He frowned. 'Your repressive tone does not bode well, Lady Tess. What is it that you see?'

'That you intend to proceed without my help.'

'I can assure you I have managed this sort of business on my own for a great many years. I will report back to you with my findings the moment I have anything of use. In the meantime, however, you and I must do the pretty, so as not to arouse your cousin's suspicions that my interest in you is anything other than honourable.'

'Do the pretty?'

'Drive out. Dance at balls. The usual sort of thing that couples testing the waters might do. Though of course you will not dance with me exclusively. There must be no hint of scandal.'

No hint of the sort of thing that had happened at Ingram Manor, he meant.

'I really think I should help you look for my brother.'

'It is out of the question, Lady Tess. No lady can go where I intend to look.'

How typical of a man to think her help would be of no use. But what choice did she have? This really was her last hope.

Duty done, Jaimie strode out for his office. For a tense moment, Jaimie had thought she was going to refuse his help. Quite a shock to his ego, if he was truthful, given the choices she was facing. But he had to admit, while he had offered to find her brother in a moment of weakness, as any man would faced with the onset of tears, he was having trouble keeping his mind off Tess and her glorious body. When he should be focused on finding the Mayfair burglar, he was thinking about the way she had come apart in his arms.

He had decided that this would be the best way to

end the distraction. Find her brother, get her settled and get back to his work.

Hopefully.

When he entered his office, he found Growler at his desk poring over what looked like another letter from the Home Office.

'Another burglary?'

'Three,' the other man said harshly.

'Three in one night?'

Growler shook his head. 'One yesterday evening, two last night.'

'Our lad is getting bolder.'

'You think it is one man acting alone then?'

Jaimie took of his coat. 'Instinct tells me it is. The only pattern is the stealth and the fact that there is no pattern. There cannot be many with his skill. Bring the report in, we will add it to the others.'

They went through to his inner office. Growler added the new crime to the others, marking the map of locations and writing down the stolen items by category and date.

Jaimie stared at the map. Up to now, nothing had made a scrap of sense on that map, but a casual, almost sideways glance had revealed something he had not noticed before.

'Look,' he said, stabbing a finger at one of the map's quadrants.

Growler peered at the spot and frowned. 'I don't see nothing.'

'That is my point, my dear Growler. The robberies are scattered all across the map, all except right here.'

Growler nodded slowly, comprehension dawning in

his face. 'I see what you mean. Do you think he lives in that area?'

'If he does then he's no ordinary criminal. He's a member of the *ton*, or close to it.'

He stared at the telltale gap on the map. There were other blanks, but they were poorer neighbourhoods. No, the robberies were definitely sprinkled around that empty space set squarely in Mayfair and Jaimie did not believe in coincidences.

'He either lives there, or is avoiding someone who does.'

'Someone who might know his face?'

'That doesn't make sense. He commits these crimes at night,' he mused. 'What was taken in these last three?'

'A couple of silver spoons. A box of tea. A candlestick from one. A rump roast, some bank notes from the second. A pearl ring and a pound of butter from the third.'

Growler stared at him. 'Why is he taking food? What is this fellow doing? Setting himself up for a fine dinner?'

'A gentleman fallen on hard times, perhaps?'

Growler went down the list of stolen items. 'Almost each and every time he's taken food of some sort, even when the other items taken don't come from the kitchen.'

Finally, they had found the pattern they had been seeking.

Now they needed to set a trap.

'You know, Mims...' Tess touched a fingertip to the image of a face she could scarcely recall. Her mother had died bearing the son that would have made all their lives so very different '…no one who saw this bracelet would forget it.' She did not show her the sketch she'd drawn of Grey.

Mims left the clothes she was folding and shuffled over. The poor old dear should have retired long ago. Hopefully Stedman did not feel the way Phin did about pensioning off his elderly retainers. She really ought to ask him. Or add it to the settlements or something. She would have to speak to Phin.

The old lady squinted at the bracelet in the portrait. 'Your pa had that piece made for your mother after the likeness of something he saw on his travels in India. Heathen, I call it.'

Heathen. Exotic. Intricate. 'It is beautiful.'

Mims sniffed. 'I hopes Master Greydon realised its worth, that's all I can say.'

The only way he could have done that was to have sold it. Which would mean it was for ever lost. But if he had pawned it, that would be another matter entirely. She had been looking for the wrong thing. Instead of seeking Grey himself, she should have concentrated on looking for the bracelet and that might lead her to information about her brother.

'Help me get ready. I'm going out.'

'You are ready.'

She rose to her feet. 'I wish to change into my mourning gown.'

Mims groaned. 'You'll be the death of me, you will, my lady. It is time to stop these mad starts of yours. They can only lead to trouble.'

'One last try, Mims.' Sandford had offered to help

her, but she just didn't trust him to follow through. In her past experience, men made all kinds of promises, but only kept those that were to their advantage. No matter how many times Father had promised to stop gambling, he always went back on his word. And besides, even if the bracelet was lost to her forever, she would dearly like to know what had happened to Grey. To assure herself he was well and happy. Any information she could find might help ease her worry.

An hour later, dressed as she had been when she first went to Lord Sandford's place of business, she entered Rundell & Bridge. She waited while the clerk attended to a dandy dithering over a tray of cravat pins. How could such a simple thing take so long?

Finally the indecisive twit made a choice and the clerk completed the sale. He smiled as he turned to serve her. 'May I help you, madam?'

He didn't seem at all fazed by the fact that he could not see her face because of her veil. She pulled out the portrait from her reticule.

'I am looking for a piece of family jewellery that I believe was sold some time ago. I wish to buy it back.'

'It was sold through us?'

'I am not sure, to be honest.'

The clerk's lips tightened. 'We do not deal in stolen property, madam.'

'No, no. That is not my meaning. A family member sold it.' Hesitantly, she put the drawing of Grey on the counter. 'This man. The sale was quite legitimate, but

I would like to buy it back for sentimental reasons. It belonged to my mother.'

The clerk glanced at the portrait and the sketch. He shook his head. 'I have never seen either of them before.'

'Are you sure?'

He picked up the portrait and inspected the bracelet through his jeweller's eyepiece. His lip curled. 'I have never seen anything like this in my life.'

She picked up the items and was about to tuck them away when an elderly man, with greying whiskers, a bald pate and a cheerfully ruddy complexion, came through a door behind the counter. 'Something wrong, Jeffries?'

'This lady is looking for a family heirloom, Mr Rundell,' the young clerk said, his demeanour changing from scornful to obsequious.

The old gentleman took out a monocle which he screwed into one eye and peered at the portrait. He shook his head. 'It has not passed through our hands, madam. I would recall it.'

'Where else might I try? My, er, my relative was rather desperate at the time.' No need to show him Grey's likeness, since he hadn't sold the bracelet here.

Mr Rundell's face furrowed with doubt. 'You think he sold it outright, rather than pawned it?'

'I am honestly not sure. He has not been in contact with me for a long time.'

'A moment, if you please.'

He disappeared through the door by which he had entered. The clerk moved off to serve a couple who had entered the shop while she was speaking with the owner.

The old man returned after several minutes. He handed her a piece of paper. 'Here is a list of where your relation might have gone to sell such an item. Gambling debts, I am assuming,' he said with a note of disapproval in his voice.

If only it was that simple. 'Quite possibly.'

He peered at her over the spectacles he had donned. 'These at the top of the list are respectable places. Below the line… Well, madam, may I suggest you send your footman?'

He had gone far beyond the call of duty. No wonder people thought so highly of this establishment.

'Thank you, Mr Rundell, you have been most helpful.'

Rundell bowed. 'I wish you well on your quest, madam. It is a unique piece. Whoever saw it will recall it. I only wish the young gentleman had come here. I would have kept it rather than sell it on, for I know how it is with these family items.'

Clutching his notes, she walked out into the street, before reading the list. Mr Rundell had printed not only the names of the business, but their addresses. As he had said, the first three were on Ludgate Hill, as he was. The rest were on streets she did not know. She hailed a cabriolet and gave the driver the first address below the line. She assumed they would get worse the further down the list she got, but if Grey had been as desperate as she assumed, then it was likely he would not have entered the exclusive shops on this street. They would have asked him too many uncomfortable questions about the bracelet's provenance.

Something she should have thought about before.

The next address was only one street over and while it was small, the neighbourhood was not too run down. 'Wait for me,' she said to her driver.

He scratched his nose. ''Ow do I know you won't skip out the back door?'

Oh goodness, clearly she had entered a whole other world by leaving the main street. She dived in her reticule. 'How much?'

'Two and sixpence, if you wants me to wait.'

Exorbitant. But beggars could not be choosers as his smug expression said all too clearly. She handed over the coins. At this rate, she would have nothing left in short order.

The man in the shop shook his head at both the portrait and the sketch, so it was off to the next business on her list.

At the next address, she once more handed over two shillings and sixpence in advance to keep her conveyance waiting.

This shop was in a narrow, rather unpleasant-smelling alley and up a flight of gloomy stairs. The three balls hanging outside the door proclaimed it was a pawnbroker. The fellow behind the counter was dressed in a flashy waistcoat embroidered with forget-me-nots and lilies of the valley. Likely something someone had pawned and never come back for. She pulled out the miniature. 'Has this piece of jewellery ever been brought into your store?' she asked, pointing to her mother's wrist.

Like Mr Rundell, he inserted a monocle into his eye socket and inspected the picture closely.

He shook his head. 'Can't say as how it has.'

'What about this gentleman?' She smiled sweetly, holding out the sketch.

The man's eyes narrowed. 'Who wants to know?'

'I am willing to pay for the bracelet's return. It is a family treasure. I am also willing to pay for information about this man who may know of its whereabouts. I am not looking to cause any trouble for anyone.'

'Never seen 'em before.'

'Might anyone else here have seen either one?'

He narrowed his eyes as if trying to divine the truth. Finally he nodded. 'Wait here, madam.' He took the portrait and the sketch through a door behind the counter. He returned within moments. 'It never came here.' He gave her an oily smile. 'We could make you one.'

She stared at him blankly.

'If you lost it, we can replace it. Make it with paste, if you can't afford stones. We does it all the time for ladies what's *misplaced* items.'

He gave her a knowing wink. He must think she had given them to a lover who had sold them off. Heat rushed to her cheeks. Thank goodness for her veil.

'Thank you, I will keep that in mind.'

The man opened the door for her and she headed back down those dark stairs.

If this unpleasant place was second on the list, what would the ones lower down be like? Her stomach clenched. She wanted to find Grey, but she wasn't an idiot. Perhaps she should give up this quest.

A man on his way up the stairs backed down when he saw her. In the half-light she could make out his shape, but not his features. She halted, waiting for him to get to the bottom so she could pass.

He glanced up and halted, staring at her.

'If you would be so kind,' she murmured, hoping to remind him of his manners.

'It is you!' a familiar voice said.

'Good lord,' she said, recoiling. Her heart picked up speed, her mouth dried. 'Lord Sandford. Fancy meeting you here.'

'I do not fancy it at all,' he said grimly. He waved an imperious hand. 'Down you come, if you please.'

'You have no right to speak to me in such a manner,' she said, the hairs on her nape bristling.

'Do I not?' His voice had a hard edge to it. 'Once more I find you putting yourself in danger, and after I told you I would look after the matter. This. Must. Stop.' Again came the imperious hand gesture.

She glanced back over her shoulder, aware of the shopkeeper having come out of his door to see what was going on. 'Very well. I will accept your escort to my carriage.'

'Your carriage?' He made a scornful sound. 'If you mean that disgusting hackney outside, I will do no such thing.'

She stiffened at the autocratic words, but couldn't help feeling relieved. He was right, it was disgusting, she'd simply tried not to notice.

Head high, she walked down the stairs and, when she reached him, he turned to allow her to pass and followed her down to the street.

'You will allow me to escort you home,' he said

pleasantly, though there was nothing pleasant in his expression as he took her arm and handed her into his carriage. 'I will pay your driver off.'

A few moments later the hackney drove away and.

Sandford climbed in beside her. He eyed her askance. 'What devil's mischief are you up to now?

Oh dear, what should she tell him? The truth. Ultimately, honesty had been the watchword of all their dealings.

He wasn't going to like it.

Chapter Eight

Staring at Tess as she lifted her veil and draped it back over her bonnet, revealing her face, Jaimie could not remember the last time he had felt quite this angry. He didn't usually let himself get angry. He solved problems using his brain, but her lack of trust in his abilities was simply infuriating.

He calmed himself. 'Well, Lady Tess?'

She sighed. 'I had another idea of how I might find my bracelet.'

He frowned. What game was she playing now? 'I thought it was your brother we intended to find?' He had men scouring the city based on the description she had provided.

She winced as if his words caused her pain. 'I thought it might lead me to him.'

Damnation. Something twisted in his chest, unpleasant and painful. Surely he wasn't jealous of her devotion to this man? He reverted to his usual bored expression. 'I thought you were going to leave the investigation to me.'

'That was your idea, not mine.'

Mouth agape, he stared at her. 'We came to an agreement. If your half-brother cares anything for you at all, as you seem to imply, he would not want you going into places like this.' He stabbed a finger in the direction of the establishment she'd so recently left.

She closed her eyes for a second. 'I know. I started at Rundell & Bridge. Mr Rundell gave me a list of possible places to look.'

'Mr Rundell suggested you come here? I am going to have a word with that worthy.'

'Jaimie, no.' She leaned forward and put a hand on his arm. Her touch sent tingles up his arm.

He stilled. It was the first time she had voluntarily used his given name.

'Mr Rundell suggested I send a footman with the portrait I showed him.'

He took a deep breath. 'A portrait of your half-brother?'

'No, the portrait of my mother.'

He was losing the thread again. 'Why—?'

She pulled a miniature from her reticule and thrust it at him. 'It includes a likeness of the bracelet.'

He stared at the intricate piece of jewellery on the wrist of the woman who looked a great deal like Tess. It was indeed a unique piece and instantly recognisable. He glanced down at the list Tess had given him, wincing at the locales. 'Which of these have you visited?'

'The first two below the line. After my visit to Rundell & Bridge where they were curious about where the bracelet came from, I decided it unlikely that Grey would have gone to anyone on Ludgate Hill.' Her voice dropped to a whisper. 'Honestly, I had decided not to go to any more of the places on the list after I left that last one. They became progressively more unpleasant.'

Imagining what might have become of her in this part of London, Jaimie felt his throat dry. He swallowed down his fear for her and shot her a glare. 'I am glad to know you have a smidgeon of sense left.'

'Why are *you* here?'

For a moment, he thought of spinning her a tale, but decided there was no reason to prevaricate. 'I am pursuing enquiries into recent robberies.'

She glanced in the direction of the shop she had left. 'He buys stolen items?'

He nodded grimly. 'He does.'

'I am not surprised.'

'You are fortunate you came to no harm. I will take your portrait to the others on your list, if you wish.' He groaned inwardly. Another distraction from his task was the last thing he needed. He could not seem to stop offering to do things for her that he would never do for anyone else.

She glanced at the paper in his hand. 'I suppose you know all of these shops.'

He frowned. 'There is one here that is new to me.'

'Do you think…?' Hope coloured her voice and filled her soft gaze.

Hope for what? An unpleasant suspicion tightened his gut. 'Out with it.'

She ducked her head a fraction. 'I would like to go with you. When you go to enquire about the bracelet.'

He recoiled. 'Certainly not. You have already seen far more than you should have of this sort of establishment. And that really is not the worst of them.'

'I realise that, but in your company—'

'No.'

'But you don't know Grey. You won't know if he had been there or if it was someone else who brought in the bracelet.'

She sounded so logical, so reasonable, when what she was asking was so absolutely beyond the pale. He dredged his mind for sensible words. The sort of words his father might have spoken to his wife had she asked for such impossibilities. He found none. He didn't know his parents well enough.

Anger spilled over. Anger at the loss. Anger that she had reminded him of it yet again. 'That is the most ridiculous thing I've ever heard.'

She shot bolt upright in the seat and grabbed for the portrait. 'Then I do not need your help, Lord Sandford.'

He easily held it out of her reach. Her personality was so forceful, he was always forgetting how tiny she was. How easily overpowered. He grasped her outstretched hand, pulling her towards him. She landed hard against his chest. He gazed down into her startled face, while inside him anger warred with fear for her safety. Her eyes hazed over and drew him down into their depths. She wetted her lips with a little dart of her tongue. His groin tightened. Instead of giving her the lecture on behaviour he had intended, he…kissed her.

She struggled for one brief moment and then she threw her other arm around him and kissed him back.

It was long breathless moments later when they broke apart and he realised his anger had fled, to be replaced by a much less complex and more demanding passion. Not something he should indulge. Not unless he wanted to find himself leg-shackled in the immediate future, which he definitely did not. He gazed down into her flushed face and was struck anew by her beauty. Damn it, despite every logical sensible reason he could come up with, he was going to let her have her way.

He gave a sigh of resignation and set her back on her seat. 'Very well, we will visit this next place on your list. I will return here later with regard to my own business.'

'Thank you. I-I am sorry to be so insistent, but I am terrified something bad has happened to Grey. He is the only real family I have left. Well, the only one I truly care about.'

He could remember his feeling of joy when Michael had returned home. The relief. A crushing weight had lifted from his shoulders. If he had been able to search for his cousin, he would have done so, but in those early years he could barely leave his bed for pain, not to mention the opium.

He rapped on the roof of the carriage. The coachman lifted the trapdoor. Jaimie gave him the next address.

'What are the items you are seeking from the robberies you are investigating?' she asked as the carriage moved off.

'Small things, items easily disposed of.' He dragged his own list from his pocket and handed it over.

'A silver spoon,' she read, 'with monogram A.R. A

salt cellar, silver. A silver cake server. These hardly seem worth the trouble of a man in your position.'

Her quick understanding surprised him anew. 'It isn't the items themselves so much as it is the way the perpetrator gains entry into the house without anyone being any the wiser. The *ton* are starting to fear for their lives.'

'Has he hurt someone?'

'Not as yet, but he walks willy-nilly through their houses at night.'

'Oh.' She peered at the list. 'I recognise this name.'

'I recognise them all. They are all members of the *ton*.'

'Yes, but, I mean, someone mentioned this person to me recently. And not in a favourable light.'

'Therefore it is all right for them to be terrorised in their own homes?'

'That is not what I meant.'

She tapped her lips with a forefinger. Plump rosy lips he had kissed only a moment ago. Lips that were pouting as she thought, tempting him to kiss them again. Damn it, she was the most annoying female.

'Oh.' The little *o* formed by those pretty lips definitely needed kissing. After all, they were alone in a closed carriage with no one to see and perhaps she needed to be reminded why it was not a good idea for a young lady to gallivant around town unaccompanied. A very gentle reminder. He slid an arm around her waist and the other under her knees and lifted her on to his lap. Something inside him finally relaxed, felt right.

'Oh,' she said again, all breathless, and this time her lips softened to sultry.

He kissed her. Or she kissed him. Whichever it was,

it mattered not one jot. His brain scrambled. His body hardened. His heart pounded so hard against his ribs he half-expected it to smash its way out. The carriage lurched around a corner. Even mindless, some instinct had him bracing his feet and holding her fast so she did not tumble to the floor. Unfortunately it also ended the kiss.

She stared at him, cheeks rosy, lips plush and red, eyes soft. 'Oh, my,' she whispered. With a touch as light as a feather, she stroked his cheek with her fingertips.

Oh, hell. No wonder parents didn't allow single young ladies to ride alone in carriages with gentlemen. Right now all he wanted to do was rip her off her clothes and bury himself deep within her body. If she'd let him. 'Tess.'

'Jaimie.'

The sound of his name on those deliciously inviting lips had him harder than rock. The invitation in her voice stole his breath. He pulled her closer, kissed her deeply, savouring the feel of her lush little bottom against his aching shaft. It would not take much—

No, not here. Not in a carriage. Awkward and fumbling. Hurried.

His manhood protested that smidgeon of sense, fought for control, demanding fulfilment. With great effort he returned her to her side of the carriage, hating the chill that replaced the warmth of her touch.

'Oh, goodness,' she said, her expression sensual, her lips moist and plump from his kisses.

He mentally cursed his lack of control with this particular woman. She'd have him dancing to her tune if he didn't get a grip on his lust and whatever else it was making her almost irresistible. Had he not sworn after Hester died never to let any woman rob him of reason? Had he not learned his lesson about headstrong females with not a thought in their heads but the instant fulfilment of whatever desire they had at that moment?

He inwardly withdrew. Wrestled his unwilling body into submission.

Expressions flitted across her face. Confusion. Disappointment. Longing.

'Perhaps I should return you home,' he said repressively, as if that kiss had been all her fault.

She flinched and coloured and he felt a twinge of guilt. She straightened her spine. 'You said I could go with you.'

He gave a long-suffering sigh which had nothing to do with her insistence about his promise and everything to do with maintaining his status as an honourable man. 'We are almost there.'

Glancing out of the window, she grimaced with distaste as the carriage turned into a narrow, filthy street.

Good, perhaps she'd change her mind and let him take her home.

Tess was doing her level best to sound ordinary when she felt anything but normal. When had she become so wanton? A simple kiss from him and her body burst into flames.

Hah! Simple did not describe his kiss. The scent of him, sandalwood and bergamot, the silken slide of his tongue in her mouth had driven all sensible thoughts from her head, except the need to be close. Closer. As if she could crawl inside his skin with him. And now he sat opposite her, looking coolly unaffected.

Kissing was certainly extraordinarily exciting. Something she had not expected. Her cheeks heated again, the warmth flooding upwards from deep inside her. Oh, heavens, she must stop thinking about it or she would be the one doing the kissing.

And that would not do at all. After all, unless they found Grey still in possession of her bracelet, which if she was honest, she now doubted they would, then she was either going to have to marry Mr Stedman or be banished to live with Phin's Aunt Marie.

She certainly couldn't imagine kissing Mr Stedman or doing those other things with him that she'd only done with Jaimie. Perhaps if she hadn't allowed herself to be tempted into those kisses and touches, she might not have minded so much. She would not have known any different. Now, the very idea of being with any other man like that made her feel ill.

Blast Lord Sandford and his delicious kisses. She should have known better than to trust any man. She should never have gone to him in the first place.

She just had to hope that finding Grey would be the answer to her problems.

She realised Jaimie was watching her, his gaze hooded. No doubt expecting her to give up her quest just because he had kissed her and made her feel all lovely and melty inside.

She leaned over and picked up his list that had fallen to the floor. She frowned. What a strange collection of items it contained. The sort of things that— She looked over at him.

'What is it?' he asked.

'Did it occur to you that all of the items on your list are usually found in the butler's pantry? And that they are all parts of a set that would likely be difficult to replace?'

He picked it up from where it had fallen on the floor and scanned it. 'Well, it didn't, but I do see what you mean. Someone trying to complete their own missing pieces?'

'Hardly likely. Many of them are monogrammed.' She absent-mindedly straightened her bonnet. 'Who steals a half-side of beef? As well as an enormous round of cheese and a twenty-pound sack of potatoes. It is as if they are feeding an army.'

'Thieves have to eat the same as other people.'

'But the amounts are extraordinary, do you not think?'

He straightened. 'Yes. You are right.'

She had half-expected him to pooh-pooh her suggestions. That he had not made her feel a different kind of warmth inside. A growing respect for his intelligence.

'I would rather you remain in the carriage,' he announced when the vehicle came to a halt.

The warmth dissipated like smoke.

'No.'

He stiffened. Clearly he was a man who was used to being obeyed. Not something that augured well for a wife if he ever married. She took a calming breath, reining in a spurt of temper. 'Don't you think they will be more amenable to talking to us if we go in as a couple looking for items to use in our home, rather than you going in there questioning them like an officer of the law, all stern and forbidding?'

'That is the same argument you used when we went to Ingram Manor.'

'It is a valid argument.'

He grimaced. 'I don't have to enter that place…' he jerked his chin towards the door with its peeling paint, grimy windows and the dangling three balls that had once been gold, but were now a rusty brown '…to know what it will be like. It is not suitable for a lady.'

She pulled down the veil. 'No one will recognise me. I might see items Grey sold that you would not recognise. Gifts from my father. You can't even accurately describe what he looks like.' She tried to ignore the folded sketch inside her glove. Someone might recognise him, poor though the drawing was.

His chin took on a stubborn slant. 'Describe him to me, then.'

Dash it, the man had an answer for everything. 'I'll come back on my own if you don't let me go with you.'

His normally cool gaze flashed fire. 'I will insist your cousin keep you under lock and key.'

She gasped. 'You wouldn't.'

'Try me.'

'Please, Jaimie. I promise I will stay close by your side. My reasons are good. You know they are.'

He let go a sigh. 'Very well. Do not go one half-inch away from my side. Let me do the talking until we see what we are dealing with.'

He reached under the seat and pulled forth a small box from which he removed a pistol. He tucked it into his waistband at the small of his back.

Her jaw dropped. 'You think that is necessary?'

'Under normal circumstances, likely not, but I am not taking any chances.'

He knocked on the roof and a moment later the footman opened the carriage door and let down the steps.

'You servants are well trained.'

'This is not the first time we have visited this part of town. They know to wait until I give the signal.'

He climbed down and helped her out. Once he had her arm safely tucked beneath his, he strode through the shop door.

A bell rattled above their heads.

Inside, the place was ill lit and there were boxes and bags piled hither and yon as well as stuff crammed on to shelves. So much stuff, from candlesticks to items of clothing. The combined smells of dust, cooked cabbage and mildew hit the back of her throat and made her gag.

The counter from behind which the shop owner peered at them was littered with an assortment of items. Behind him, a glass-fronted cabinet held trinkets and what looked like more valuable objects.

The shopkeeper's grizzled eyebrows drew down and his pointed nose seemed to twitch as they approached him. 'How may I help you, madam, sir?' he asked in a hoarse voice.

While she was trembling inside with fear as the place was so intimidating, Jaimie was the very picture of insouciance and aplomb.

'We are setting up our home.' Jaimie gave her a dazzling smile and patted her hand. He so rarely smiled and her stomach did a little somersault at the sight. 'We were told you carry items that are within our budget.' He pointed to one of the shelves. 'That candlestick, for example.'

Tess felt a thrill run down her spine as he embellished the scenario she had suggested.

'That is right, my dear,' she said softly.

Huffing and puffing, the shop keeper climbed a stepladder to reach the candlestick, dusting it on his sleeve as he brought it down. 'Nice piece this. Solid silver. Worth a bit.'

Jaimie looked it over. 'It's not solid. No hallmark, and look, you can see here where the silver is worn away. This is brass showing through.'

The man cocked his head on one side. 'Ah, I can see you are a sharp young fellow.' He grinned, showing stained and broken teeth. 'I only want a crown for that there. Worth a lot more it is.'

Jaimie looked at her. 'What do you think, my dear?'

She bit her lip. 'It's a bit expensive. I wonder if they have any salt spoons. We need those more than a candlestick.'

'Always so practical, my sweet lady.' He raised a brow.

'Got hundreds,' the old man said, pulling out a box. 'Have a look at these.'

He plonked the box in front of them. 'Sixpence for one, a shilling for three. Take your pick.' Tess turned them over, looking for monograms, while Jaimie leaned over the counter to look in the cabinet behind the old man.

The box contained a great many little spoons, but none as described on Jaimie's list. She smiled. 'I like this one.'

She held up a plain one.

Jaimie clearly understood that she hadn't found anything. 'My darling, it is yours.'

The old man rubbed his mitten hands together, making a dry rasping sound.

'Anything else for you? Got a nice collection of carving knives. A silver bowl that has only one dent in it.'

He set the items before them. Tess inspected them.

'What about that bracelet in there?' Jaimie asked.

Tess froze, every sense on alert as the man turned to see where Jaimie was pointing.

'Ah, expensive that be, sir.'

Tess finally saw what Jaimie was looking at. It was a pretty item, but nothing like her mother's. Then she saw what he had really been looking at. 'I like the one beside it.' She held her breath. Could it be?

The old man took a key from his pocket, unlocked the cabinet, took out the item and relocked it before bringing the bracelet for them to see.

Tess's heart thumped loudly in her chest with an excitement she could scarcely contain. But when he spread it out before them, it was a huge disappointment. Yes, there was a bit of filigree work, but it was quite obviously a very poor paste imitation of oriental design and not nearly as intricate as the one she sought.

'It is nice,' she said. 'But it is missing several stones.'

'Can have them replaced for you. Cost a bit more, of course.'

'I will think about it.' She glanced around the shop. She had been so wrong, thinking she could find anything in a place like this. It would be like looking for a needle in a haystack. 'Show him the portrait, my dear,' Jaimie said. 'He may have seen something like it.'

Tess dug it out and handed it over. She winced at the way the old man put his grimy hands on her mother's picture.

'It would have been brought in by a man of about twenty, with dark hair and eyes. He has a small scar on his cheek in a crescent shape,' Tess said.

He finally shook his head. 'I ain't never seen nothing of this quality. Nor a man such as you describe.' He narrowed his eyes. 'It's not stolen, is it?'

'The picture?' Jaimie asked.

'The bracelet. I don't deal in stolen stuff.'

'I'd be prepared to pay a goodly sum to make my little lady here happy.'

Jaimie had not answered the question. He was making the man think it was stolen.

The man shook his head. 'Sorry, guv'nor. This item hasn't come my way.'

'And there is nothing else here I like.' She didn't have to pretend to be disappointed. She was. Terribly.

'Well, thank you for your time, good sir. We'll be on our way as soon as we pay for the spoon.'

He presented his coins. The old man wrapped their purchase in a bit of paper.

Back out on the street, Tess inhaled a big breath of fresh air. Fresher than in the shop anyway.

'Now you know why I wanted you to wait in the carriage,' Jaimie said tersely. 'But I have to admit I was glad of your presence. You were right, the shopkeeper was not nearly as suspicious as those fellows usually are when I speak with them.'

The surprise wasn't so much that she had been helpful, she knew she had. It was his admission of her value. Perhaps he wasn't as arrogant as she had thought. They visited two more shops and at each they were disappointed. No one had seen either the bracelet or anyone answering to Grey's description.

When they entered the carriage the third time, he pulled out his pocket watch. 'What time are you expected home?'

'Before five.'

'It is nearly five now. I will take you back.'

'We have only one place left on our list.'

'We will have to visit it tomorrow.'

He was right, she should not be out too late. Phin would only start questioning her. 'I'm not sure I can sneak out again.'

A small smile curved his lips. 'You really should not be sneaking anywhere.' He put up a hand to halt her objection. 'I will take you driving tomorrow. Leave your veil with me and we'll change carriages once we are out of sight of your house.'

Finally he was recognising the importance of her search and including her in its execution. Seeing her as a partner in the hunt. The urge to kiss him hovered on her lips. She settled for a smile. 'That will be wonderful.'

When his gaze settled on her mouth, a gaze that she felt like a touch on her skin, she thought he might also be overcome by the idea of kissing her again, but instead he turned his head to look out of the window.

Perhaps he didn't find their kisses as entrancing as she did.

'A note for you, Lady Tess,' the butler said.

Wilhelmina put out a hand with an arch look. 'Let me see.'

Containing her ire, Tess put her needlework aside. It didn't take long for her cousin to scan the paper and then hold it out for Tess to take, forcing her to rise. 'From Sandford. He regrets your outing must be postponed until tomorrow.'

Tess wasn't in the least surprised, but she was still disappointed as she glanced at the note written in a bold scrawling hand. Short and to the point. No regrets.

'I was expecting it,' she said calmly. 'Given the weather.' The dratted man must think she was made of icing sugar. Men couldn't see what was in front of their noses.

'He's hardly lover-like,' her cousin said with a titter.

Tess froze. 'Why would he be lover-like?'

Wilhelmina's plucked brows climbed her forehead. 'Is he not a suitor for your hand? One would expect something a little more endearing.'

Oh, that. Tess flushed red. She hated the lie. And flushed even darker at the recollection of the kiss that had almost got out of control in the carriage on the previous day. That had been far *too* lover-like.

'My goodness, Tess. You are blushing.'

Tess went to the window and looked out. The sky was leaden and the rain light but steady. 'I really should return my book to Hatchard's and I need to stretch my legs.'

Her cousin sighed. 'Always so restless. I hope Sandford will not be put off by your odd ways. Phin would be very disappointed. Perhaps while you are out you can pick up the bracelet, should it be ready.'

'Mr Rundell said he would send a note round.'

They'd had this conversation at least three times in the last two days. Tess suspected that Phin had decided to lay claim to the bracelet for the estate. No doubt he wanted it as a gift for his wife. It was just the sort of thing he would do, even after Tess had explained to him that it was her mother's personal property. He'd simply asked her to prove it, knowing she couldn't.

Wilhelmina sighed. 'Well, I hope he will not charge overmuch. It has cost Phin a fortune for your come out.'

Not quite the truth. Her gowns she had made herself and she had worn them all more than once. But there had been expenses Phin had covered. Expenses that ought to have been provided for in Father's will. She should have guessed they would try to make her feel guilty and give up her mother's bracelet in recompense. After all, she really should not have been their responsibility.

The pain of her father's lack of care hit her anew, but she forced herself to say nothing. 'Do you have anything you would like me to collect while I am at the bookshop?'

'Not that I can think of at the moment.'

'Then I will see you at afternoon tea.'

On her way up to her room, Tess let the butler know she would need Mims to go with her to Hatchard's.

A few minutes later Mims came puffing into the room. Tess had already put on her hat and spencer. 'You are going and want me to go with you?' Mims looked distressed, but bravely determined.

'We'll take a hackney when we are out of sight of the house.'

'And where are we going?'

'To visit Lord Sandford.'

Mims frowned. 'Your father may have let you run riot at Ingram, but this is London and that is not the behaviour of a proper brought-up young lady.'

'I am not a proper brought-up young lady. I am an Ingram. Brought up to solve my own problems. Believe me, you would like the alternative much less.' She could have decided to take Mims with her to visit the rest of the pawnshops. No. She would not. It wasn't safe. She might be reckless in the pursuit of an objective upon occasion, but she was not a fool.

'I don't think your father would be pleased,' Mims said.

'It is Father's fault we are in this mess.'

Mims frowned. 'Your pa might have been reckless with his coin at times, but he wasn't one to shirk his duty. Look how he took in Master Hammond.'

Tess grimaced. 'Gambling away the family fortune is hardly living up to one's responsibilities.

The old lady sighed. 'I suppose not.'

Tess swept downstairs, took the offered umbrella from the footman at the front door and made him get one for Mims. Outside, the air seemed to have an acrid tang. Rain and coal smoke. She walked at a gentle pace with Mims hobbling a foot or so behind. As soon as they turned the corner, she flagged down the first carriage for hire to come along.

Chapter Nine

Jaimie wiped his dirty hands on a rag. 'Is she alone?' he asked his butler who had brought in her calling card.

'No, my lord.' The man sniffed. 'Brought her maid along.'

Thank the Lord for small mercies.

He glanced down at the worktable where he was in the midst of a critical graft. If he left it now the stems would dry and the graft would fail. If that happened, he'd have to wait another six weeks for the right shoot to appear. 'Offer tea to the maid in the kitchen and bring Lady Tess in here.'

'Here, my lord?' He sounded scandalised.

As well he should. Jaimie glanced around his conservatory. It really was not the best place to entertain a lady, but really, he hadn't asked her to come here. Why could she not simply wait for him to get in touch? He was busy. He glared at his butler. 'I am sure I can rely on you to be discreet, Rider. After all, any gossip and I would know from where it came. And send up a tray of tea with biscuits and cake, would you please?' He was starving. He glanced at the clock on the far wall. No wonder. He'd missed luncheon, though he was pretty sure it had been announced. He'd been too engrossed in what he was doing for it to register.

The butler left with another sniff.

He was certainly going to have a word with Tess about upsetting his servants with her madcap ways.

He began the careful work of binding two stems together at the precise point where his knife had removed the outer layer of bark. Focusing on the intricate task was all that was stopping him from losing his temper. The more he thought about Tess's folly, the higher his ire rose. And the last time he'd truly lost his temper the result had been utter disaster. He'd stomped off to London after a blazing row with Hester about her lack of driving skills after she'd scraped the paint off his brand-new curricle. Just to prove she was better than he, she'd then driven the horses he'd forbidden her to have put to and had ended up with a broken neck. He should have known better than to have left her alone and angry. He had known better.

But he'd been unreasonably angry himself and had lost his wife as a result…

'Lady Theresa,' the butler announced. He directed a footman to put the tray on the end of the workbench and the two men left.

'Sandford,' she said.

He preferred it when she called him Jaimie. He nodded and continued inspecting his handiwork to the sound of tea being poured.

It pleased him that she got on with things without

waiting for the formalities. It also irritated the hell out of him that she thought nothing of taking charge. 'Why are you here, Lady Tess? I thought we agreed this would not happen again.' He took up another piece of twine. You could never use too much in his opinion. He carefully wound it around the joint.

'Because apparently you could not call for me in this weather.'

He fumbled and the thorn he'd been avoiding stabbed his thumb. He cursed and stuck it in his mouth.

She walked up behind him and peered over his shoulder. 'What are you doing?'

'Grafting two roses.'

'That is nice.'

Nice. A milk-and-water sort of word. It wasn't how he would have described it. It was more of an obsession.

'Tea is ready,' she said.

He picked up his magnifying glass and inspected the joint again. Perfect. 'Give me a moment.'

He replanted the cutting and tidied up the implements while she wandered up and down the conservatory, inspecting the pots and plants set on benches along its length. She leaned in to sniff at a bloom. 'No scent.'

'No. Something about crossing them seems to rob them of perfume.' He washed his hands using the bowl set on a washstand at the other end of the long room.

'Not an improvement, in my opinion.'

Nor in his. He made his way to the tray and picked out his favourite biscuit.

She handed him a cup of tea and they sat down side by side on the old sofa he'd had placed in here.

'You weren't expecting me to make my horses stand around in a downpour so you could visit the Seven Dials, were you?' he asked when she had taken a sip of her tea.

She sighed. 'I wasn't sure. Your note said, *in my phaeton*. I wondered if you meant that we could go if we went in the closed carriage, but that you couldn't very well drive up to the front door and expect Wilhelmina to let me drive out in it.'

And here he'd thought he'd been making the reason for his non-appearance clear. Something she could surely have figured out for herself. 'I meant exactly what I said. Our drive will need to be postponed until tomorrow.' The woman needed a husband to keep her in check, though he'd pity the poor fellow. Well, perhaps envy him, too…

Her gaze wandered the room. 'You spend a lot of time with these plants.'

'I do. I started working on creating my own rose when I was twelve.'

'An unusual hobby for a boy.'

'When I was young I was unable to go about much. I was recovering from an injury and this was a way to pass the time. These days, I find it helps me think.' Though his brain hadn't had much chance for thinking recently because his body seemed to have taken over.

'Think about what?'

'Well, for example, your comment about the objects stolen. I have been thinking about that.' Or trying to. He'd also been thinking a lot about Lady Tess and her delicious kisses.

Indeed, right now he was having a hard time not focusing on her cleavage. He took another biscuit to keep his hands busy. Shortbread. His second-favourite.

'What sort of injury?'

Damn, he had left that door open, had he not? His brain really did seem to be working at less than full capacity. Hell, what did it matter? The fire was common knowledge. Better that he tell her some of the true story than have her listening to gossip. 'Our house caught fire when I was a small child. I was not burned. At least not much.' He held up his hand and she could see the odd way the little finger stuck out and that the skin there was scarred. 'Unfortunately, I inhaled a lot of smoke. My lungs were badly affected.'

'You are fully recovered now?'

'For the most part.' He was fit and healthy, but he could not run any great distance without falling into a fit of coughing.

She touched his arm. 'I am glad. Fire is a terrible thing.'

Fire was his worst nightmare. 'I lost nearly all of my family in that fire.'

'Oh, no! I'm so terribly sorry, Jaimie.'

He remained silent. The guilt was his to bear alone. Only his cousin Michael knew the full story and he insisted none of it was Jaimie's fault. It had simply been an accident.

Jaimie and Tess sat side by side on the sofa in companionable silence, sipping their tea and nibbling biscuits. An odd feeling of contentment slid over him. *This* was the sort of marriage he hoped for. Something peaceful. A haven he could come home to as a respite from his work.

'Can we not visit the next shop on the list now?'

He hurtled into the present. 'We will go tomorrow.'

'But what if it is raining again tomorrow? Who knows how much longer Mr Stedman will remain away? He has been gone three days already.'

Why could she not trust him to make the necessary arrangements? 'If it rains tomorrow, then I will offer to escort you to visit the two remaining members of my family. Lord and Lady Hawkhurst. They rarely come to town and it would make sense, since we wish my intentions to appear honourable, for me to take you to meet them. In the company of your maid, of course. We will visit the last shop on the list on the way back.'

'You have it all thought out, don't you. But how do you know I am not busy tomorrow?'

This was exactly the sort of argument Hester would use to tie him in knots. He'd been too young to handle her then. Too besotted with her beauty and the fact that she had chosen him of all the fellows to marry. Likely because she'd thought she could wrap him around her little finger. Well, that would never happen again.

'Are you busy tomorrow? Because if so, then we will go the *next* day.'

She heaved a sigh. 'As it happens I am not. My cousin is going for a fitting for a new gown and I am at a loose end.'

'Then there is no more to be said. As soon as you are finished your tea, I will return you home in my carriage.'

'Oh no! I wouldn't dream of putting you to such trouble.'

'No trouble at all.' He glanced at the clock. 'I was going out shortly anyway. The carriage should be ready in five minutes or so.' Damn, he really should have had lunch. Still, there would be sustenance to be had at his club.

She half-turned in the seat, her face alight with anticipation. He had the sudden urge to kiss her again. All over this time.

'Why do we not go now then, so that tomorrow we can think of what to do next if nothing useful turns up?'

A dash of cold water killed his desire. It was not him who had her looking all enthusiastic after all. He put aside his cup.

'We go tomorrow.'

Her eyes narrowed. 'Were you intending to go there now, without me? Is that why your carriage is ready?'

Damn, but her suspicions struck him on the raw. 'If you think so badly of me, Lady Tess, I am surprised you risked coming here at all.'

Her eyes widened. 'Oh, I do beg your pardon. That was terribly rude of me. It is just that every man I having dealings with seems to let me down.'

He stiffened. 'I can assure you I am a man of my word, my lady. I have offered to take you there tomorrow and that is what I will do. However, it will be the last such place we will visit.'

She gasped. 'What do you mean?'

'I was wrong to expose you to such ugly surroundings. It is not fitting.'

'You think I should pretend not to know that such

places exist? That I must not see or hear anything unpleasant because I am a woman?'

'A gently bred woman does not...'

Her eyes glittered with anger. 'Does not what?'

His own anger sparked. 'Does not needlessly endanger
herself. She leaves things of a questionable nature to her
responsible male relatives.'

'Hah.' It was the most scornful noise sound he had
ever heard. As if he had just made the most ridiculous
statement, instead of speaking simple common sense.

Her chin came up. 'Then we must suppose I am not at
all gently bred. I can assure you, Lord Sandford, I have
no intention of giving up my quest to find my brother,
with or without you.'

A bitter smile curved his lips. 'I must say, I am starting to pity old Stedman trying to keep you in line.'

'In line? Oh, you are the rudest man I have ever
met—and the most arrogant!'

'Thank you.'

She bit her lip. 'I beg your pardon. That was rude
of me. You seem to bring out the worst of my temper.'

She brought out the worst in him, too. Because every
time she showed that flash of temper, he wanted to kiss
her and explore all that fire and passion.

He must be losing his mind, because the only way
that could ever happen again was if they were married.
But she was the last woman he wanted for a wife. And
she was right. The sooner they visited this last establishment, the sooner he could be done with her.

There was not a doubt in his mind that if they did not
go now, the moment he set her down at her front door,

even if he carried her inside, she would be off to visit that shop on her own—and that he would not allow. It was dangerous in the extreme.

'Very well. Have it your way. We will go now.'

She smiled in triumph, but then she shook her head. 'It won't work. What will Wilhelmina think when I arrive home in your carriage? You will have to set us down before we get to the square.'

'Nonsense. Having seen you out walking in the rain, I offered you and your maid a ride. What could be more normal?'

A shrug greeted his words 'I suppose it would work.'

'I'm glad you approve. Let us be off.'

Why had he given in so easily? Tess worried the tip of her gloved finger. Was he going to take her home and reveal the whole to Rowan as he had threatened? It was just the sort of thing a man would do. They wouldn't see such behaviour as dishonourable when dealing with a woman.

She could not help but watch his lithe figure as he walked briskly to the other end of the room and rang the bell. He looked gorgeous in his shirtsleeves. Good enough to eat. And the scent of earth and growing things mixed with the delicious scent of his cologne sent warmth trickling through her veins. It was a good thing he had rung for the butler or she might be tempted to do something quite untoward, like twine her arms around his neck and kiss him. She loved the feel of his wonderfully hard body against hers. She had dreamed of it last night.

The butler, when he had received his instructions, shot her a most disapproving look, then left.

'Your butler is exceedingly high in the instep,' she observed.

'Somewhat.'

'Has he been with your family a long time?'

'No. I hired him a couple of months ago.'

How strange. In her experience servants stayed with one forever, if one was reasonable. Was he a harsh employer? Was that cool calm exterior merely a front?

'The carriage will be at the door momentarily,' he continued. 'Let us go.'

Swept along by his obvious impatience, she let him escort her to the front hall, where Mims was already waiting. At the sight of the dear old stick, he hesitated.

'Mims,' Tess said, 'this is Lord Sandford. He is going to drive us home in his carriage. He has an errand to run along the way.' Mims's gaze sharpened. There wasn't much that escaped her notice, but nevertheless, she bobbed a curtsy. 'My poor old feet thank you, my lord.'

Jaimie made an odd sound. Was he laughing?

A moment later they were climbing into his town carriage, the porte cochère making it unnecessary for them to use their umbrellas, and, once settled in the vehicle, Jaimie engaged in pleasantries about the weather with Mims.

Surprised at this spectacularly unusual unbending, Tess watched Jaimie with interest. She'd thought him arrogant, but he was going out of his way to be nice to an old lady. And since it was likely only Mims's presence that had convinced him to take this journey this afternoon, she could not help wondering if that was because he didn't trust himself to be alone with her, or because he didn't trust her not to be wanton. Whichever it was, the thought intrigued her. Set up little flutters low in her belly.

Desire he had made sure she could do nothing about.

It did not take them long to reach their destination. They left Mims inside the carriage and entered the shop. Tess had thought nothing could be worse than those they had visited the day before, but she had been wrong. The smell that assaulted her senses as she entered this one robbed her of breath. Her eyes watered and the stink from the man behind the counter caused an involuntary contraction of her throat.

Sandford, blast him, gave her an I-told-you-so look. No wonder Mr Rundell had been so firm about her sending a footman.

The greasy-haired moustachioed man rose from his stool behind the counter.

'Wot do you want?' Clearly he didn't like the look of *them*, either.

'We are looking for—'

'Don't give me that load of rubbish,' the man wheezed. He wiped his sleeve under his nose. 'What? You think we don't talk to each other? You visited three shops yesterday and now you is visiting me. Well, I ain't got whatever you is looking for, so you can tell *that* to the Runners.'

Tess twitched Jaimie's sleeve and shook her head.

No matter how bad things were, she was quite positive Grey would never set foot in such a place as this.

'My good man,' Sandford said, ignoring her silent appeal that they leave, 'you will answer my questions or you will find yourself facing a magistrate.'

The man shrank back. 'Now let's not be too hasty, sir.'

'My lord,' Jaimie corrected.

The fellow's eyes shifted back and forth as if he was looking for an escape route. Finding none, he cringed and bowed low. 'Whatever you require, my lord.'

Jaimie outlined the items they sought. The ugly fellow frowned. ''Tis not me you should be asking, your lordship, 'tis that woman at Covent Garden. Undercutting me, she is. Selling on the cheap. Selling those sorts of things wot you is asking about.'

Sandford tilted his head. 'Unlikely you would be intimidated by a woman.'

'Ah, well, me and the boys thought we might show her the error of her ways, but she's got a feller. Quiet as a cat he is and as lethal as a snake.' He shook his head. 'They's up to no good, I'll bet a guinea to a monkey.'

Talk about throwing your competition under the proverbial carriage wheel.

'Covent Garden, you say?' Tess asked, a strange feeling invading her chest. A sort of knowing. How very strange.

'At the Friday market, miss, er, my lady.'

She glanced at Sandford, who was poking around one of the shelves. He picked up an ornate candlestick and inspected it closely.

'All right, guv'ner, I'll admit I might have the odd file or two who asks me to sell items for him, but it's honest business. This woman and her hoity-toity ways is cutting the legs right out from under shops like mine, pretending to be honest and charging pennies for top-quality goods. Up to no good, she is, you mark my words.'

It was the strangest thing Tess had ever heard.

Sandford scratched at his chin. 'This candlestick, now. Where did it come from?'

The man shivered. 'Bought it.'

'From whom? The truth now.'

'From her. Mrs Plunkett. I can make a tidy profit on it, I can. Had to send one of me girls to buy it. She wouldn't sell it to me. Oh, no, I was not the sort of person she wanted buying her goods.'

Jaimie tucked it under his arm. 'I'll be taking it with me for evidence.'

The man looked as if he wanted to howl a protest, but one look at Jaimie's face and he backed away and gestured for him to help himself.

'I don't think we require anything further at the moment,' Sandford said, giving her an enquiring glance.

Tess shook her head.

He held out his arm and they departed.

Tess had never been so glad to leave anywhere in her life. It took her a moment to recover her breath. 'Is that one of the items on your list?'

'It is.'

'Then we need to pay Mrs Plunkett a visit this Friday.' She glared at him. 'Together.'

'You heard what he said about the ruffian she employs.'

'I am sure you have men equally rough.'

He frowned. 'Yes. Very well, I will take you with me. We will simply go as if we are shopping. It works well enough. If that does not succeed, then we will think of something more drastic. While our friend in there and those we visited yesterday might talk amongst themselves, I doubt they will be passing along any help to this outsider, Mrs Plunkett.'

Four days from now. 'What if Mr Stedman comes back before Friday?'

'I doubt that he will. Growler has arranged to keep him occupied for a while.'

She gave a sigh of relief. 'Still, perhaps we should ask the man in there if he knows where Mrs Plunkett lives. If we could question her before Friday, it would not be a bad thing.'

Jaimie raised an eyebrow. 'Good idea. Wait in the carriage.'

Well, finally he had accepted that one of her suggestions was a good idea. This time she had no objection to returning to the carriage while he went back to enquire. She sank gratefully into the spotlessly clean squabs with a heartfelt sigh, waking a napping Mims in the process.

'Everything all right, deary? You look a little pale,' Mims said.

No surprise there. It was a wonder she hadn't been physically ill in that shop. 'I'll be better soon.'

Mims narrowed her eyes, peering at her stomach.

'Not been up to any hanky panky with his lordship, have you?'

Heat rushed to Tess's face. 'Certainly not.'

Mims looked as if she didn't believe a word. Fortunately Sandford's arrival forestalled any further questioning along those lines. For now.

He gave Tess a slight nod. 'I will have one of my men follow the information I was given.' He set the candlestick on the seat between them.

The old lady eyed it askance.

What on earth could she be thinking? She didn't dare ask, since Mims had no trouble offering her opinion when asked. No matter how scathing.

When Sandford dropped them off, he declined her invitation to come in for tea, merely escorting them to the front door and seeing them safely inside.

Dash it. They hadn't made any arrangements for Friday. Oh, but she would have plenty of time to talk to him when they went driving on the morrow.

Wilhelmina bustled into the hallway. 'Goodness, where have you been, Theresa? Surely you did not forget we are attending the Foggartys' ball this evening.'

No, she had not forgotten. She simply hadn't known they were going. 'What time are we leaving?'

'In an hour. We are to dine with the Petersons and go on from there.'

Mims shot her a look that said she had known nothing of this either. How typical of Wilhelmina.

'I will be ready,' Tess said. 'Mims will work her usual magic.'

Mims trundled up the stairs. Tess removed her hat and coat, giving the maid plenty of time to get up there and catch her breath.

Wilhelmina glowered at the maid's arduous progress up the stairs. 'It is time you found someone younger and more up to snuff. At the very least you need a change of hairstyle.'

Thanks heavens she'd insisted Mims be paid from the small allowance left her by her mother, something that had been in place before her father died. 'I am perfectly happy with my hair.'

'Is Lord Sandford attending the Foggartys' ball?'

Tess gritted her teeth. 'I'm not sure. He didn't mention it.'

'Tell the truth, Tess. You forgot to ask him. Such lack of interest might well drive him away and then where will you be?' The threat was clear. She'd be back expecting an offer from Mr Stedman.

Tess smiled her sweetest smile. 'Why don't you let me worry about Lord Sandford, Wilhelmina.'

'Well, I hope you know what you are doing.' Wilhelmina flounced off, no doubt annoyed that Tess hadn't buckled under her carping.

Tess raced up stairs. It was going to be nip and tuck if she was to be ready on time.

Why it hadn't occurred to him to set a watch on Lady Tess's movements before, Jaimie wasn't quite sure. If she had been a person under suspicion he would have done it without thinking. While he'd felt a little uncomfortable having men posted near her house after her arriving at his house yet again, he'd deemed it imperative. Their instructions were to report on arrivals and departures from the house as well as follow Tess whenever she left the house. It had clearly been the right thing to do. This evening she would be attending a ball she hadn't seen fit to mention to him, for some reason. In his experience, Tess never did anything without a reason.

The butler took his card and bowed him in to the Foggarty residence. 'I know I am late,' Jaimie said. 'No need to announce me. I'll see myself up.'

Unfortunately, he knew the house well. Lady Foggarty was an old flame. His first. Fifteen years his senior, she'd taken him in hand, literally, when he'd first arrived in town. Her husband spent all his time hunting, shooting and fishing and left his wife to her own devices. She liked her men young. As a twenty-year-old, he'd been hurt when she'd dropped him for an even younger, less worldly fellow. It would be awkward seeing her again with her husband present as well as her most recent *cher ami*. Back in those first halcyon days, after years of loneliness, he'd honestly thought he loved her. It had taken him a long time to realise that for her their affair had been nothing but dalliance.

Despite the fact that his cousin Michael had warned him not to take things too seriously, explaining that all young men went through stages of calf love, Jaimie had been sure she cared as much for him as he did for her. In those days, though, he needed affection badly. It was a weakness he now despised.

Then Hester had come along. After her, he'd learned

never to wear his heart on his sleeve. It made a man too vulnerable.

He climbed the stairs to the first-floor ballroom to the sound of music, laughter and chatter. Somewhere amongst the throng he would find Lady Tess. It would be interesting to hear why she had not mentioned she was coming here tonight. Avoidance? Was she up to more of her mischief?

If so, he could not think what it could be.

The Ingram party had gathered to the left of the orchestra. Careful not to appear too eager, he made his way around the room, greeting old friends and nodding to acquaintances. The moment Tess spotted him, he felt her attention like a touch on his skin. A soft brush of fingers across the nape of his neck. The same feeling he got when he had a criminal in his sights and they had no means of escaping his net.

Damn. It was all in his imagination. She wasn't even looking his way.

He spotted Michael and his wife not too far off and sauntered over to them.

Michael's face lit up at his approach. 'Jaimie. You never said you'd be here tonight when I saw you at the club earlier.'

Jaimie bowed to his wife. 'Lady Hawkhurst. You look lovely tonight.' He shook his cousin's hand. 'I only decided to come at the last moment.'

Alice smiled warmly. 'What a pleasant surprise, Jaimie. You so rarely attend parties.'

These people were his family. Their pleasure at seeing him gave him a rare warm feeling inside. A feeling he sometimes felt around Tess, now he thought about it. How odd since he'd thought his feelings for her were mostly lust and impatience.

His emotions regarding Michael and his wife were different. Simpler in some ways and in others more complex. At a basic level, Michael was family and that was all that needed to be said.

They were the only family each other had left. When Jaimie had dropped the candle, while he hid behind the curtains watching the guests at a party hosted by Michael's parents, the house had burned down. Both sets of parents as well as Michael's siblings had died in that fire. Michael's forgiveness brought Jaimie a measure of redemption, though he would never stop regretting that one foolish act as a six-year-old.

Now Michael had a wife and two small children who called Jaimie uncle, when he was really only their cousin.

'I don't suppose your attendance has anything to do with the lady I have been hearing about?' Alice asked with a hopeful little smile.

He should have guessed the rumour mill would have started turning. Likely Rowan was already counting his chickens before they were hatched.

His gaze wandered over to where Tess stood with her cousin. The urge to show her off to the Hawkhursts took him by surprise. 'I presume you mean Lady Tess Ingram? I admit, I sought and received permission to call on her, but as to where it will lead, I am not yet sure.'

Alice looked puzzled. 'Oh, dear. I had such hopes that at last you had found someone—'

'Would you care to meet her?' he interrupted, not wishing her to continue along those lines.

Inwardly he groaned. This had all the makings of a disaster if he wasn't careful.

Alice smiled, but her eyes were regretful. 'Naturally, if you wish us to.' She sounded doubtful.

Michael glared at him, making several of the men nearby shift uncomfortably. 'Not toying with her, are you, Jaimie?' Michael had a strong protective streak.

'Of course not.' He lowered his voice. 'Look, she is a client of mine, looking for a lost relative, and she doesn't want Rowan to know of her search, so I beg your discretion.'

Michael's eyes widened a fraction. 'Going behind a man's back with one of the female members of his family? Not like you to play such games.'

Jaimie swallowed his chagrin. Now Tess's shenanigans were making his cousin think less of him. 'I am simply trying to aid a lady with a problem of a private nature.'

'I imagine Rowan will be most disappointed when he learns you are not a suiter,' Michael said. He frowned. 'Are you sure she's not trying to put your head in the parson's noose? You are a good catch, Jaimie. And from what I understand the lady is both penniless and desperate. Be very careful.'

Jaimie stiffened. 'I will thank you not to malign the lady or me. I am not a fool, Cousin.'

Michael looked unimpressed.

Alice tilted her head as if hearing some hidden meaning in his words. 'I hope she might have you in her sights. For your sake. It is a long time since Hester—'

He tensed. He hated talking about Hester. All the old guilt rushed back. The terrible feeling that he should have known better than to have forbidden her anything. Her father certainly had thought so. An opinion he was at great pains to express at the funeral. Jaimie could not deny that he should have been there, protecting his wife, despite his duties for the Prince of Wales that had called him away. He had known how headstrong she was, but he'd never imagined she would endanger her life to make a point.

'Leave it, Alice,' Michael murmured. He knew the full story that had poured forth from Jaimie one night after too much brandy. His guilt. His anger at Hester. He had been so ashamed of that anger.

'I simply want to see Jaimie as happy as we are,' Alice said with an arch look at her husband.

'I have no doubt that he will not appreciate your attempts at matchmaking.'

Jaimie forced himself to smile. 'I am perfectly content as I am at the moment. And I know it is my duty to marry again and will do so, at some time in the future.'

Alice shook her head. 'Duty. Marriage is not just a duty, Jaimie. It is far more than that.' She frowned. 'This story you are setting about could easily ruin Lady Tess's reputation.'

'I've been on the town long enough to know how to handle such matters.' Since Hester died most of his affairs had been brief discreet flings with willing widows and never a hint of scandal.

Lady Tess was a completely different matter. A girl of marriageable age with a family who wouldn't hesitate to insist he observe the proprieties if they were given the chance. He had no intention of giving them any such opportunity. And yet not to introduce her to his family would look strange. He had no wish to embarrass Tess. 'I'll bring her over at an appropriate moment.'

'Very well. We will meet this young lady.'

And hopefully Alice would give up matchmaking for the present.

Michael smiled fondly at his wife. 'I see that they are striking up a waltz and it is an age since I danced with my wife, if she would do me the very great honour.'

Alice beamed. There was no mistaking the genuine affection between the couple. It was what he had sought all those years ago with Hester.

Jaimie felt a pang behind his breastbone. A strange sense of longing directed towards Lady Tess.

Nonsense. He knew exactly what sort of wife he required this time around. Jaimie had had enough drama to last him a lifetime. He wanted peace. A well-ordered life with a nice quiet wife was what he needed. There was nothing quiet or peaceful about Tess.

Michael gave him an impenetrable look and leaned close to murmur in his ear. 'You could do worse than Lady Tess Ingram, Jaimie. She might not have money, but from what I've heard she's a sensible girl. Did an excellent job caring for her father's estate.'

Shocked, Jaimie stared at him. '*Et tu, Brute?* Where did you hear such a thing?'

Michael smiled his enigmatic smile. 'I have my sources.' He bowed to his wife and held out his hand. 'My lady.'

She took it and the two of them strolled on to the dance floor.

Chapter Ten

Tess could not believe the way her heart had picked up speed the moment she saw Jaimie enter the ballroom. She had done her best not to stare at his beautiful lithe form as he meandered through the room. Several other ladies were also covertly admiring him. And why would they not? The way his tight black coat drew attention to the width of his shoulders and the leanness of his waist and hips was enough to draw any woman's eye. Long legged, loose limbed and supremely confident, he exuded masculine grace.

Recalling what lay below the elegant tailoring, she felt her breasts tighten and little pulses flutter at her core, sending heat streaming through her blood.

'He is here, after all,' Wilhelmina said.

Was that disappointment in her voice?

'Who?' she asked, looking around as if she had not yet seen him.

'Sandford.'

'Oh?' She tried for insouciance, but feared she

sounded breathless, eager. She finally let her gaze land directly on him, though he'd not been out of her sight for a single moment. The couple he was talking to seemed pleased to see him. The lady was beaming at him in a most particular way. Irritation slid a blade between her ribs when he smiled down at her and the lady patted his arm with her fan.

The man, presumably her husband, did not look pleased. Tess had not taken Jaimie for a flirt. He never ever flirted with her. She swallowed her chagrin and looked away. How could she possibly be jealous?

'He's coming this way,' Wilhelmina hissed.

She pasted a smile of welcome on her face, but it felt stiff and awkward.

'Lady Rowan. Lady Tess.' Jaimie bowed. 'Good to see you again, ladies.'

They greeted him in unison. He gave Tess a cautious look. 'Would you take a turn about the room with me, Lady Tess?'

Disappointed he had not asked her to dance, Tess looked to her cousin, who tittered, 'Run along, do.'

She took Jaimie's arm and he led her away. 'I beg your pardon for not asking you to dance, but I wished to introduce you to my family and I did not want to include your cousin in the introductions. It would look too particular. This way we can be casual and not arouse undue interest.'

He only had to draw in a breath to arouse her interest, but his expression mirrored concern. Her stomach pitched. 'Something is wrong?'

He winced. 'I informed them of our true arrangement. I did not want their expectations raised.'

The warning in his voice was unmistakable. He did not want her to have raised expectations either. As if she would! She lifted her chin. 'Why is it that all families can think about is marrying off their single relatives? Is it that they wish us to be as miserable as they are?'

He looked startled at her vehemence. 'Well, some of them are happy. My cousin and his wife are, I am sure.'

'No one knows what goes on behind closed doors.'

'True.'

Well, at least they agreed on something.

'I would prefer it if you do not mention your visits to the pawn shops.'

She raised her eyebrows. 'I wouldn't dream of it.' He must think her a fool if he had to warn her of that. Typical male. Always assuming women couldn't figure out anything for themselves.

'Good.' He made a face of distaste. 'My cousin would be astonished if he learned of it. He certainly would not approve any more than I do. And if it ever got out...'

He was ashamed of her? Mortification filled her. While there was clearly never any intention on his part to make her an offer and nor did she want him to, the thought that he held her in such low esteem hurt.

She had a very real urge to drop her hand from his arm and flee the ballroom. But that would only make things worse. She stiffened her spine. The sooner they found Grey, the sooner she could rid Sandford of her embarrassing presence.

'Was it your cousin to whom you were talking a few minutes ago?'

'It was.'

Jaimie had been warning them about her. She wanted the floor to open.

'They are dancing. Perhaps I should meet them some other time.' Or never.

'No. I told them I would bring you to meet them. It would look strange if I did not.'

Sandford strolled towards the couple the moment the music finished. The woman had lively hazel eyes and a smile that lit her face to the point of loveliness. Her husband, on the other hand, a handsome broad-shouldered fellow with hard blue eyes, stared at Tess as if she had crawled out from under a rock.

'Lady Hawkhurst, Hawkhurst, I don't believe you have met Lady Theresa Ingram.'

'Lady Theresa,' Lady Hawkhurst said. 'Such a pleasure.'

Both of them were studying her intently. What on earth had Jaimie told them?

'It is a pleasure to meet you,' Tess said, refusing to be intimidated. 'Please, call me Tess. Everyone does.' She grimaced. 'Except my cousins. But I hope you will not follow their example.' Dash it, she sounded like a featherhead. How could she be so nervous at a mere introduction? It wasn't as if she would ever see them again, once Grey had been located.

'And you must call me Alice,' Lady Hawkhurst said.

Lord Hawkhurst bowed, but his expression did not invite informality. 'Lady Tess.'

'What is your home county?' Alice asked. 'We reside in Derbyshire when we are not in town, not far from Sandford's estate.'

'I come from Kent, a small place near Sevenoaks.'

'I love the southern part of the country. My family's home is in Oxfordshire.'

Her husband made a sound like a growl.

Tess jumped.

Alice shook her head at him. 'It was a bone of contention for a time, but we overcame it, did we not, Michael?'

He took her hand and raised it to his lips for a brief kiss on her knuckles, but his eyes held a possessive glint. 'Thanks to you, my love.'

Alice laughed and tapped his hand with her fan when he seemed inclined to keep it. She turned back to Tess. 'Perhaps you and your cousins would do us the honour of dining with us next week? What do you think, Jaimie?'

Jaimie looked nonplussed and then irritated.

'It is very kind of you,' Tess hastened to say, 'but I cannot speak for my cousins.'

'I will send round a note,' Lady Hawkhurst said brightly.

'There is no need, Alice,' Jaimie said repressively. Well, he would. He knew that by next week all pretence of a possible alliance would be over.

A pang stole into Tess's heart. She would miss him...

Oh, yes, she would miss his arrogance all right. The same as she might miss a stone in her shoe. With relief.

Lord Hawkhurst narrowed his eyes. 'Why don't I speak to Rowan? He belongs to my club.'

'That won't be necessary.' Jaimie and Tess spoke in harmony.

A grim smile flickered on Hawkhurst's lips. Dash it. The man was bedevilling them. His wife, on the other hand, seemed genuinely disappointed.

'I will speak with them,' Jaimie said calmly. 'Unfortunately it might be a week or so before I am free of my current engagements and I believe you plan to return to the country long before then.'

Lady Hawkhurst's lips tightened and she looked as if she would like to say something, but after a glance at her husband's face, she remained silent.

How interesting, the way they communicated without words. Tess had never seen that before.

'We will look forward to hearing from you, Jaimie.' There was a great deal of dryness in Hawkhurst's tone. He turned to his wife and smiled. 'Won't we, my dear?'

'I most certainly will,' she said firmly.

Dash it all, Sandford should never have introduced them. Clearly they did not approve of what they were doing.

The orchestra struck up another waltz. 'May I have this dance, Lady Tess?' Jaimie asked with an elegant bow, clearly deciding to extract them from the awkward interview.

'I would be delighted.'

He escorted her on to the dance floor with calm reserve.

She, on the other hand, was thrilled. Though she would never admit it to Jaimie, she loved the feel of his hands on her body, no matter how lightly they rested and how polite the distance he maintained.

He, on the other hand, clearly felt none of the thrills that were skittering down her back. As he whirled her around the floor, a strange lump formed in her throat. She could scarcely believe her reactions to this handsome, elegantly masculine man. Each time her gaze wandered over his person her breath caught in wonder.

What would it be like to have such a man for a husband? She could almost imagine… How foolish to even think of putting her trust in a man who she knew had no tender feeling towards her. A man like Sandford was not the sort to consider the opinions of a woman. Not when it came to matters of importance. He thought he knew best on every count. And if he took it upon himself to gamble away his fortune or drink himself into a stupor there was nothing a wife could say about it. He would expect her to be silent. Accepting. Obedient.

As she had been with her papa. She could not go through that again. She had loved her papa and his betrayal had hurt her badly. It would be far better to marry a man for whom she had no feelings than a man she cared for and who would betray her on a whim. A hollow sensation filled the space behind her ribs. To trust Jaimie would be foolish in the extreme.

'What unpleasant thoughts are going through your mind, my dear Tess?' His voice was cool and distant, but the words were a shock.

How had he known her thoughts were unhappy ones? Was she so transparent? If so, she must be more careful with her thoughts when around him. And perhaps it was time to give him some of his own back.

'I was thinking about how much I dislike this pretence of ours.'

He looked startled. 'Now you think this? You have been keeping secrets from your family since the moment I met you.'

'That was different. That concerned none but myself. But this pretending that things between us are something they are not and knowing that the Hawkhursts know it, too? Well, it just feels horrible, that is all.'

'I see.' The fluidity of his movements as they waltzed to the music did not change, nor did his expression, but something in the air around them changed. Little prickles raced across her shoulders. Had she somehow insulted his honour? Men were so sensitive about some things that never made much sense to her at all. Papa had been just the same. Let the roof fall down around their ears so long as he paid a debt to a man with whom he had wagered the outcome of a race between a couple of stag beetles.

Not that she thought Sandford quite as foolish as Papa, but the principle was the same. You could not trust men to be sensible about important matters.

'Lady Tess, it might be a pretence, but it is one we agreed upon. And with every eye in the room focused upon us right now, it might behoove you to attempt a little friendliness in your expression,' he said. 'A smidgeon of a smile would not go amiss or there will be rumours of a rift reaching your cousin's ears before morning.'

And then Mr Stedman would be back in the running. Or Tante Marie. She forced a smile that felt more like a grimace.

His brows drew together, a frown quickly smoothed away. 'I believe we need to talk.'

'I thought we were talking.'

He turned her under his arm, guiding her without the least appearance of doing so. 'Talk about Friday.'

About visiting Covent Garden. She had almost forgotten, she'd been so caught up in her worries about their charade. 'Oh, that.'

He glanced around the room. 'Yes, that, and there is not a scrap of privacy to be had here. Meet me in the library in twenty minutes.'

The music drew to a close and he walked her back to her cousin.

Jaimie lounged in the library and sipped at his whisky. He'd taken the liberty of pouring himself a glass from a decanter on the console by the window. He wasn't even sure Tess would turn up. She had looked so dismayed at the suggestion. Indeed, she had been looking unhappy all evening.

The door swung open and Tess strode in, looking about her, seeking him out. For a brief moment her face lit up and he basked in the warmth of her gladness. It disappeared so quickly he wondered if he had imagined it.

Once more she looked worried.

He rose to his feet. 'You had no trouble leaving your cousin?'

'Heavens, no,' she said, sitting down on the sofa opposite the chair he'd been using and sinking back against the cushions with a sigh. 'I told her I was going to the withdrawing room. You wanted to discuss going to Covent Garden on Friday?'

'That, too. But, Tess, are you truly so unhappy with our arrangement?'

She sat up, her face suddenly alert. 'It is not *our* arrangement. I knew nothing of your plan until I was faced with a fait accompli. The longer it continues the more uncomfortable I feel. I suppose I should be grateful you told your cousins the truth, but honestly, I think they do not approve of it in the least.'

Dammit all. 'Did you have a better idea, then?' He knew he sounded annoyed, when he really had intended to set her mind at rest. Usually he was able to keep his emotions buried. With Tess she always brought out the worst in him.

She clasped her hands in her lap. 'Isn't it somewhat too late to ask?'

'Not at all. If you have a better idea of a way a single gentleman can escort an unmarried lady all over London, I would really like to hear it.'

'Why, so you can use it another time?'

'I cannot imagine there would ever be another occasion where it would be required.'

'Oh, you are impossible.'

He was impossible? He sat down beside her. She moved as far along the sofa as space would permit and turned her face away.

God help him! Do not say she was going to cry.

He forced himself to speak quietly. 'I am sorry, Tess. I honestly thought you would be pleased that I found a way for us to work together to find your brother.' And escape the looming betrothal to Stedman—something he did not think he should mention. Because once they found this brother of hers, they would go their separate ways and her cousin was just as likely to insist on the match. The thought of her marrying Stedman made him feel ill.

Damn her cousin for laying those debts on such slender shoulders. A man inherited and then he dealt with the outcome; he didn't push the problem on to someone else to solve.

'Tess.' He put her arm around her shoulders. 'I can understand why you feel uncomfortable about this, but it really was the only way.'

Apart from actually offering for her hand. Would that really have been so bad?

The thought hit him like a bolt of lightning out of a cloudless sky. He tried to push it away. To pretend it had never occurred to him, but it simply sat there, like a recalcitrant child, refusing to be dismissed.

Oh, hell. He'd had one bad marriage, he certainly didn't want another just because he felt sorry for the woman.

If only that was all it was. He *liked* her. He liked her loyalty to her brother. He liked her determination to find him, even if he didn't quite like the way she set about the search. He certainly found her alluring. Irresistibly so. But was passion a firm enough ground on which to build a future? She certainly was not the sort of woman he had envisaged taking as a second wife.

Nor did she seem particularly keen on the idea of marriage, so far as he could tell.

When she finally turned and gazed at him, her eyes were clear and dry, but sad. 'I should never have embroiled you in my affairs.'

'Well, you certainly know how to make a man feel like a knight in shining armour, my lady.'

Her eyes widened and then she laughed.

He gave a sigh of relief.

'I am sorry,' she said. 'I had no wish to sound ungrateful. But you know, despite your best efforts, Rowan is quite likely try to force us into marriage if this arrangement continues.'

'Is that what is troubling you?'

'In part, I suppose.'

He took and deep breath. 'And if it came to pass, would it be so very awful?'

She stared at him and an emotion he could not read flickered in her eyes. 'Are you mad? You do not want this marriage any more than I do.'

He hid his wince. He hadn't realised the notion would be so distasteful to her. 'I cannot imagine you would prefer the alternative.' He hoped he sounded logical, not hurt. Of course he wasn't hurt. Not exactly. Not when she echoed his own thoughts on the subject of matrimony.

'Stedman, you mean? Of course you are better than him! But the whole reason for looking for Grey was to find a way *not* to get married.'

He should have guessed she would be different to any other woman he had ever met. 'Never?'

'I suppose if I met the right man, I might feel differently. But honestly, I am not sure I want the responsibility.'

He stared at her. 'The man of the house is the responsible one.'

She looked at him askance. 'That is what they say.'

The dryness in her voice gave him a little twinge in his gut. He knew a lot of irresponsible men. He hadn't exactly done a stellar job with Hester, had he? And Michael had not been a saint with Alice in the early days of their marriage. 'So it is all the more important we find this brother of yours.'

'I suspected when you said you wanted to talk, that you had decided to cry off going on Friday. Or at least to go without me.'

He ought to. 'I never go back on my word.' He had gone back on his word to Hester with disastrous results. He had promised to take her out in his curricle, but had been called away to attend the Prince Regent. He'd never had a chance to keep it.

And clearly several men had already broken their word to Tess. Not that he trusted Rowan in the slightest. The man was desperate for money, willing to do whatever it took to get it.

Well, he wasn't going to let her marry Stedman. She would have to marry *him* instead. Surprisingly, Jaimie found himself rather pleased with the idea, now he had actually come up to the mark. He had been young and naive when he'd married Hester and spectacularly ill prepared for marriage. Michael had advised him to wait. But ever since he could remember, he'd wanted someone he could call his own and he'd charged ahead.

He was older now and wiser, and truthfully, Tess wasn't nearly as madcap as Hester had been. The difficult thing would be convincing Tess that she wanted to marry him...

There was one sure way to make certain she would come around to his way of thinking. A very pleasurable way for both of them. A pang of guilt assailed him at the thought of using her passionate nature against her, but it was the right solution. The only answer.

Tess looked doubtful, her lips pouting adorably as she still considered his promise not to go back on his word.

Those irresistible lips...

He leaned closer until he could feel her breath against his mouth, see the quickening of her pulse in the hollow of her throat and the rapid rise and fall of her chest. She was no more immune to him than he was to her.

He brushed his mouth across hers, teasing lightly. Her eyelids fluttered closed. Her small hand came up to rest against his chest, hesitant at first, and then boldly creeping up to settle on his nape, her fingers tangling with his hair.

He deepened the kiss, stroking her lips with his tongue. Her scent filled his nostrils, her lovely lush form melded into him.

What had been intended as something sweet flared into something searing. His body hardened. He wanted her closer, but should anyone walk in the door, they would be in full view, a subject of sordid gossip and titillation.

He lifted his head and her soft moan of protest went straight to his bollocks. Painful pleasure. He scanned the room. There. An alcove sporting a bloody great map table.

'Hold on, sweet,' he murmured, rising to his feet, lifting her, his hand under her gorgeous bottom. She clung around his neck, her legs hampered by skirts curled around his calves. He staggered the few feet to the table and perched her on its edge.

She pressed little kisses to his cheek and chin and nose, then nuzzled into his neck as he worked her skirts up her legs and under her bottom to her waist.

A soft hiss of shock escaped her, when her bared bottom encountered the cool wood tabletop. He had never heard anything quite so erotic.

She wiggled closer to him, clasping her thighs around his waist, bringing her hot little centre tight up against his groin. He swallowed a growl of pleasure.

The table was an inch or two higher than he would have liked, but where there was a will… He pulled her closer to the edge, stroking through the soft curls at her core.

His shaft strained towards that soft damp centre, as if it could thrust its way through his clothing. He rocked his hips against her and let the waves of pleasure wash through his body and numb his mind.

This was what he had wanted since they had parted in her chamber. He'd been punishing them both by denying the truth. And now that he had decided he wanted her for his wife, he felt a sense of freedom, an anticipation for the future. Provided he could convince her to walk down the aisle.

Of course he could.

Her soft pants and sounds of excitement were all the encouragement he needed.

A small hand burrowed into his waistband, busy fingers finding his shaft and curling around it the way he'd shown her.

His brain nigh exploded with the pleasure of that bold but slightly awkward little hand. Deliberately, he thrust into the tight circle of her fingers, while he located the little nub of pleasure hidden deep within her folds.

Her hiss of pleasure had him surging forward, wanting to bury himself deep in her wet heat.

Her hand released him and he felt the loss of her touch as keenly as the bite of a northern wind, yet when she went for his buttons, he had enough brain left to ease away and grant her access. In moments, his falls were undone and his breeches pushed down his thighs. He broke their kiss to watch as she lifted his shirt the better to gaze upon his erection.

Her eyes darkened. Her tongue flickered across her lips. A groan rose from his chest as he imagined her tongue licking him where her gaze rested. Dammit. That was surely not the sort of thing one did with a virgin or a wife.

He pushed between her thighs and ran his tongue around the rim of her ear, feeling her quake against him. 'What I would not give to be inside you,' he whispered as he rubbed his thumb against that hard little nub in tight, quick circles.

Her head fell back as if her neck could no longer support its weight. Complete surrender from a woman who never gave up. The sight almost unmanned him. He caught her around the shoulders before she fell backwards. Damn it, the table was no harder than he was. And this was neither the time nor place to…

'Yes,' she whispered. 'Yes, please.'

His foggy mind might have trouble comprehending her words, but instinctively his hand pulled her closer until the head of his penis was nudging her delicate folds aside and inching into her delicious silken heat.

Instinct took command and he thrust up into her, tortured by the difference in their relative heights. He wanted in to the hilt. He was barely halfway, her tight little sheath contracting around the head of his shaft, driving him mad with the need to be deeper.

So tight. And resistant. She gasped. A sound of shock, rather than pleasure.

He drew in a shuddering breath. First time. Gently. Slowly. This was a gift of monumental proportions. He wasn't going to ruin it by being impatient. Nor must he let it go too far. He could not rob her of all her choices.

He slowed the pace, easing into her one small fraction at a time, while using the ball of his thumb to keep her languid and receptive to the invasion of her body.

She shuddered, a miniature quake of pleasure. Dear sweet heaven, she was so responsive and she was building again.

His own orgasm fought for release deep within him.

He took a deep breath, slowed his rhythm, took it down to a manageable level, and decreased the depth of his entry. The pain of denial was so achingly sweet, it rocketed him back to the edge of the precipice.

He had to hold back.

'Put your arms around my neck,' he whispered in an urgent plea.

Her eyelids fluttered upwards as if they were weighted by lead.

Incomprehension filled her gaze. 'Arms around my neck,' he demanded. If she didn't hurry…

Languidly she draped her arms over his shoulders. It would have to do.

He braced and lifted her off the table.

His shaft slipped out of her body and she muttered a protest.

With one hand under her, with the other Jaimie guided himself home. For a second she looked puzzled, then she lifted her legs and grasped him around the hips, letting her body sink on to him, in a long, slow outrageously delicious slide.

All control left him. Using the table to support a fraction of her weight, he thrust upwards. Burying himself deep. His mind went black, comprehending nothing but the pleasure and the sensations of her body's slide over his, her weight and her delicious perfume drawn in with every breath. No longer able to prevent the drive of his lust, he pumped his hips, her cries encouraging him to thrust harder, drive deeper, until she had taken it all.

He thrust again, going a fraction deeper as her body opened to him. Twice she fell apart with soft cries and deep shudders. The third time he finally unleashed his tight control and buried himself so deep inside her, he had no notion of any separation between them.

She cried out his name at the same moment his body shattered into a million separate pieces of bliss.

Legs weak, he put both hands on the table to support her weight. She clung on around his neck for dear life, until he was able to seat her back on the table edge.

'Oh, my,' she breathed against his neck. 'Oh, my goodness me.'

Panting, chest heaving, body glowing, knees trembling, he leaned against the table and her, and somehow she held him up.

Strong. This tiny woman was stronger that he ever could be.

His mind slowly cleared. Damnation, he really had not intended they take it quite so far. He'd simply wanted to show her the pleasures of being a wife that lay ahead. *His* wife. Now the die was cast.

He pulled up his breeches. What they had done must already have shocked her nigh to death. When she was decent, he lifted her down and set her on her feet.

Limp and languid and breathing hard, she clung to his shoulders.

He lifted her chin with one hand, looking down into a face so hazy with sensual pleasure something seized inside his chest, making it impossible to breathe for a moment.

'Are you all right?'

She nodded vaguely. 'You will still help me find Grey, though?'

Inside, he stiffened at her lack of trust, yet he should not be surprised that her brother was more important than himself. He had to earn his value in her eyes. 'I gave you my word. I will keep it.' And then she would trust him.

He could not stop himself from adding a truth. 'I cannot promise we will find him.'

She drew in a deep breath, stepping back and smoothing her skirts. 'I understand. In the end, it might be futile, but I cannot be content unless I know I tried my best.' She peered into a nearby mirror and tucked up a stray tendril of hair. Such a very personal, feminine thing. And he hoped that soon it would be his right to see more such intimate activities.

A strange softening occurred deep in his chest. He realised that he truly *wanted* this marriage. And he wanted it to work. It would mean an end to a loneliness he hadn't even known was part of his life, until now. He filled his days with work and his nights with tending his roses, but this was a completely different kind of fulfilment that he hadn't known existed. It was like…coming home after a long absence. Something like that. Perhaps?

When Tess turned to face him, her expression contained anxiety. 'We should go back before anyone comes looking for us.'

Her anxiety was his fault. Somehow, he would make her see he would never allow her to come to harm. He also had to convince her that marriage to him would answer all her problems, whether or not they found her elusive brother. For some strange reason, he wanted her to come to that conclusion by herself. Not that he was wearing his heart on his sleeve. He'd never do that again, but still he did want to relieve her of her worries.

He kissed the tip of her sweet little nose. 'You go on ahead. I will follow in a few minutes so as not to engender gossip.'

With a brisk nod, she left the room. An unwelcome cold feeling settled in the pit of his stomach. A warning something was about to go horribly wrong. He ignored those flashes of insight at his peril.

For once, there was so much going on in his life, he could not pinpoint from whence came the danger.

As he had promised, Jaimie collected Tess at eleven in the morning on Friday. They would not have a lot of time to spend at Covent Garden, since the stalls generally closed at noon, but leave home any earlier and they might have aroused suspicions. As it was, it was very early to go driving and he'd asked Michael and Alice to agree to meet them at Gunter's for an ice to give them the excuse.

They were to meet them at half-past twelve. Luckily for them, the weather had decided to co-operate for a change. Rainy days outnumbered fine ones by three to one according to Growler who seemed to keep track of such things.

Tess looked lovely in her carriage dress of mint green-and-white stripes, with frothy lace at the neck and at her wrists. But then she always looked sumptuous to him. The way the dress emphasised her lovely curves heated his blood.

Right at that moment she glanced at him and caught him staring at how well her figure filled out her bodice. He raised a brow. She blushed and looked away. He frowned. It wasn't like her to be shy. 'Is something wrong?'

'Oh, no. Not at all.' Her expression, however, belied her words. She looked uncomfortable.

Not what he was aiming for. He wanted to woo the girl, not frighten her off. He could do better than this. He took a breath. 'You look lovely today. That colour suits you.'

Her eyebrows shot up, her pretty mouth opened a fraction. If anything, she looked even more on edge.

Damn, had he said it wrong?

'Why are you being so nice to me?' she asked, lifting her chin a fraction.

That was certainly more like her usual direct self. He manoeuvred between two carriages stopped at the curb on each side of the road. 'I am simply saying what I think.'

A brief smile curved her lips. Small though it was, it relaxed him. There was a comforting familiarity in the emotions she evoked inside him, yet they also made him feel restless. Not quite his usual self. Lust he understood perfectly, but this desire to please her had him at sixes and sevens. He wanted her to see that marriage to him would work. That she needed him.

He pulled his vehicle over to one side on Bedford Street opposite St Paul's church and his tiger went to the horses' heads. Jaimie hopped down and helped Tess to alight.

If he'd been thinking rationally, the way he usually did, he wouldn't have brought her here, but on the other hand, he certainly didn't want her coming here by herself. He'd not wasted his time, though. He'd already set Growler doing a thorough investigation of Mrs Plunkett and her market stall.

Clearly there was something odd about the woman. She charged very little for the goods she sold and had a great number of persons coming and going, yet rarely did anyone purchase anything. Perhaps Tess's quest to find her bracelet—and her brother—was also bringing Jaimie closer to solving his case? A fortuitous alignment of the stars. If it wasn't for the nagging feeling that something was going to go very wrong, he would have been a contented man.

As he and Tess had agreed on the drive over, they wandered through the stalls, gradually closing in on their target.

They stopped at a flower-seller's stall and Jaimie bought a bouquet of lilies of the valley. Tess buried her face in the flowers and inhaled. The rise of her bosom within the confines of her light summer carriage dress was enough to drive a man mad. He glowered at a couple of fellows who were also regarding her with admiration…and lust. *Mine*, his glare said.

Both looked away. He resisted the urge to pound his chest in triumph. What the devil?

'They are lovely.' Her smile was wider this time, lighting up her face, but there was a wistfulness in her voice. Did she not understand the meaning of these particular flowers? Should he tell her? He would feel a fool uttering such nonsense. *You make my life complete.* What sort of fellow would ever say such a thing? Or perhaps he was misunderstanding the situation. 'If you don't like them, I can get something else.' He scanned the flowers, looking for something appropriate, deliberately skipping over the roses. He did not want to give her any false ideas.

'This is the first bouquet I have ever received.'

Well, that wasn't right. When they were married he would see to it that she got one every single day. Hell! Why wait until they were married?

He brushed a dusting of pollen from the end of her nose. 'The first of many.'

She sneezed and laughed, and it was the sweetest sound he had ever heard. He wanted that for her every day, too. Perhaps he was up to snuff on this wooing thing, after all. Unfortunately, they were not here purely for pleasure.

He took the bouquet and handed it to a scruffy little lad who was taking in the interaction with a strangely inquisitive look. 'Take this to the tiger with the black carriage in front of St Paul's.' He flipped the child a coin. The boy caught it and dashed off on his errand while the shopkeeper thanked them effusively for their business.

He took Tess's arm and this time their steps led them to the stall at the end of one of the rows. Little more than a barrow, it had only a few items on display.

The woman beside it smiled at their approach. She was in her early thirties, he judged, though she could be younger for she had the world-weary look about her of someone who had struggled hard, but her hair showed no signs of grey. Her clothes were shabbily genteel and had been mended several times. In a basket beside her lay a baby. The baby glowed with health and its accoutrements were spotlessly clean.

'How can I help you, sir, madam?' the woman said with a bob when they paused at her display.

She clearly had not been forewarned of their coming, she was behaving far too naturally.

'Oh, what a pretty little spoon,' Tess said. She held it up for him to see. The monogram was an intricate T and one he recognised from his list.

Wariness filled him. This seemed a little too easy. Tess, meanwhile, moved on to a salt cellar of unusual design.

He shook his head. It was not on his list and besides it had a pepper mill beside it.

'What about that?' He pointed to a sack at the woman's feet, shoved mostly under the cart, but the mouth had fallen open and the arm of a candelabra poked out.

The woman followed his gaze. 'Oh, that is already bespoken, sir. I am sorry.' Another customer has ordered it.'

'May I not see it? It seems to be just what we were looking for.'

'My dear,' Tess said, 'if another customer has already purchased it—'

He frowned. 'You are right, pet.' He gave the woman a charming smile. 'Give me the name of this other customer of yours and I will offer him more than he paid, if I like the piece.'

The woman paled, then swallowed. 'If you want it, sir, I could always give the other gentleman his money back. He left a deposit only. He said he would return with the rest before the end of the day. I fear he may not even come.' She bent and opened the sack. Inside were other items of silver, but she quickly hid them from view. Only his greater height allowed him to see them over her shoulder.

She set the candlestick in front of him.

'Do you like it?' Tess asked, picking it up and turning it over and around. 'It looks old and is very heavy.'

He ran a fingertip over the intricate design. 'It looks like one of a pair. Do you have the other?'

The woman blanched. 'Only one, sir.'

He scratched the tip of his nose, a signal to Growler who was somewhere in the crowds wandering around the stalls, that what he had in his hand was what they sought. He shook his head. 'It is certainly a nice piece. Genuine silver, judging by the hallmark, and made by a craftsman. How much did you want for it?'

Jaimie entered into a round of bargaining. Strangely, the woman wanted nowhere near as much as it was worth, usually a sign it might well be stolen.

Bargain almost complete, Tess tugged on his arm. 'I am not sure I like it as much as the other one we saw, after all, my dear. And there were two of them. They were not nearly as expensive either.'

The woman named a lower price.

Easy to do when you had paid nothing for the item in the first place.

Jaimie pursed his lips as if considering his options.

'I think you are right, my love, the other pair was precisely what we require.'

The woman looked relieved. She scurried to put the candlestick back in the sack.

'Do you have any jewellery?' Tess asked. 'I am looking for something to wear with a new gown. A bracelet, perhaps?'

The woman shrugged. 'No, madam, no jewellery.'

Tess drew forth a small scrap of paper. She held it out to the woman. 'Have you ever seen this man?'

The woman took the paper and studied the drawing closely. 'No, madam. I have not.'

Jaimie could see Tess wanted to press the woman. 'We will look somewhere else,' he said in the manner of a husband comforting a wife.

Tess frowned, but to his relief did not argue.

They wandered off. A few yards from the stall, Tess stopped. The look of distress on her face was like a blow to the gut.

'I don't believe we are ever going to find the bracelet. Or Grey.'

'It is not like you to give up,' he said, hoping to put heart into her. 'We haven't exhausted all possibilities yet.'

She shook her head and continued walking. 'I was so sure that this woman would provide the answer.'

'She lied about not having any jewellery. There were a couple of rings on that table.'

'They were tawdry rubbish. Not real jewellery. No, I think she was telling the truth about that at least. I have this sinking feeling in the pit of my stomach that she was our last hope.'

'Will you give me your miniature and let Growler take it around to places where you and I cannot go?'

She sighed. 'I think it hopeless, but, yes, I will do that.'

He nodded, but the lump in his throat at her obvious sorrow made it hard to swallow. 'Time we set off to Gunter's.'

'Do we have to go?'

He couldn't quite understand why she looked so anxious. He'd thought she'd be pleased to become better acquainted with members of his family. 'We do,' he said firmly. She needed something to take her mind off her pesky brother. If they ever found him, Jaimie was going to have strong words with the fellow about worrying his sister so badly.

Chapter Eleven

Meeting Sandford's cousin, Hawkhurst, was like being inspected under a microscope. The man's piercing blue eyes seemed to miss nothing. And everything about him was intense and watchful. Tess had the feeling that if she so much as whispered a word against Sandford, Hawkhurst would tear her to shreds without blinking an eye. Why he would be quite so protective of his adult cousin she could not imagine.

Alice, on the other hand, was a sweetheart. Tiny and sweet and kind.

The gentlemen seated the ladies at one of the tables in Gunter's. They perused the menu. Alice leaned closer to Tess and lowered her voice. 'I cannot remember the last time Sandford escorted a lady out in public.' She made a little gesture with her head and Tess became aware that a great many people in the crowded restaurant were observing them with avid interest.

Oh, dear. Did the poor woman still have the wrong idea about her and Jaimie? 'I thought he told you. I am a client,' she whispered.

Jaimie raised his gaze from his menu and Lady Hawkhurst fluttered hers in front of her face like a fan. 'My word, it is hot in here, Jaimie, can you not open that window and let in a little breeze?'

The look Jaimie sent her was one of disapproval, but he got up and did as she bid.

Again, Lady Hawkhurst leaned close. 'He has had many clients who are women. Not once has he introduced them to his family.'

Tess felt heat rise in her cheeks, but tried to look calm. 'It was the only way we could think of not to give rise to gossip.'

Lady Hawkhurst smiled sweetly, but there was a knowing glint in her eye. But there was no more to be said since Jaimie returned to his seat.

Sandford and Hawkhurst entered into a discussion about the wording of a bill before Parliament. Lady Hawkhurst watched them with a fond eye for a moment. 'You know, I would not like to see Sandford hurt. He has a soft heart and his first marriage was a disaster.'

Tess's jaw dropped. 'He was married before?'

'His first wife died under tragic circumstances, driving Jaimie's carriage. I don't think he has ever forgiven himself for what happened.'

'Oh, I am sorry to hear that.'

Lady Hawkhurst's mouth tightened. 'They were not married long, but after her death, I feared he might never set foot in matrimonial waters again.'

Tess swallowed. 'Please, do not think for a moment that Jaimie and I—'

'Oh, I know. You are engaged in a matter of business. But it would be so wonderful if he could find someone with whom to share his life. He does seem to like you.'

Tess flushed. 'And I like him.' A little too much for comfort. Every time she remembered what they had done in the library, she wanted to do it again. Which was terrible of her. Thoroughly wanton.

'Poor man. He really has not had an easy life. What with the fire and then his wife's death, it is no wonder he is cautious.'

Tess cast her eyes down. 'Yes, he told me about the fire.'

'Both Michael and Jaimie lost their families. Jaimie has always blamed himself for that, too.'

'Why?'

Alice glanced over at the two men, but they were deeply engrossed in their conversation. 'He dropped the candle that started the fire off. He was so scared he ran and hid and didn't tell anyone about it until it was too late.'

Tess shuddered, trying to imagine what it would be like to have a tragedy like that on her conscience. 'Poor Jaimie.'

'Of course, he never talks about it. He was very young at the time, only six, I believe. No one blamed him, least of all Michael, but I know it troubles Jaimie still. To lose nearly all his family in one fell swoop must have been awful.'

It had been awful losing her parents one at a time and in neither case was Tess to blame. 'He didn't elaborate on the details.' They really hadn't spoken very much at all about things of so personal a nature, but she could imagine how he must still feel.

She felt terrible about losing contact with Grey and he was still alive—or at least so she hoped. She should certainly have never involved Jaimie in her troubles to the point that people were expecting him to make her an offer of marriage. It was the last thing she wanted. Wasn't it?

Of course it was. The man was impossibly arrogant. He expected women to follow his instructions as if they were mindless beasts. The fact that making love to him had been delicious and lovely was neither here nor there. It was only a very small part of married life, after all.

It would be best if she put an end to it before things got completely out of hand. If they hadn't already, given what had happened in the library.

Tess decided, sadly, that she would have to give up searching for Grey. If he had wanted her to find him, she would have by now. She'd simply have to tell Phin she had managed to lose the bracelet between the jeweller's and home, and that would be an end to it.

Then she would have to find some other way to avoid marriage with Stedman. Perhaps a visit to Yorkshire was best after all. It would be a very long visit. Likely permanent.

Misery stole into her heart. A sadness she did not understand. Or perhaps she did, but there was no one in her life she could trust enough to share her worry.

'Is something wrong?' Jaimie's deep voice murmured in her ear.

She started. Then blushed. Dash it, now she looked

guilty. 'No. I beg your pardon. I was off gathering sheep's wool.'

'A penny for your thoughts, then.'

'They are hardly worth that.' She smiled vaguely. 'Have you and Lord Hawkhurst finished solving the political problems of the day?'

Hawkhurst's piercing blue stare cut her way. 'We have indeed. And you?'

She froze, staring into those eyes that seemed to see her very thoughts. 'Me?'

'And my wife,' he said drily. 'You looked as if you were sorting out a matter for the ages.'

'Enough, Michael,' his wife said placidly. 'We were merely discussing the odd traits of men and how much they needed our guidance.'

He laughed, the hardness going out of his face and a dimple appearing in his cheek. 'I shall look forward to your words of wisdom, my dear.'

His wife flashed him a saucy smile. 'I will hold you to that.'

At that moment, to Tess's relief, the ices arrived. And the melee of getting the right dish in front of the right person turned the conversation in another direction.

'Sandford says you will be returning home in a few days,' Tess said to Alice.

'Yes. We really must get home to the children. I am missing them terribly.'

Her husband glowered. 'We could have been gone a week ago had you not insisted on having a completely new wardrobe.'

Alice laughed. 'You know very well it was you who

did the insisting. And glad I am that I did, or I would not have made Lady Tess's acquaintance.' She cast Jaimie an arch glance that seemed a bit too knowing.

Tess glanced at Jaimie, expecting him to refute the teasing innuendo, but he merely smiled that rare smile of his that made him look good enough to eat—far more tasty even than the strawberry ice in her dish. 'More likely you want to see me firmly leg-shackled so you can cease worrying about your wayward cousin,' he said.

Michael grinned. 'How did you guess?'

'Michael!' his wife scolded with a laugh.

'You of all people should know better,' Jaimie said, but he was looking at Tess, his gaze warm. Her heart gave an odd little kick.

Afraid of what she might give away, she lowered her gaze to her dish and moved the strawberry ice around with her spoon.

'Is your ice not to your taste?' Jaimie asked.

She smiled. 'No, indeed. It is quite delicious.' She proved it by eating a spoonful.

He took a taste of his own lemon ice.

'How are your investigations into these robberies coming along,' Hawkhurst asked. 'Made any progress?'

'Not at much as I should have,' Jaimie said.

No doubt because she had taken him away from his investigations. He would be glad to hear she had decided to give up her search. It was the right thing to do. She could not have people expecting him to make her an offer. It would be just too embarrassing when they parted.

Jaimie gave her a brief smile, but his eyes held puzzlement. Had he sensed her change of mood? 'If you have finished, Lady Tess, I believe your cousin mentioned something about an appointment with a modiste this afternoon.' He smiled around the table. 'You ladies and your clothing. I don't know how you find time for anything else.'

Tess rose and everyone stood. 'Thank you for keeping track of the time, Sandford. It was a pleasure to meet you again, Alice, Lord Hawkhurst.' She dipped a curtsy.

'I do hope we will see you again,' Alice said. She smiled fondly at Jaimie. 'Spend a week with us later in the summer, I am sure Hawkhurst would be delighted to have some company. Particularly since the rivers are stocked and the fishing is excellent.'

'My work keeps me busy,' Jaimie said stiffly.

'Your work is important,' Hawkhurst said. 'But all work and no play makes Jack a very dull boy, remember. I would very much like to see you at Hawkhurst, if you can stand to come to us.'

'Fields and acres and cows. No, thank you.' Jaimie shook hands with his cousin.

Hawkhurst gave him a hearty slap on the back. 'Wait until you wed. Cows and fields will hold great charm then.'

Somehow Tess could not imagine the sophisticated, elegant Lord Sandford being at home in the country. Much as she loved it herself, she was resigned to living in London with her husband. *Whoever that might be*, she added to herself with a start.

The woman who sat at Jaimie's side in the carriage clutching the bouquet he had bought for her earlier was not the bold piece who had first come to his office in a veil. Something was wrong. Was she regretting their lovemaking on the map table? It was too late for regrets.

He had to allow her to be convinced they should marry. To do anything else would be dishonourable. For a very brief moment, he wished she had not come to his office.

And then he was glad that she had.

What the devil was wrong with him? His thoughts were wandering, his wits scattered and he badly wanted to kiss the lady sitting beside him.

He pulled up outside her cousin's house and helped her down.

'Would you like to come in?' she asked.

He definitely wanted in, but not to her cousin's house. 'I'm afraid I have a meeting this afternoon.'

She nodded. 'Then I will see you later.'

'Yes. I hope to have more news of Mrs Plunkett and her nefarious doings very soon.' Along with the man responsible for the thefts. If they were careful.

He saw her into the house and returned to climb up into his carriage. Now to apprehend the man who was almost certainly responsible for the burglaries that had the King writing to him every day.

And in the meantime, he was going to woo Tess until she had no alternative but to agree to their marriage.

'More flowers? Where on earth are we to put them?' Wilhelmina sounded thoroughly peevish. 'Perhaps you would drop a hint in Sandford's ear that I am running out of vases.'

Jealousy made people cruel, but really—what *was* Sandford up to? They should be drifting apart. Getting Rowan used to the idea that the marriage would not go ahead, not giving him hope… Or her.

Tess smiled at the butler. 'Put them in the library, please, Carver.'

Carver handed her the accompanying note and trotted off.

'Anyone would think it was a love match,' Wilhelmina grumbled, 'rather than a marriage of convenience.'

Love had never entered into Tess's dealings with Sandford. Each day the language of the flowers he sent spoke of loyalty and fidelity and innocence and desire, even courage, but never of love. Never once was there a rose in the bouquet. She was surprised Wilhelmina hadn't noticed the lack. Perhaps Tess herself had only noticed because Sandford grew his own. Still theirs was not a love match, therefore she should not give it a moment's thought. Yet foolishly her heart had ached a little more with the arrival of each bouquet.

Surely she did not fancy herself in love with Sandford? Yes, beneath that haughty arrogant exterior he had proven to be a kind and loyal friend. And, yes, she was attracted to him. Wildly. He just had to glance her way with a certain heat in his eyes and her pulse picked up speed and breathing became difficult. But *love*? Simply because her heart seemed to lift at the sight of him did not mean she was in love. Did it?

And in any case, they were not truly going to be married.

She sighed.

Wilhelmina rifled through the invitations and other mail Carver had delivered a half-hour before. 'Tomorrow seems to be a choice between the Frobishers' annual moonlight picnic or an evening of cards at the Melthorpes'. I know which dearest Phin will prefer.' She tossed the invitations aside. 'And then he will scold because I will have lost this week's pin money.'

Wilhelmina had no head for cards. She could not keep track of what had been played. All her friends knew this and took shameful advantage.

'I think Lord Sandford said he would attend the card party,' Tess said casually.

'I have no doubt of it,' Wilhelmina said stiffly. 'But it is to the picnic we shall go. I am sure I told Mrs Frobisher we would attend when I met her in Bond Street the other morning.'

Tess hid her smile. The last thing she wanted to do was sit and watch Wilhelmina at the card table. Without her own money, she could never participate, unless they were playing for pins which the Melthorpes would never do. Besides, Sandford had told her he would be at the picnic and he expected her to dance with him. He had been most attentive these past few days and had not missed a single opportunity to dance with her at least three times at each event they attended.

People were beginning to talk, especially since Phin had trumpeted the 'secret' to anyone who would listen. Nor did she understand why Sandford was sending her flowers every day.

'What is the matter, Tess? Surely you are not pining for Mr Stedman.' Wilhelmina gave her a rather sly smile. 'Shall I tell Phin you have changed your mind and to fetch him back from Yorkshire?'

If things went on much longer it would be impossible to end this without making Sandford look like a fool. Nor did she want to end it. Not really. She would miss him terribly. As a friend. Indeed, she would miss him as a lover.

'I do not pine,' she said repressively.

Wilhelmina tittered. 'You owe Phin this marriage. It is your duty to your family. Do not go putting off Sandford the way you clearly must have put off Stedman, seeing as he has not returned.'

Tess's spine stiffened. 'I know my duty, Wilhelmina.'

Her cousin waved a dismissive hand, as if her words meant nothing. 'What is this I hear about Sandford taking you to Hampstead Heath fair this afternoon? Phin mentioned it when he visited me this morning at breakfast. Surely you have more sense than to risk going to such a low place? It will be infested with the veriest hoi polloi. Phin said you had asked Sandford to take you. What can you be thinking of? His lordship will think you a terrible hoyden.'

His lordship already did.

'The aeronautist is to attempt to travel from Hampstead all the way to Scotland, sketching views of the countryside as he goes so that all may share in his adventure.'

'It sounds like a great deal of hot air to me,' Wilhelmina said caustically.

'So it does, given his mode of transport.'

Wilhelmina looked blank.

Tess swallowed a groan. 'Flying away in a balloon must be very exciting. Would you not like to try it?'

'Good heavens, no. What a ridiculous notion. Look how many people have died in the stupid things. I prefer to keep my feet firmly planted on terra firma where they belong.'

'Lord Sandford, my lady,' Carver announced.

The gentleman in question sauntered in. As usual he was a picture of sartorial elegance. His piercing gaze caught hers and a slight frown appeared as if he sensed Tess's tension.

'Sandford,' Wilhelmina declared. 'Why on earth would you take my cousin to some horrid fair on Hampstead Heath? It is really not suitable. The place will be crawling with pickpockets and cut-throats and...' she shuddered '...cits.'

There was nothing worse than people who worked for a living in the city apparently.

Sandford's brow cleared. 'Lady Tess will be quite safe with me, I assure you.'

'Well, don't let her go up in the balloon,' Wilhelmina said. 'Dearest Phin would be most displeased if she was to make such a spectacle of herself. As would you, I am sure, my lord. Not the behaviour a peer of the realm expects from a wife.'

'Should I have a wife and she wished to fly in a balloon to the moon, then I can assure you everyone would agree it would be a most suitable endeavour for any lady of quality.'

Wilhelmina's jaw dropped.

Tess suppressed the urge to laugh or give Sandford

a round of applause. It would be rude to do so, but the twinkle in his eyes said he had interpreted her feelings exactly. It almost made her wish they *were* going to be married.

'I must thank you for this morning's bouquet, my lord,' Tess said warmly.

He smiled and bowed. 'My pleasure.'

Tess waited for Wilhelmina to ask him not to send any more, but all she did was give Tess a pointed stare.

'Are you ready for our jaunt?' he asked Tess.

'Mims must go with you,' Wilhelmina said.

'I believe not,' Sandford said immediately. 'We will be accompanied by Hawkhurst and his wife. And since I plan on taking my curricle, there is no need for a maid.'

'What if it should rain?' Wilhelmina said.

'It is not going to rain,' Tess said firmly. 'One only has to look at the sky to see it is set to be fair for the rest of the day.'

Wilhelmina pouted. 'Very well, but if you should get soaked to the skin and catch an inflammation of the lungs I beg you will not complain to me.'

'I believe I am able to engage shelter for my party should it be necessary, Lady Rowan,' Sandford put in smoothly, clearly wishing to be gone as much as Tess did.

'I will fetch my hat and coat.' Tess left before Wilhelmina could voice some new objection. Or put any more of a damper on the outing. One thing was certain, banishment to Yorkshire had one advantage. She would not any longer be subject to Wilhelmina's carping.

Chapter Twelve

Jaimie kept a firm grip on Tess's arm as they wandered along behind Michael and Alice. Michael, naturally, had scoffed at the idea of taking his wife to a fair on Hampstead Heath, but Alice, bless her, had insisted. Somehow she had sensed the outing was important. How she had, Jaimie didn't know, because he wasn't exactly sure why it was important himself. He just knew that Tess had expressed a desire to see a balloon ascension and he had wanted to fulfil that wish.

In front of them, Hawkhurst intimidated anyone who so much as looked in their direction while Jaimie kept a sharp eye out for incursions from the rear. He didn't blame the poor for trying to relieve those better off of handkerchiefs and coins, as long as they didn't try it with any of those under his protection.

'Oh, look,' Tess said. 'It is already going up. We are going to miss it.'

At the centre of the fairground, still some distance off from where they were, the balloon was slowly rising above the heads of the crowd. 'I would say it is barely half-full yet,' he said, patting Tess's small gloved hand where it rested on his sleeve. 'There is still lots of time.'

'It is already huge.'

'It has to be, to lift a man.' He caught a whiff of burning straw. His stomach gave an unpleasant lurch. 'He's using fire?'

Tess glanced up at him, her expression full of interest. 'I thought that was what a hot-air balloon meant.'

It did. He just hadn't thought about it. 'Most aeronautists these days use hydrogen. It is easier to manage. Less dangerous.'

'Oh.'

Hawkhurst continued to press forward until they were at the front of the circle surrounding the balloon. The opening of the balloon was being held over a fire while its ropes prevented it from lifting off the ground. The envelope, a blue-and-red striped affair, was gradually swelling up. It bobbed and flapped when caught by the light breeze. Beside it sat the gondola in which the aeronautist would ride and another smaller brazier which would be suspended beneath the neck of the balloon once it was airborne.

'Why on earth is he using fire?' Jaimie asked.

Michael gave him a sharp look. 'I suspect its cheaper than hydrogen and easier to replenish once he's far distant from human habitation.'

'Makes sense.' The uneasy feeling in the pit of his stomach would not be stilled. He hated the smell of smoke, no matter how much his rational mind told him there was absolutely no danger. The wind wasn't strong enough to carry sparks any distance, but this sort of barely controlled burning was enough to drive him mad. God willing, the idiot would get the thing started and be on his way.

'Have you ever wanted to go up in one?' Tess asked.

He stared at the contraption. A feeble thing made of paper and silk and varnish. He'd watched several ascend when they'd first made headlines in the newspapers. 'Yes. I would.' But not if they were using fire as the means of ascending. He had too much respect for his life to be throwing it away. At least, he did now. At one time, not so much.

'Me, too,' Tess said.

'Do you think he will offer rides?' Alice asked.

Hawkhurst growled a warning.

'It is perfectly safe,' his wife said. 'As long as the balloon is tethered.'

'It is perfectly unsafe,' Hawkshurst said. 'Half the balloons launched result in loss of limb or life. You have children at home who need you, madam.'

Jaimie shot his cousin a look of sympathy, but knew better than to join in a marital squabble.

Alice pouted, then grinned. 'I was thinking of Tess, not me.'

Jaimie felt his face drain of blood. If Tess went, he would be obliged to go with her.

'Me?' Tess said.

Jaimie steeled himself.

Tess glanced up, an expression of something flitting across her face. Did she sense his disquiet? He waited for the mockery that would come next.

'I think I would prefer to watch this first time,' Her

smile was too bright for it to be the truth, but he took the out, none the less. Coward.

He eyed the scene, judging the diameter of the circle around the expanding envelope. This distance from the fire seemed safe enough. 'It shouldn't be long now.'

The crowd around the perimeter of the ropes pressed in tighter, but both Tess and Alice were sheltered by the stalwart and braced bodies of their escorts. Compared to the size of the balloon, that was now lifting clear of the ground, the little basket in which Mr Phipps would travel seemed almost minuscule, but it was more than large enough to carry several people.

What would it be like to fly up in the sky like a bird? Did she really want to try? Both men seemed to agree it was highly risky. And indeed she had read about several accidents.

The balloon lifted skywards. The crowd gasped. It bobbed about on its ropes almost as if it was alive. The gondola now righted itself and sat beneath it. The man in charge of the whole affair stepped forward, yelling about the glories of flight, and the wealth of knowledge to be gained from his endeavour, while his minions began passing among the crowd collecting donations. Both Hawkhurst and Jaimie tossed coins into the hat pushed in their direction.

Mr Phipps climbed into the gondola.

'So he is not offering rides,' Tess said, half-disappointed and half-relieved.

'Apparently not,' Sandford said. 'I gather this is a serious endeavor, not a display for entertainment.'

The minions continued to harass the crowd, seeking more funds. Finally, they returned to their employer, who blithely pocketed the money. The men then worked at the ropes attached to stakes in the ground. At Phipps's signal they set them free and the balloon rose into the air.

The crowd fell silent as it lifted slowly. Tess stared upwards, almost dizzy as it went higher and higher directly above them.

Phipps leaned out and waved his hat.

The crowd broke into applause.

Someone jostled against Tess. A tug on her reticule made her look down. Sandford grabbed the arm of a little ragamuffin who looked up at him with shock and fear on his face.

'What the devil?' Sandford exclaimed.

Hawkhurst reached for the lad who slipped his arms free of his coat and burrowed his way through the press of the crowd. In seconds he'd disappeared.

'Blast it,' Sandford said. 'He got away. Are you all right, Lady Tess?'

'Perfectly fine.'

Hawkhurst's lips thinned. 'Did he take anything?'

'Oh, he could not have. He was only beside me for a moment.'

'Check, please, Lady Tess.' Sandford looked furious. 'Blasted little thief. Damn clumsy.' He was staring after the boy. 'I feel as if I have seen him somewhere before.'

Tess dug in her reticule. 'All I brought with me was my handkerchief and a coin purse containing a few pennies.' All she had left of this month's pin money. Her fingers encountered both items along with something that had not been there when she'd left home. *A note, folded in a triangle.*

She gasped.

'What is missing?' Hawkhurst asked in a tight voice.

'Nothing,' Tess said, her heart beating so fast the word came out jerky. 'Everything is here.'

Sandford gave her a strange look. 'If he did steal something, we really should go after him. If we catch him, we might be able to save him from committing worse crimes. Even find him gainful employment.'

Her mind whirled at her discovery. Only one person ever folded his notes in that particular way. Grey. Was it possible? Desperate to go home and read his message in private, she glared at Sandford. 'Is that really your intention?'

He looked down his nose. 'Why would I lie?'

'Oh, dear,' Alice said. 'If Lady Tess says nothing was taken, then there is no more to be said.'

Sandford meanwhile was gazing into the distance, as if he could somehow divine where the boy had gone. The last thing Tess wanted was for him to find him. At last she had the hope of finding Grey.

She glanced up at the sky, where the balloon was little more than a speck in the distance. 'Did you not promise us luncheon, Sandford?'

He turned back to her, suspicion rife in his gaze and his smile mechanical. 'I did. Shall we go?'

'You sent for me, me lord?'

Jaimie straightened and stretched his back. He gazed

regretfully at his latest attempt at a graft, then poured water in to the bowl and washed his hands. 'I did. It came to me an hour or so ago. A boy. You sent him to discover where Lady Tess lived, the first day she came here. Do you remember?'

Growler looked affronted. 'Of course I do.'

'Who is he?' Jaimie asked.

'Who?'

'What is his name? Where does he live?'

Growler scratched the end of his nose. 'Just one of the lads, he is. A hey-you or a you-there sort of fellow. He hangs about with some of the regular boys sometimes, so I give him a copper for doing this and that. I was thinking we might take him on permanent, maybe. He's bright enough.'

But who had his loyalty? 'Hangs about with the other lads?'

'Chin wagging. Larking about.'

Everything Growler said made the heaviness in his gut grow worse. 'Can you find him, do you think?'

Growler grimaced. 'I ain't seen hide nor hair of him for the last couple of days, me lord.'

'He was the lad who stumbled into Lady Tess. I thought he was a cutpurse.'

'What?' Growler's gravelly voice became even more raspy. And louder.

'He didn't take anything.' So she had said. But something had happened. Something he couldn't quite put his finger on that had caused Tess to be silent on the way home and positively anxious to be rid of him. 'I have seen him at other times. He held my horse once. Outside a pawnbroker where Lady Tess was paying a visit. And he ran an errand for me at Covent Garden Market. Not until today did I realise it was the same boy.'

'What in hell's name—?'

The answer flashed across his mind. 'He is a spy. He looks ragged, but his fingernails are spotless. His teeth, too. Why did I not notice before?' Because Tess was a constant source of distraction to him, that was why.

Growler's brow lowered. 'His togs were filthy. Torn to shreds. I gave him a shirt when I asked him to run a couple of messages. His was so raggedy I thought he might get arrested if he went anywhere near any of our clients.'

'Part of his disguise. Find out what the lads have told him. No blame, mind. And tell them to let me or you know if they see him again. Treat him as they always do, but come to one of us at the first opportunity.'

Growler walked up and down the rows of plants. He stopped at one. Bent and inhaled. 'Now that's what I calls a flower.'

Surprised Jaimie joined him. 'Saints in heaven.' He stared at the bud starting to unfurl.' He couldn't quite believe it. He'd given up on this one weeks ago. About the same time Tess had arrived in his life.

'I want you to follow Lady Tess, Growler. You and no one else. And have one of the regular boys, one you would trust with your life, shadow that maid of hers.'

Growler's beetle brow lowered. 'Still don't trust her, Guv?'

Jaimie winced at the disapproval on Growler's face. But Tess had lied to him. Again. No doubt she was off on another of her starts and heaven only knew what sort of trouble she'd end up in. But he had a strong feeling it had something to do with that boy.

And there was no denying the bad feeling in his gut. The sense of being played for a fool.

Chapter Thirteen

Sipping at her morning chocolate, leaning back against the pillows and still snug beneath the covers, Tess read and reread the short note from Grey. Each terse syllable. *Cease your search.* No signature, but the note could have come from no one else.

Her heart twisted painfully at the lack of any sort of greeting or assurance of wellbeing. The lack of an expression of a desire to meet. Grey had never treated her that way before. Something was wrong.

'My lady!' Mims sailed into the room. 'Still abed? I thought you were to be out shopping with Lady Rowan in less than half an hour and your bathwater is getting cold in the dressing room.'

Heavens, Wilhelmina would be furious if she wasn't ready. She folded the note carefully and looked up to find Mims watching her with narrowed eyes. 'Is something wrong, my lady?'

'No.' She gave a light laugh. 'Why would you say such a thing?'

'I've know you long enough to know when you look worried, my lady.'

'I simply do not want to be late, that is all. You know how my cousin is when things do not go exactly as she has planned.'

Mims gave a little sniff but said no more on the matter.

As Mims helped her dress, Tess continued to worry. Why hadn't Grey contacted her before? Why was his note so lacking in warmth? At least he was alive. What could have happened to him over the past year since she'd seen him? But above all, would he still have her bracelet? Surely he would return it if she asked? If she could find a way to actually speak to him face to face.

'My lady?'

'What? Yes.'

'You didn't hear what I said.'

'Of course I—' She lifted her gaze to meet Mims's eagle eye. 'Oh, dash it! What did you say?'

'Blue-sprig muslin or primrose gauze.'

She'd worn both of them several times, but not on any of her outings with Sandford as yet. How clever of Mims to remember. She really was a treasure, even if she did take advantage of her position from time to time.

Someone tapped on the door.

Mims shuffled over and staggered backwards a moment or two later with a neatly tied tangle of honeysuckle. Fragrance filled the room. Why on earth would he send her wild honeysuckle? Her heart sank as she recalled its meaning. Inconstancy.

Mims handed it to her. 'I'll fetch a vase.'

Tess inspected the bouquet more closely. In addition to the honeysuckle, he'd added sprigs from the bough of the cherry. Deception. Clearly he had guessed she had not told him the full truth yesterday. Guiltily, she glanced at Grey's note.

She should have trusted Sandford and told him about the note. After all, he'd shown himself to be nothing but honourable. But how *could* she when she had no idea of Grey's current circumstances?

Yet something in her heart was telling her to seek help from Sandford.

Her heart? Really? She had to admit these past few days she had seen a very different side of the arrogant handsomer-than-sin lord of all he surveyed. His good looks were overshadowed by an unsuspected kindness and generosity. Not to mention he made her laugh with his dry wit.

Perhaps her heart had opened up a fraction and allowed him a place inside. Did that mean she could trust him enough to tell him everything? Perhaps it did. The moonlight picnic tonight might be the perfect opportunity.

Hopefully she would not have cause to regret giving him her trust. She did not think she could bear it if he, too, let her down.

A month ago Jaimie would not have imagined attending the annual Frobisher moonlight picnic. To be honest he'd almost cried off. His investigations into the mysterious Mayfair intruder were coming to a conclusion. Usually he liked to be in at the arrest of the culprit, but he'd given his word to attend this affair with Tess, so here he was doing his duty, escorting her across the grass to watch a game of croquet under the stars. Well stars, and the few hundred torches that turned night into day.

What surprised him most was that he would far rather be here with Tess instead of presiding over the arrest and confinement of yet another poor wretch who had fallen into criminal activity. Unfortunately, the oddity of the circumstances surrounding this particular fellow had him on edge and thinking he should maybe be there instead of here. By all accounts, the burglar, who he'd discovered was known as The Smith, was a hardworking blacksmith revered for his honest dealing and generous spirit. He was also a popular bachelor at whom many of the local young ladies had set their caps.

None of the information Growler had garnered fitted with his nefarious night-time activities. But after following him from Mrs Plunkett's establishment for several days and nights in a row, Growler had been positive they had the right man. And a clever man he was, too.

He had set one of his lads to watch Jaimie and garner information about his investigations. No wonder they'd had such trouble catching him in the act. Tonight, surprise would be on their side and they would spring the trap.

Once more he ran through the instructions he had given his men, as well as going over the plan one last time. He feared there was something, some little thread, he was missing. If so, the whole plan could go awry.

For example, why had a boy connected to a criminal attempted to rob the companion of the man out to catch that criminal? It did not make any sense. And therefore there must be a reason behind it.

'You are very quiet this evening,' Tess remarked.

He dragged his mind back to his companion. 'I do beg your pardon.'

'Your work?'

He nodded.

'It is a big responsibility.'

Enormous. The Home Office was at its wits' end and demanding blood. He had to admit, though, that he'd enjoyed talking things over with Tess, getting her input. Growler was all very fine at taking orders, but he'd never indulge in the sort of give and take Jaimie enjoyed with Tess. Their minds were in tune, thought they each came at problems from a different direction. He had also reached a level of comfort with her he had never before known with a woman. He was beginning to rely on her sharp mind almost as much as he relied on his own. In addition, his attraction to her seemed to be growing rather than fading with time and familiarity.

They halted at the edge of the croquet field where several laughing couples were knocking balls through hoops. The men were becoming overbold and the young ladies' mamas were becoming restive.

After a few moments he drew Tess away, towards the perimeter of the torches. 'Have you seen the fountains?' he asked. 'I am told they are quite something to behold.'

She must have heard the deepening of his voice as he thought about Tess alone in the dark, for she glanced up sharply. A small secret smile crossed her lips. 'I have not.'

With everyone on the lawn focused on croquet, he took his chance and guided her to a path that led away into the dark. He was after all a man with wooing on his mind and he still wasn't sure she would accept a proposal if he made one. Not sure she really trusted him. There had been that business of the boy at the hot-air balloon ascension. She had not told him the truth of that matter, he was sure of it.

'How are your investigations coming along?' she asked lightly and somewhat breathlessly as they strolled among the shrubbery. Moonbeams lit their steps on the pale flagstones.

He allowed her the courtesy of letting her distract him from the main purpose of their excursion. At least for the moment. 'Exceedingly well. Indeed, I am expecting the final conclusion this evening.'

'That is wonderful news.'

'It will be a relief all round.'

That was an understatement. According to the Home Secretary, the King was frothing at the mouth after yet another incident two nights ago. The impudent rogue had actually stolen items from the householder's bedroom while he was lying in bed asleep. A snuff box and, of all things, a chamber pot. He was looking forward to questioning this 'blacksmith' fellow. Though it was likely to be no more of an intriguing reason than the fellow needed to make use of it and decided to take it with him in case he woke his victim.

The path divided, circling a huge round stone fountain decorated with three elegant Greek women who seemingly poured water into the pool at their feet from the urns they held. Above them a dolphin spouted high into the air. The droplets, as they fell, look liked rare sparkling jewels.

'How lovely,' Tess murmured.

He swung her about to face him, moonlight playing over her features. Her lips parted, her eyelids drooped seductively. His body hardened. 'You are what is lovely,' he said huskily, the words escaping before the thought was formed.

Her eyes widened a fraction in surprise.

He walked her backwards until she was up against the edge of the pool. 'I mean it, Tess. You look beautiful. I have been dying to get you alone like this for days.'

She laughed, a little throaty sound that spoke of surprise and pleasure.

Ha, he was getting better at this. Perhaps because he was actually telling the truth. He bent his head and kissed her lips. She kissed him back so openly, so honestly, so boldly, it stole his breath. He broke away. 'I've been wanting to kiss you like that ever since we got here.'

Her breathing quickened. 'I, too,' she gasped.

He pressed his thigh between hers. 'Do you want me, Tess?' he growled. Wanting the admission. Needing it on some deep feral level. A desire for possession. He stilled and began to draw back in case she felt he was going too far. But one small hand curled around his nape and drew his head down, to press a kiss to his lips.

Who possessed whom?

He groaned as she rocked against his thigh and he felt her hot centre through the fine fabric of their clothes. He wanted to be inside her. Now. Right at this moment. He broke the kiss and let his lips wander the tender softness of her cheek, the delicate curve of her ear, the vulnerable pulse at her throat.

'I have missed you,' she said softly, turning her head to give him better access.

He'd missed doing more than just kissing her. Every time he saw her he wanted her and this was the first opportunity they'd had to be private for some days. If it was possible, he hardened inside his breeches just thinking about being alone here with her, in the dark on a warm summer night.

The urge to pleasure her rode him hard.

Quelling the urges of his body, he stepped back, looking around for...seclusion. Somewhere safe from prying eyes.

There were seats all around the edge of path, but anyone walking here would be instantly aware of them. No, he needed... *There!* Another statue shadowed by shrubbery, barely visible but for a soft gleam of white in the moonlight. Eros, balanced on the ball of one foot, ready to fire his arrow.

He swept her up in his arms, knowing if he didn't move now, he would be tempted to take her where she stood and to the devil with onlookers. He pushed into the encroaching bushes. The plinth was solid and wide. As close to a bed as he could get at this moment. He set her on her feet.

'You are very resourceful, my lord,' she said, her eyes sparkling with mischief.

Damn, but that marble was going to be hard and rough on her delicate flesh. He stripped off his coat and laid it on the marble.

She lifted her skirts to climb up, revealing a delicious glimpse of a lush bottom. Unable to resist, he stroked the silken flesh and dipped a finger into the dark shadow between, finding her hot and wet. Ready for him. One knee on the plinth, one foot on the ground, she stilled. He moved in close behind her, replacing his exploring finger with the head of his aching shaft, rubbing it along her slit, bathing it in her moisture, feeling the shock of her heat on the sensitive tip.

She gasped as he rubbed it against her little hard nub of pleasure. She leant forward, supporting herself on her hands, opening herself to his probing shaft. He inched in.

Damn, but that felt utterly amazing. His balls drew up tight. The tingle of orgasm rippled outwards. He fought it, distracting himself by reaching forward to position his coat to better cushion her knee. He cupped her breast in one hand, taking the weight, teasing the nipple through the material of her gown while steadying her with his other arm around her waist. He surged into her welcoming heat.

She moaned, widening her stance, encouraging him deeper.

Careful to support her weight, he obeyed her wordless demand. She shivered with pleasure. Her body tensed. He thrust harder, deeper, driving into her, his

hips a sensual slap against her bare bottom. She reached
down, a fingertip stroking the base of his shaft at her
entrance. A sensual little exploration that made his mind
go blank and his body tremble. He was going to... He
hauled in a breath. Forced himself back from the brink,
even as her palm cupped his bollocks. 'Touch yourself,'
he whispered hoarsely, knowing she needed external
stimulation he could not provide given that his hands
were already full of gorgeous, tempting, delicious Tess.

She hissed in a breath of shock. Shock, but also titillation. Her hand moved away and he felt her quiver as
she must have touched that sensitive little bud. Her head
dropped forward and he bent over her, kissing her nape,
nuzzling against the delicate skin and then... He opened
his mouth and closed his teeth on that vulnerable nape.

With a cry, she fell apart.

He followed right after, control utterly eluding him.

He pounded against her three more times, shuddering with the release as his seed poured into her. Somehow he managed not to collapse and held her up despite
his own body's laxness.

Carefully, he lowered himself onto the plinth and
pulled her on top of him. They lay there, her head on his
chest, his hand supporting her, breathing hard for what
felt like hours, but must have been only a few moments.

There was something he had needed to do. Something he had planned to do when he had asked her to
join him here in the dark and they'd been overwhelmed
by passion. He fumbled for his jacket pocket where it
lay beneath him and pulled out a small velvet pouch.

'Marry me, Tess.'

'W-what?' She sat up, leaning against him.

'Before we go any further, I am asking you to marry me. I believe we will suit very nicely. You won't need to worry about the bracelet and money any more. I will settle up with Stedman. We can even work on my cases together.'

'Oh.' She looked dumbfounded and doubtful. 'You mean it? You want to marry me? It's not because you feel you must? Because of this...' She waved vaguely at their surroundings.

'It will solve all our problems. I need a wife. You don't want to go to Yorkshire. And we can do *this* whenever we want.'

'I really wasn't planning on getting married at all.'

He stilled. 'I see.'

'You *don't* see. Every man in my life has let me down. Father. Grey. I should have been able to rely on them. By marrying, I put myself in yet another man's hands.'

So that was why she was so independent. He should have guessed. 'You can rely on me. I swear it.'

She stared at the pouch in his hand. 'I would like to believe you,' she said softly. 'I really would.'

'Have I done anything that says you cannot?'

She lifted her gaze to his face. 'No, you have not.' She swallowed. 'You are not suggesting this is a love match, are you?'

Shocked, he glanced away. A love match? That was what everyone had called his marriage to Hester. The whole thing had been a disaster. 'No,' he said slowly, bringing his gaze back to meet hers. 'I am not suggesting that. I am saying our marriage would make perfect sense. We are friends, we have passion in common and we will both benefit.' He flashed a grin. 'And I am clearly a much better match than Stedman.'

She chuckled. 'Or Yorkshire.'

It wasn't the most romantic proposal a girl could receive, but in their circles marriages were mostly practical arrangements and Tess could certainly see the advantages. She smiled at him 'Yes. I will accept your proposal.'

'You will?' He stood, grasped her around the waist and spun her around in a circle. 'That is stupendous.' He set her on her feet and kissed her, then placed the ring from the pouch on her finger. 'It was my mother's,' he said softly.

She glanced down at it gleaming in the moonlight. 'Thank you. It is beautiful.'

He kissed her again until they were both breathless.

Oh, he was going to like being married, now that he'd finally come to terms with the idea of taking the plunge yet again. Tess was perfect—and once they were wed thank heavens they would have regular access to a bed. Though as places went, moonlight and Eros would be hard to beat. Perhaps he'd have a similar statue installed at Sandford...

Tess broke away. 'Do you think anyone has missed us?'

Back to reality. 'If not, they soon will.'

They helped each other to straighten their clothes, and arm in arm they wandered back past the fountain and out on to the lawn.

Growler loomed out of the shadows right in front of them.

Tess gave a squeak of surprise. Jaimie bit back a curse. Growler never sought him out in public.

'Dammit, man, how long have you been there?'

The man hung his head. 'A while, Guv. Saw you go in. Thought I'd better wait here for you,' Growler said. 'I need a word.'

Foreboding like nothing Jaimie had ever experienced before ripped through him. Something had gone wrong tonight. They must have lost their quarry. Damn it. For a brief moment, he toyed with the idea of telling Growler it could wait. *What?* When had he ever been so irresponsible? Since he'd met Tess. He sighed. It seemed she had turned everything on its head. He gave her brief smile. 'I hope you will excuse me, Tess. I'll take you back to your cousin and then see what Growler wants.'

The quick nod of Growler's head indicated he agreed that the matter wasn't so urgent as to need him right that second, but he quickened his pace regardless.

'If it is urgent, I can find my own way back,' Tess offered.

His bride-to-be was nothing if not perceptive. He slowed his steps. 'It is nothing that can't wait for me to do my gentlemanly duty.'

'You care about doing your duty, don't you, Jaimie?'

'It was something my father drummed into me and Michael whenever we misbehaved.'

'A good lesson for boys, I think.' She sounded a little sad. Thinking of that brother of hers again. Who had clearly not done his duty by her. 'Grey didn't come to us until he was seven. Father said he'd learned a lot of bad habits in his previous situation.'

There it was again, her knowing what he was thinking, as if she was completely attuned to him and he to her. Marrying her wasn't going to be a duty at all, it was going to be a pleasure on a great many fronts.

'Tess, can we perhaps not announce our betrothal until after I have closed this current case? I want to shout it from the rooftops, I really do, but the King is most adamant that this take priority over everything else. I don't want him to think I've been neglecting my duty to go courting.'

'Of course it can wait. After all, who is more important than a king?' She slipped the ring off her finger and into her reticule.

He patted her hand. This was why he liked her so much. She was sensible. Most of the time. 'Thank you for your understanding. I am hopeful it will be finished tonight, but sometimes things go wrong.'

Lord Rowan and his wife were on the dance floor when they arrived at the terrace. Stemming his impatience, Jaimie found Tess a seat at one of the little tables scattered around the room and called a waiter over to get her a drink.

'Go,' she said with a smile. 'You know you want to.'

She couldn't come to any harm sitting here, with her cousins nearby. And if some other young buck asked her to dance, well, she deserved to dance, if she wished. Though he'd much prefer she danced only with him.

* * *

The next morning, Tess awoke feeling happier than she had for a very long time. When Mims arrived, she looked pale and drawn. *How very strange.* She'd seemed perfectly all right when she'd brought the breakfast tray up only a half an hour before. 'Are you all right?'

'Yes, my lady.'

She didn't sound all right. Tess frowned. 'Is that the newspaper you have there? Has Phin seen it already?'

Phin didn't like anyone touching his newspaper before he was finished with it.

'Yes, my lady. No, my lady.'

Confused, Tess stared at her. 'Well if he hasn't read it you had best take it back downstairs.'

Mims looked at her like a lost sheepdog. 'It's Master Hammond.'

Tess straightened. She put her cup aside. 'Let me see.'

Mims handed the paper over. 'He were arrested last night. Carted off to Newgate. Oh, my word. What are we to do?'

Tess scanned the article. 'This doesn't say anything about Grey. This is the man Lord Sandford has been seeking. The one robbing all the people in Mayfair. Apparently he's known as The Smith.'

The maid pulled out a handkerchief and dabbed at her eyes, then blew her nose. 'Master Hammond *is* The Smith.'

Tess let the paper fall from nerveless fingers. 'What?'

Mims nodded, her mob cap flopping madly. 'Yes, my lady.'

A dreadful suspicion entered her mind. Along with anger. 'You knew about this before today, didn't you?'

Mims backed away.

'You knew about this and said nothing to me, knowing I was looking for Master Hammond all this time? Knowing how worried about him I was?'

'He swore me to secrecy, my lady.'

'Why on earth would he do that?'

'Because of Mister Phin...Lord Rowan, I mean. You know how he is about Master Hammond.'

'Surely Grey wouldn't think I would betray him to Phin?' She looked down at the paper again. Every bit of happiness she'd felt upon waking that morning had fled. 'Are you telling me my brother is a common criminal?' Not only that, but it was he whom Lord Sandford had arrested. Her heart took a long swooping dive.

'He isn't a criminal.' The maid's fierce voice took Tess by surprise.

'He most certainly is. He's been going into houses and stealing people's property.'

'Those people stole from their servants. All he did was get back what was owed. No more, no less.'

Tess closed her eyes. That sounded so like Grey. The Grey she had known as a child. But he was a man now. 'He can't go around pretending he is some sort of Robin Hood. And besides, even if those employers were unfair to their servants, they hardly owed them a candlestick or a snuff box.' She glanced down at the article. 'None of the property has been recovered either. It is robbery, plain and simple.' And punishable by death or transportation.

She felt nauseous.

Mims wrung her hands. 'Oh, my lady, you have to help him. Not a penny has he taken for himself. It all went to those who deserved it. Perhaps if you could just see Master Hammond, make him promise to stop, perhaps his lordship could see his way clear to giving him another chance. Master Hammond would keep his word. You know that, my lady.'

She knew it about the Grey she had known as a child. But what about the man he had become? 'I am not sure I have that much influence over his lordship.'

Her stomach gave a sick little lurch. When his lordship learned the truth about Grey, that The Smith was her brother, he would likely call the marriage off. What peer of the realm would want to admit a common criminal to the ranks of his family? Nor should he. Her heart gave a horrid little squeeze. After all, he was only marrying her to save her reputation. Now it seemed she didn't have one worth saving.

She tried to imagine going to Jaimie and asking him to release Grey. She could see herself asking, but she could not see him saying yes. It was surely beyond the realm of possibility. Oh, heavens above, she needed to get to the bottom of exactly what was going on. 'Help me dress.'

Mims looked relieved.

'No promises, mind.' Another thought crossed her mind. 'Who is the boy who put a note in my reticule?'

'What?' Mims looked guilty. 'There is a boy, my lady. Mrs Plunkett's lad. He occasionally brings me messages since we've been in London.'

'Messages?'

'Yes. Grey were keeping an eye on you, like. Keen to know what you were doing. You and his lordship, too.'

'And you told him, of course?'

Mims beamed. 'I told him everything he wanted to know, my lady. I was sure he would come back to us one of these days. And now he has.' Her face fell. 'In a manner of speaking, since it is somewhat too late, I suppose.'

So that was how Grey had always managed to avoid capture. He'd used her own servant to gather information to ensure his freedom. He knew she'd always talked things over with Mims. 'It is a great deal too late. Why did he not speak to me?'

Mims gave her a blank look. Shook her head. 'He didn't say.'

What on earth would *Jaimie* say? The ache in Tess's chest seemed to intensify. She threw back the covers.

No sense in putting it off.

Chapter Fourteen

'Lady Theresa.' The butler stared down his nose in disapproval.

Tess ignored him, pushing past him into the hall with Mims hard on her heels. 'Where is his lordship?'

'In the conservatory, my lady.'

Well, at least he wasn't in bed. 'No need to announce me, I know the way. Mims, see if the kitchen can rustle up a cup of tea.'

The butler drew himself up in affront. 'I will have tea brought in to you, my lady.'

Tess nodded her thanks and headed for the conservatory. She found Jaimie sitting at the bench staring at one of his plants. Though he was in his shirtsleeves and looked positively rakish, his attention was somewhere way off in the distance. He looked far from happy.

He looked up at the sound of her steps on the marble tile and straightened. 'Lady Tess.' He glanced up at the clock in the corner. 'To what do I owe the pleasure of your visit at this early hour?'

On the walk over to his house, Tess had decided that telling him the truth was the only option. 'The man you arrested last night is my brother, Greydon Hammond.'

Jaimie looked down his arrogant nose. 'I know.' He frowned. 'I recognised the small crescent-shaped scar on his cheek from the sketch you showed Mrs Plunkett.'

He knew? 'I had no idea Grey was the burglar you were seeking. You do believe me?'

His expression tightened. 'Someone was passing him information about my plans.'

Oh, dear. She could not tell him about Mims. She did not want her arrested as an accomplice.

'What are you doing here, Tess?' Realisation dawned on his face. 'Have you come to ask me to set him free?'

He also got straight to the point. 'Would you?' she asked.

He shook his head, but more than the denial, the look of disappointment in his eyes hurt. Could he not under-stand her loyalty to her brother?

'You would be asking me to free a criminal who has been terrorising half of Mayfair,' he said, 'and ruin my reputation.'

'I quite understand,' she said briskly. Though she had hoped he might do this for her. But then men al-ways let you down when you needed them the most. 'I would like to see him, if I may.'

'See him?'

'Yes. I need to ask him something.'

'You want to know about your bracelet. I wouldn't hold out any hopes in that direction, if I were you.'

'You are not me. I trust Grey.'

'You also received a communication from him, did you not, and you did not tell me.'

'I—' She halted her denial. 'I am sorry. I wasn't sure what to think. He wanted nothing to do with me. I thought it might be because of my association with you.'

He took a deep breath. 'You should have trusted me, Tess. Told me what was going on.'

'I apologise. I was going to tell you at the picnic, but we became otherwise...occupied.' He didn't look in the least mollified. She plunged on. 'Will you take me to see him? I would go myself, but I fear they will not let me into the prison.'

He glared. 'I should hope not. Newgate is no place for a lady.'

'But surely in your company...'

'Not under any circumstances.'

She rose to her feet. 'Then I will simply have to go on my own.'

He stared at her. 'You really are headstrong, stubborn and wilful. I kept making excuses for you, but I am a fool.'

What was he talking about? 'He is my brother.'

He stilled. 'One of the things I admired about you, Tess, was your loyalty; however, in this case it is misplaced.'

He clearly wanted her to choose. Grey or him. She stared at him in disbelief. 'I cannot walk away from him in his greatest time of need.'

'It would be better for all concerned if you did.'

Better for him, no doubt. He would not want to be aligned with a woman related to a criminal. She pulled out the engagement ring from her reticule and placed it beside one of the flowerpots. 'It is a good thing we did not tell anyone about this.'

His mouth hardened into a flat line. 'You will do anything to get your own way, won't you?'

'I need to speak to Grey. I must thank you for all your kindness and help these past few weeks.' Her voice caught in her throat. The pain around her heart was almost unbearable.

'Devil take it, Tess, there is nothing you can do now to help your brother. He clearly has no intention of providing his real name. No one will ever know you and he are related. Let it go.'

She could not expect Jaimie to sacrifice everything he held dear for her sake. His reputation. His honour. 'If I do not try to help him, *I* will know.'

She headed for the door.

'*Were* you passing information to him? Details of my plans? Helping him avoid capture?'

The blood drained from her head, making her feel dizzy. He thought she had been working against him all this time. 'Does it matter? You have captured him at last.'

Disappointment filled his expression. He glanced over at the ring and back at her. 'No. It doesn't matter. Come. If you are that determined to speak to him, I will take you.'

The ride over to Newgate was accomplished in silence. Tess stared silently out of one window and Jaimie out of the other, while Mims sat beside her mistress, twisting her handkerchief in her hands and glancing from one to the other of them.

Jaimie didn't want to believe that she had deliberately betrayed him. Used him for her own ends. Clearly, he was a fool. Because if she had not, she would have denied it.

Dammit, he would never understand women. And to think he had begun to believe she was the best thing that had ever happened to him. Actually offered to marry her! Thank God she had given him back his ring. Except that it hadn't made him feel the slightest bit glad.

If only she had trusted him…

A sick feeling came over him. He'd been fooling himself. Making out he was only marrying her out of duty with a little bit of friendship and a lot of lust thrown in. Telling himself the wooing had been simply smoothing the path. He'd wanted far more than a dutiful wife. He wanted a helpmeet. He wanted the sort of marriage enjoyed by his parents, what he remembered of it. Honestly, he'd never thought he'd find such happiness after Hester. Never thought he'd deserved it, in truth. And then Tess had come along and given him hope.

Hope she'd now crushed. He should have known better. She had never trusted him from the start. Never given him the full story. Well, he would learn the full story now, because he would not allow her to be alone with this brother of hers. The man was as brutal a fellow as he'd ever met. A bruiser of a man. And tougher than the horse nails he spent the other half of his life pounding into shape on an anvil.

The carriage drew up at the entrance to the prison. 'Wait here.'

She stared at him, her eyes large in her face and full of questions.

'I'll have him brought up out of the cells to a room where you can meet with him alone.'

Shock filled her expression, followed swiftly by understanding. 'Yes. Yes of course.' She swallowed. 'I will wait.'

Well, at least she was trusting him that far.

'I will be as quick as possible.' And it was going to cost him a pretty penny to grease the right palms to make sure she didn't have to walk amongst the scum that inhabited the prison.

Luckily for him, the prison governor was in his office and the arrangements were made in short order. When he got back to the carriage, Tess had draped a thick veil over her bonnet. Thank heavens for that bit of discretion and her cleverness. One never knew when a newspaper reporter might be hanging about. There had certainly been enough of them outside the prison the previous evening when news had spread that he had finally captured the notorious Mayfair burglar. If they weren't very careful, Hammond's link to the Ingrams would soon be known to everyone in town and Tess would be ruined. It was the way it worked.

They entered the prison through the governor's private door. The guard who opened it led the way down a corridor and up a flight of stairs. Even here the smell of the inhabitants lingered, musty and stale and unpleasant.

At the top of the stairs, the guard unlocked a heavy wooden door. 'In here.'

It was gloomy inside and only a small window high in the wall let in any light. It took a moment for Jaimie's eyes to adjust and pick out the figure standing in the shadows in the corner.

Tess threw back her veil and stared about her.

The man shifted, the clank of his chains drawing her attention as he moved into the light. He had a split lip, a black eye and a gash across his cheek.

Jaimie frowned. The fellow hadn't looked nearly that bad when he'd left him here yesterday.

'Oh, my sainted aunt!' Tess said, sounding horrified, shooting an angry look at Jaimie. 'Grey, what have they done to you?'

'Tess?' He jerked backwards, lifting his hands as if to ward her off. He glared at Jaimie. 'What the devil are you thinking bringing her here?'

'I made him bring me,' Tess said defiantly.

'What is he? A man or a mouse?'

Jaimie swallowed his temper. 'Tess, some of those bruises are because he resisted arrest. But not all of them.' He glared at Hammond. 'Have you been fighting with your fellow inmates?'

The man said nothing.

Indeed, it seemed out of character. Though he'd tried to escape, once he realised he was outnumbered, he'd surrendered when he could have done some major damage to his captors before they finally had him subdued.

'Grey,' she said brokenly. 'Why did you never contact me? You know I would have helped you, if you needed money.'

The prisoner gave her a look that was not quite loathing, but was not in the least friendly. 'Did you not get my note? Did I not tell you to leave me alone? I don't want you here.'

Tess flinched. Hurt filled her expression.

Jaimie's ire rose another notch. 'Mind your manners, convict.'

Tess shot him an angry look and turned back to the prisoner. 'I came to see if there was anything I could do to help you.'

'There isn't. They caught me fair and square. Go back to your nice life, Tess, you are not wanted here.'

'Be civil to your sister,' Jaimie said. 'She's been beside herself worrying about you. Not that you deserve it.'

The younger man shot him a look of dislike. 'If not for her, I wouldn't be in this situation.'

Jaimie frowned at the odd choice of words. 'Your sister wants to know what have you done with her diamond bracelet.'

Beneath the grime, Hammond paled. He curled his lip. 'So he was right—you are going to lay that at my door.'

'What do you mean?' Tess asked, shocked. 'Who else would have taken it?'

Hammond turned his back on them. 'Go away.'

Tess shot Jaimie a glance of appeal. 'May I not talk with him alone?'

Desperate men did desperate things, but the look in her face was so full of hurt, so full of betrayal, he found himself acceding to her wish. 'I'll go, if you promise not to get any closer to him than you already are.'

She gasped. 'What? Why?'

'Because I'm chained to the bloody wall,' Grey said, his voice harsh and full of loathing. 'And if you stay where you are, I can't reach you and take you hostage.'

Tess gave a little start. 'You would never do that to me.'

'Can't be too sure of that, can you, your bloody lady-ship?'

'Mind your language, in front of a lady,' Jaimie said.

Hammond gave a bitter laugh. 'Why should I? Those rules are for gentlemen. I'm nothing but a common thief. A bastard common thief.'

A common thief with the accent of a well-educated man.

Jaimie focused on Tess. 'Do I have your word? It is the only condition under which I will leave this room.'

She nodded. 'I promise.'

Against every instinct he had, he walked out and left them alone.

The moment the door closed, Tess approached Grey. He'd changed since she'd seen him last. He was taller, broader and angrier. The fury in his eyes was painful to see. He'd always been devil-may-care as a lad. Cheerful and friendly. Could he really have altered so much? She stepped closer and held out her arms. After a moment of hesitation, he walked into them. Rested his forehead on her shoulder. 'Dammit it, Tess. You should not be here.'

'Bad as it is,' she said softly, 'I am happy to see you.'

He made an odd sound and pushed away. 'Don't get so close. I'm filthy.'

She gestured to the chair at the table. 'Sit down.' She took the one on the other side. 'What happened, Grey? You never stole a thing in your life before.'

'Tell that to your cousin.'

'Phin?'

'Who else?'

'What happened, Grey?'

'If I tell you, he'll have you behind bars, too.'

Her heart rose in her throat. 'Tell me.'

He shook his head and stared at his hands. 'That man, that Lord Sandford, what is he to you?'

'A friend.' Barely a friend.

'I led him a merry dance.' He grinned and then hissed in a breath. He touched the cut on his lip. 'Phin sent men over here last night.'

'Why would he do such a thing?'

'The night he kicked me out, he followed me. To make sure I never came back. He had that groom of his give me a serious beating. I still came back.'

She could scarcely believe what he was saying. 'Did Phin know you took my bracelet?'

He gazed at her, hunched a shoulder and turned away. 'Thank you for coming, Tess. Now if you don't mind I'd like to go back to my nice cosy cell.'

'What did I say?'

A thump came on the door. 'Five more minutes that means,' Grey told her.

'Oh, no,' she protested. 'We've barely begun talking. I still don't know how you turned into a burglar.'

'I'm a bastard, remember. It's in my blood.'

None of this made any sense. 'Mims has explained that you were using the money to pay people who were wrongfully dismissed and shopkeepers who were going broke. Like the people Father owed money to when he died. Is that what you used the diamonds for? Is that why you stole them and didn't come back?'

'Believe what you like. Just get out.' He stood and clanked back to the corner, turned and faced the wall.

She got up and started towards him. She remembered him like this when he had first come to live with her and Papa. It had taken her a long time to get him to trust her. 'Grey, this is me, Tess. I'm here to help. Please don't turn your back on me.'

'Warder, we are done here,' he shouted.

The door swung back. 'Time's up,' the warder said. Behind him a grim-faced Jaimie stood waiting.

There was nothing more she could do or say.

Jaimie led her out the way they had come in. 'I have arranged for a private cell for him,' he said, 'rather than the stinking hole where they put him. He'll get a bath and food.' It wasn't much comfort to offer, but it was better than nothing.

'Thank you.' She sounded distracted, almost as if she hadn't heard a word he had said.

When they were finally outside and could take a deep breath, she turned to face him.

Jaimie knew what was coming, of course, because he had been standing at the listening post in the room next door. There was no privacy in a prison.

'Is there nothing more you can do?'

He inwardly cursed the hopeful note in her voice, at the appeal in her gaze, and gestured her towards his carriage. 'Let us not discuss this in public.'

He helped her into the carriage and sat down opposite. 'There is nothing to be done. The *ton* wants justice.'

She shivered. He wanted to comfort her, but he wasn't sure she would accept it coming from the man who had arrested her brother. 'If I'd had any inkling that he was your brother, I would have approached this from a very different angle.' The irony of the fact that they had both been looking for the same man for very different reasons and the fact that she had helped both of them was not lost on him.

She gave him a narrow-eyed stare as if she did not believe him. 'You would have let him go free because he was my brother?'

Would he? He shook his head. 'No. But honestly I would have been a little more discreet.' He'd contacted the newspapers at the request of the Home Secretary. 'The government has been bashed repeatedly for not catching the Mayfair burglar. They wanted to broadcast their success far and wide. It would be better if no one knows he is related to you.'

She stared at him, her eyes wide, her face a picture of misery. 'I should never have looked for him. I could not believe he had stolen my bracelet. I was sure he intended to use it for collateral of some sort and then planned return it. When we were children we used to talk about setting up house together when we were grown. I thought perhaps he had used it for that and eventually he would send for me to join him. Instead, he is nothing but a common criminal.' The note of betrayal in her voice was hard to hear.

'I'm sorry, Tess.'

She squeezed her eyes shut briefly. 'It serves me right for being such a trusting fool. Grey of all people. I refused to believed it.'

'I'll do my best to contain the information that you are related.' Had done so already to the best of his ability. 'You might be seen as an accomplice.' Unfortunately, Jaimie hadn't been the only one listening in to her conversation with Hammond. Her brother had signed his own death warrant and it would be difficult to keep Tess's name out of the mire. 'What I don't understand is why he admitted to his crimes when he must have known we'd be listening in.'

'What? How could you? It was supposed to be a private conversation.'

In some things Tess was such an innocent. He shrugged. 'Normal practice. Your brother is no fool, he must have been aware of it.'

'No, he's not stupid.'

A frown appeared in her forehead and Jaimie wanted to kiss it away. What he wanted to do was kiss her into forgetting all about her brother, but there was no chance of that happening. She had made her choice.

She looked at him with an odd expression. 'Why *would* he admit to everything?'

'I am guessing he wants it over and done with as little fuss as possible.'

Tess stared out of the window. 'I think it is better if we do not see each other again. If my relationship to

Grey comes out, you can say you used our friendship to get to Grey. That way you will not look like a fool.'

A cold fist seemed to close around his heart. For a second he could not draw breath for the pain of her hard words. 'Do you really thing I would do that, Tess?'

'I don't know what to think. Yes. Why not, if it suits you?'

Clearly she would never trust him. It was hopeless. 'You must think as you please. What will you do now?'

'Go to my cousin's aunt in Yorkshire. I think it is my only option.'

It was a damnable waste was what it was. And bloody wrong.

The carriage pulled up at the Rowan town house.

'Ah, good,' she said briskly, although her voice was huskier than usual. 'We are home.' The moment the footman let down the steps, she and her maid were gone.

Jaimie sat, frozen, at a loss.

Clearly the only way she'd marry him was if he managed to save her brother. Would she be satisfied if he managed to get the sentence reduced to transportation or would she insist on a full pardon?

He certainly wasn't going to allow her blackguard of a cousin bundle her off to the north of England.

Chapter Fifteen

Tess clenched her hands tightly in her lap as she sat in the drawing room waiting to be summoned to Phin's study, having asked to see him this morning. She'd spent the whole of the previous day on her return from visiting Grey trying to decide what to do. There were two possible courses of action, neither of which were likely to be fruitful, but doing something was better than doing nothing at all.

She swallowed the dryness in her throat. Bearding the lion in his den was always a daunting prospect. But she was going to confront Phin about both his attack on Grey in the prison and sending his groom after him a year ago. It didn't make any sense.

'His lordship will see you now, my lady,' the butler said.

She hurried to Phin's study. Her cousin rose upon her entry. He frowned. 'What is it, Theresa?'

'I prefer to be called Tess.' She reined in her temper and sat down on the visitor's chair. 'I need to speak to you on a matter of importance.'

He sat and, with his elbows on the table, steepled his fingers in front of his lips. The image of a man prepared to give proper due to anything she said. It was simply a front. 'Important, you say?'

She ignored the urge to reach across the desk and sweep his arms away so he cracked his chin on the tabletop. 'Yes.' She hauled in a deep breath. 'I want to know why you sent men to attack Grey, both a year ago and in prison recently.'

He recoiled. Sitting upright against the chair back. His gaze dropped briefly to the newspaper folded neatly to the right of the desk. His cheeks reddened. He glared at her. 'What sort of accusation is that, may I ask? Who told you such a thing?'

'I wonder.' She smiled sweetly.

His jaw dropped. 'You cannot possibly have gone to visit him. Have you no sense? The man is a common criminal. He is going to hang.'

Now why would he look so pleased at that thought? 'The man is my half-brother.'

'Your father never acknowledged him as such.' He smirked. 'I find it quite ironic that the man who is pay-ing you court is the man who captured him, don't you?'

She'd always thought Rowan a bit of a priggish boor ,but now he was being plain nasty. 'I have told Sand-ford we do not suit.'

The colour drained from his face. 'What have you done?'

She had expected him to be annoyed, but this was utter shock. And horror. 'What did *you* do, Rowan?'

He picked up a quill pen from the desk and snapped

it in half. 'After everything I have done, you turn around and stab me in the back. Whatever you have said to him, you will apologise. You will make it right or I will banish you to Yorkshire.'

'I have no problem with that.'

His jaw dropped. He blinked a couple of times. 'But—you will never marry. You will be a spinster all your life. A poor one at that. I'll see to it.' He threw the two halves of the quill aside. 'Better yet, when Stedman returns, you will accept his proposal. His offer was most generous. This interlude with Sandford was nothing more than that. Stedman is the man we want.'

'Why is it so important to you, Rowan? I don't understand.'

A knock came at the door. 'Lord Sandford to see you, my lord,' Carver said.

Confusion filled Rowan's face 'I thought you said he— Tell him to wait.'

'Sorry, old chap.' Sandford strolled into the study. 'My business is rather urgent. It occurred to me that Lady Tess might take matters into her own hands. I thought I ought to offer her my support.'

A rush of moisture behind her eyes made Tess blink. Dash it, the man knew her far too well. 'I do not need any help, Lord Sandford. Indeed, I believe I was about to ask my maid to pack my trunks. I am going on a repairing lease to Yorkshire.'

Phin cursed foully.

Jaimie looked down his nose. 'Not the words of a gentleman in front of a lady.'

'She's no lady. She's a hoyden. Always has been.'

Sandford's expression changed, hardened. 'There is a certain matter of a missing diamond bracelet to be settled, Rowan. I believe it is in your possession.'

Tess wasn't sure she had heard right. 'My bracelet?'

Rowan glared at Sandford. 'I have no idea what you are talking about.'

'Yes, you do.' He turned to Tess. 'I went back and had another word with your brother. Took a bit of doing, but I managed to get him to tell me exactly what happened when he left Ingram Manor. It seems he caught this *cousin* of yours stealing your bracelet while you were in Bath. I presume he was using your window to gain ingress to the house and caught him in the act.'

'Rubbish,' Rowan said. 'You cannot believe the word of a criminal over the word of a peer of the realm.'

Sandford raised an eyebrow and picked a piece of lint off his sleeve. 'I believe what I see.' He reached into a pocket and pulled out a velvet pouch. 'I found this in a drawer in your bedroom last night, Rowan. While you were at your club.'

Tess gasped.

Sandford shook the contents on to the desktop.

'You stole it?' Tess said. 'Why?'

'How dare you go prowling around my house! I'll have you arrested, sir.'

'Me and the Bow Street Runner I brought with me, also? A Runner with the appropriate legal documents.'

Rowan collapsed against the back of his chair as if he'd been pricked with a pin and all the air had rushed out of him.

Tess frowned. 'How did you manage that? And *why*?'

'As to why,' Jaimie said, 'I believed your brother's story, once I heard the whole of it. I also located the men who beat him when he arrived at the prison. They had threatened to harm you if he talked, Tess, which is why he wouldn't say anything. And when I threatened *them*, they told me who had sent them.'

'Why?' Tess asked Rowan once more. 'What did Grey or I ever do to you that you would steal my bracelet and force him to leave his home?'

Rowan ran a hand through his thinning locks. 'Wilhelmina wanted the bracelet the moment she saw it and it should have been hers. It was part of the estate, but you refused to give it up.'

Wilhelmina. She might have guessed. No doubt her cousin's wife had repeatedly asked Tess to produce the bracelet just for her own cruel amusement at witnessing her panic. 'And Father's debts?'

'A means of forcing you to agree to be parcelled off to the highest bidder, I should imagine,' Jaimie said. 'I had my lawyer look into it. The state of your father's finances was dire, though not as bad as was claimed by your cousin.'

Rowan cursed.

'There is more,' Jaimie said. 'I found something else.' He turned and stuck his head out of the door. 'I'll take those now please, Growler.'

He came back with a sheaf of papers.

Rowan rose, looking around wildly, as if he wanted to run away.

'Sit down,' Jaimie commanded sternly.

He sat.

Sandford smiled at Tess. 'It is a codicil to your father's will.'

'Liar,' Phin said. 'It is a forgery and so I will say before the courts. It is a plot to do me out of my inheritance cooked up between you and that bastard brother of hers. I am the title holder. The courts will side with me.'

Sandford looked at him with distaste. 'I am sure the lawyer who drew it up will be quite happy to testify as to its validity. He will no doubt have a copy in his files.' He shot Phin a warning glance.

A semblance of a grin split Phin's face. 'Hardly likely, unless you know how to bring him back from the dead.'

The hope that had been building in Tess's chest, leached away. 'He's right. Father's lawyer died not long after he did. There was a fire in his office when he was working late one night. The office burnt to the ground.'

Sandford frowned. 'How odd. He's someone I know quite well. He was as healthy as a horse when I had dinner with him a few weeks ago.'

Phin spluttered. He snatched up the document and opened it with a shaking hand. His face paled. 'His son?'

'Yes,' Sandford said. He turned to Tess. 'Apparently, your father was in town when he decided to have this drawn up. He wanted it done right away, so he went to his lawyer's son who has his office in Lincoln's Inn, not far from mine as it happens. Growler mentioned the name of your father's lawyer when he did his investigations. I was so engrossed in other matters it did not occur to me that there might be a connection. I checked with him this morning before I came over here.'

Phin threw the document down. 'Lies. All lies.'

'I think you will find it is all completely legal. My quick reading of it indicates that Ingram Manor has been left to Tess, along with her mother's jewellery. There is a legacy for Greydon Hammond, too, and some bequests to the servants.'

'Legacy? Bequests? He didn't leave any money,' Phin protested.

'Well, as the title holder you will be legally obliged to sell something. Your own estate is not entailed.'

Phin's face had gone as red as a beetroot. He sank down into his chair clutching his chest. 'I will be ruined.'

Tess couldn't even feel a little bit sorry for him.

'Oh, one more thing,' Lord Sandford said softly, glancing at Tess for a brief moment. There was an odd expression on his face. A warmth she had never seen there before. He turned back to Rowan. 'I would not be threatening to send Lady Tess anywhere. The King wishes to meet her, since she has managed to solve the mystery of the Mayfair burglaries. She is to present herself at court tomorrow. And if you know what is good for you, you will make sure she is happy.'

With that, Jaimie turned and walked out, leaving Tess and Phin alone.

Phin opened his eyes and looked at her. He straightened in his seat. 'You! You did this. You and that snake in the grass, Greydon Hammond. You've ruined me.'

She smiled at him. 'I did.' Though it would not help Greydon in his current plight, at least he would know their father had not forgotten him after all. That had to count for something. 'And don't think to try to marry me off to the highest bidder again, because I won't do it.' If she wasn't marrying Sandford, she certainly wasn't marrying anyone else.

She froze. Had she really just thought that?

Oh, heavens, it seemed as though she had made a terrible mistake. She'd told the man she didn't want him, yet he'd gone out of his way to get to the truth on her behalf.

She picked up the papers from the desk and walked out.

She had to put things right.

Jaimie stared at the rosebush. Or rather at the single rose it had produced. A lovely deep shade of pink. It was a triumph of hybridisation. A rose from China and an old English rose had begotten a remarkable blossom. He was so pleased with it, his first thought had been to show it to Tess. Naturally that was out of the question. The jilted suitor did not go calling on the woman who had given him his congé. Damn, but he had missed her this past week. He couldn't help wondering how she was getting on with her aunt, the one who lived in Bath, who also, under the codicil to her father's will, had been appointed her guardian until she came of age. The woman had come to London the moment she'd heard about the legal changes. This aunt was exceedingly wealthy, childless and in alt at being able to spoil her niece, so he'd been told.

The butler entered. 'A Mr Greydon Hammond to see you, my lord.'

'Thank you. Show him in.'

As usual the butler looked scandalised that he would entertain a guest in his conservatory in his shirtsleeves. He smiled as he recalled Tess's visits. She'd certainly had the fussy old gentleman looking as if he'd smelled something nasty. Yes, he'd definitely missed Tess stirring up his life…

Not one of the cases that Growler had brought to his attention since she'd left had piqued even a smidgeon of his interest. Something that had never happened before. And not one word of advice had his parents offered him either. Strangely though, while he did not hear them any longer, he was able to recall their faces much more clearly before. Perhaps because he'd gone up to the gallery and looked at their portraits.

Why he'd done that he wasn't quite sure. He had never wanted to do so before.

Now he thought about it, he wasn't even sure that the words he'd put in their mouths had ever been words he'd heard them speak. They seemed more like words he wanted to hear.

He rose as Greydon strode into the room. He was still a big burly fellow, but now looked more like a gentleman than a blacksmith or a pugilist. He'd cleaned up well. Getting a pardon for him from the King had cost Jaimie a great deal of money and time, but after explaining Greydon's history, the King had taken a fancy to the idea of a modern-day Robin Hood, particularly when the victims had been well recompensed and he'd received a substantial contribution to his own personal wealth.

The expense had proved worthwhile since Greydon had agreed to use his remarkable talent of getting in and out of buildings without being seen in service of the law of the land. He'd joined Jaimie's business and already Growler could not say enough good things about him.

'My lord,' Greydon said with a bow. He clearly had not forgotten the lessons in gentlemanly etiquette from his youth.

Jaimie got up and went to greet him with a handshake. 'Hammond. To what do I owe the pleasure?'

Hammond looked grim, but then his natural expression seemed to be mostly on the bleak side. 'I want to know when you and my sister are going to resolve your differences.'

He stiffened. 'I beg your pardon?'

'She's no more than two streets from here in her aunt's London house, pining for you, and you are sitting here pining for her. It doesn't make any sense.'

She was still in London? 'Pining?' Jaimie could not imagine Tess pining. If she had a problem, she would be out and about solving it. No, Tess had made it perfectly clear she didn't want to marry him and he certainly did not want her to take him on out of gratitude. 'I can assure you—'

'*Pining,*' Hammond repeated. 'Mims said she has to be forced to go out into company and keeps talking about retiring to Ingram Manor.' He glowered at Jaimie. 'She's not happy, Sandford, and I expect you to do something about it. My life isn't worth living in that house at the moment.'

The thought of Tess being unhappy did not sit well in his gut.

'It was she who rejected my suit, you know.'

'Too proud are you, too important, to bend your knee before a woman? To apologise?' Hammond said with a curl to his lip.

Jaimie glared at him. 'I have nothing to apologise for, as far as I know.'

'I've said my piece; it's all up to you now.' He stomped off.

Jaimie sighed. What was he supposed to do? The whole thing was completely illogical. Just like a woman to—

That was the problem, wasn't it? The past kept getting in the way of the present and messing up the future.

He glanced over at the rose.

'Lord Sandford to see you, my lady,' her aunt's butler said.

Tess's heart gave a flutter. Jaimie? Here?

She put aside her stitching, expecting Jaimie to be accompanied by her aunt. Gentlemen were not permitted to be alone with single young ladies. They might get up to mischief. Though she'd got up to so much mischief with Jaimie, no gentleman was ever going to be permitted anywhere near her ever again.

When Jaimie entered, he was alone.

'Lord Sandford.' She held out a hand and he took it in his, touching his lips to the back of her bare hand, a sensation of silk and butterfly wings. His other hand he kept behind his back as he bowed. So utterly elegant. So completely cool and unreachable.

A shiver ran down her spine. Again she looked beyond him, expecting her aunt to appear. What was the butler thinking?

Jaimie straightened. 'Lady Tess, I have taken the liberty of asking your aunt for a few minutes alone with you.'

Her heart beat rapidly. Suddenly she felt as if she could not breathe. 'I—Oh?' She forced herself to think rationally. 'Is something wrong? Has something happened in regard to Greydon? Please do not tell me the King has changed his mind.'

'There is indeed something wrong, but I can assure you your brother was perfectly fine the last time I saw him, even if he was at war with the written report I had asked him to prepare.'

'Oh, dear. Greydon was always more about doing than about studying.'

'So I have learned.'

'It was very kind of you to speak to King George about him and to give him a place in your agency.'

'Not at all. I believe I have come out ahead of the game, despite what the King believes. He has already proved very useful to us in our investigations.'

His kindness knew no bounds. She just wished she could find a way to thank him properly. She had missed him so much these past few days, in ways she had never expected, but it was his kindness that she missed the most and the way she could rely on him to keep his word. Something she wished she had realised earlier. And his lovely kisses, of course. And the way he looked when he fell apart in ecstasy… Oh, dear. 'I am glad he is being of service to you. Please sit down. Let me ring for tea. Are you working on any interesting cases at the moment?'

'Nothing of interest to me, Lady Tess.'

She frowned.

'Things are only interesting when you have someone to share them with. Someone you care about.'

Her heart gave an odd little hop. 'I see.'

He brought his left hand around from behind his back. He was holding a single rose of the deepest shade of pink she had ever seen. It was a perfect blossom with a delicious scent. Was she mistaken, or was this his way of speaking of something in his heart? Hope unfurled, but it was too precious, too tender to be exposed if she was wrong.

'Is it one of yours?'

'It is,' he said. 'This rose is remarkable and the result of hours of experimentation. Yet with no one to share it with, it is merely a rose.'

She swallowed. 'It is beautiful. What did you call it?'

'I called it Lady Theresa.'

It was the first time she had ever liked the sound of her full name.

He held it out to her.

'Oh, really, no. I could not take it.'

'It is yours. It would give me great pleasure were you to accept it.'

She took it and held it under her nose. The scent was heavenly, sweet yet dark with promise. And it was a rose. The very first one she had received from him. 'Thank you.'

He went down on one knee and she felt heat rise in her cheeks.

'Lady Tess, will you do the honour of becoming my wife?'

She swallowed. 'You are asking me again? Surely—'

'Last time I asked you because it was the right thing to do. And because I had some foolish arrogant notion that if I married you, I could form you into the wife I wanted you to be. This time I am asking because over these past few days I have come to realise that I have fallen in love with you, exactly as you are. My life is empty without you. Incomplete. I feel as if I am only half a person.'

Now she really couldn't breathe or speak.

'I have missed you, Tess. You drove out the shadows of my past and filled a void in my life as no other person ever could. I will certainly understand if I am not the sort of man you had in mind for a husband. I am not a particularly dashing fellow most of the time. My attempts at wooing are undeniably hopeless, but I did want you to know that I do love you with all my heart.'

'Oh, Jaimie.' Her throat filled with tears.

'If this is too sudden, say you will think about it. Give me leave to hope that you might some day change your mind. With practice, I am sure I shall improve my wooing skills.'

He sounded so confused, so undeniably hurt that she leaned forward and kissed him full on the mouth. He pulled her into his arms and held her tight, kissing her until they were both utterly breathless.

'Tess?' he finally said.

Her eyes burned. She breathed in a little sip of air. 'Oh, Jaimie, I was a such fool not to have trusted you, even though you never once let me down. I never gave you a chance to prove you were not like Papa. I even assumed the worst of Grey when he had done nothing wrong. I let past hurts play upon my mind instead of trusting my heart. The moment I returned your ring, I knew I had made a mistake. I thought, after that, you could never forgive me.'

'Sweet, there is nothing to forgive. I was an ass.' He rose. 'Will you then give me leave to court you? To woo you as you deserve. Give me a second chance, as it were.'

Joy bubbled up deep inside her. 'No, Jaimie.'

His expression shuttered. 'Oh. You know I will always be your friend, do you not? If there is anything I can—'

'Jaimie,' she said softly, sinking to one knee and grasping his hand in both of hers. 'I love you with all my heart, too. Will you do me the very great honour of becoming my husband?'

He stared at her for a moment. His expression changed, and she basked in the glory of that wonderful smile.

'You never ever cease to take me aback, Tess Ingram.' He pulled her to her feet. 'Marriage to you will be one long surprise.' He kissed her.

'I hope so,' she whispered against his lips. 'I wouldn't want you to become complacent.'

He laughed and kissed her again.

Epilogue

Joy, excitement and worry built in equal amounts in Tess's chest, making it hard to swallow the tea the servants had brought out on to the lawn for her and her guests after their tour of Ingram Manor.

It was a year since her marriage to Jaimie and, because of his generosity, Ingram Manor was finally ready for occupation once more. Ingrams had lived in this house since the time of Good Queen Bess. Hopefully there would always be a descendant of the family taking care of it long into the future.

'It is a beautiful old house,' Michael said. 'You have done a good job with it, my Lord and Lady Sandford.'

Tess felt a surge of pleasure at his words and the sincerity in his eyes as he raised his cup towards them in the way of a toast.

'Thank you,' Jaimie said, with a fond glance at her, 'but it is all down to my wife. She knew exactly what was needed.'

'And it was your generosity that brought it about, Husband.'

How they loved using those words. Wife. Husband. It brought a smile to her lips every time. And Michael was right, the house seemed to radiate contentment and well-being now the ivy had been cut back, the roof repaired and the lawns and gardens tended. Inside the floors gleamed and the wood shone from the care and attention they had received.

She glanced over at Grey and worry outweighed joy and excitement. With his dark brows drawn down and his attempt to keep his distance from the rest of the party by sitting a little apart, he looked horribly uncomfortable. As if he'd sooner be anywhere else but here. Yet he bore himself as any gentleman would and his accent was also that of a well-educated man, as it had always been. She didn't want him to feel uncomfortable in his own home, though it had taken all her powers of persuasion to convince him to join them today.

He had refused to stay overnight, citing his work for Jaimie as being too important to be away for more than a day.

His employment was another bit of generosity from her husband for which she would always be grateful. Grey was a proud man and he had refused any other form of help from Jaimie. He was determined to earn his keep. Her heart sank. Would he refuse her, too?

She took a deep breath. 'Listen, everyone. I have an announcement to make.'

Every eye, even Grey's, turned in her direction. Faces filled with anticipation.

'Ingram Manor has been my home for most of my life. But I have a new home in the north, with Jaimie.

This place needs the care of someone who loves it as much as I do. So, with Jaimie's full agreement, on this my first wedding anniversary, I am making a gift of it to my brother, Grey.'

Silence greeted her words.

The confusion on Grey's face turned into something else. Anger? He shot to his feet. His chair fell back on to the lawn. 'What nonsense is this?'

Beside her, Jaimie stiffened. She placed her hand over his, feeling its warmth against her palm, begging him with her touch to be silent. As usual he understood without the need for words, but still she could feel his tension.

'It is not nonsense, Grey,' she said calmly, smiling at him. 'It is what Father would have wanted.'

'If he wanted it, he would have seen to it,' Grey said, a red flush staining his high cheekbones, even as he tried to sound as if he didn't care, when she knew the lack of formal recognition from her father of his paternity had hurt him terribly.

'Please, Grey?' Tess implored.

'Very well,' he growled. 'I will take over the care of Ingram Manor, but it will be returned to you or your descendants upon my death.'

'A gloomy thought for such a fine summer day,' Michael remarked with a slight curl to his lip, which indicated he was far from pleased with her brother's response.

Grey bowed and strode off in the direction of the servants' quarters, no doubt off to see Mrs Leggat, who had been persuaded to return to her old post. She'd always been his good friend.

While Jaimie walked ahead with Alice, she and Michael strolled behind. Indeed, he seemed to be slowing his pace. She lowered her voice. 'Was there something you wished to say to me in private?'

Michael shot her one of his unreadable looks. 'Jaimie is correct. You are a very perceptive woman.' He slowed his pace even more. 'You have been good for my cousin, my dear Tess. I wasn't sure about you at first, but it is clear you make him happy.'

'Why, thank you, sir. You are very kind.'

'He has been a source of worry to me for years. First the fire and his long recovery from illness, then the loss of his wife. More recently he was becoming so withdrawn, I thought we would surely lose him to his roses and his voices from the past. Honestly, I feared you were yet another mistake. But you are exactly what he needed.'

More compliments and from a man who rarely said more than a word or two. 'He makes me happy, too.'

A small silence fell. Michael walked along, looking at his shoes.

'There is something else, isn't there?'

He huffed out a breath. 'There is. I am not sure how to broach this.' Now he simply looked uncomfortable.

'Simply say it. I prefer directness.'

'Very well. Not so very long ago, Jaimie had the idea that he would leave Sandford to me and my descendants. As a sort of penance for what happened when he was little more than a baby. I assume he has told you about the fire he caused as a child.'

'He has.'

'Well, he had the idea that if his title came to my branch of the family it would somehow make up for what he did. I believed I had talked him out of that guilt nonsense, but...' He tugged at his neckcloth. 'What I mean to say is...'

Understanding dawned. She swallowed the urge to giggle. 'Oh, you want to know if we are planning to have children.'

'Blast it, woman. Put me out of my discomfort here.'

'We are. Indeed, I—'

'You are?' He stopped, his face suddenly alight with joy. 'You are?' His voice increased in volume. It now became the man used to making himself heard across the deck of a ship in a gale.

Oh, dear, she had not intended to say anything to anyone until she had told Jaimie. And only today had she been sure. 'Hush.'

Jaimie whipped his head around. 'You are what?'

Clearly they had not got far enough out of earshot. 'Blast it. I intended to tell you tonight, when we were alone.'

'Tell me what?'

'We are going to have a baby, Husband.'

'A baby?' Jaimie exclaimed, completely ignoring the other two and coming back to her side. He picked her up and spun around in a circle. 'We are having a baby, Wife?' He put her down gently and held her in the circle of his arms, looking both happy and excited.

'We are,' she managed, before he kissed her enthusiastically.

Laughing, Alice tucked her hand in the crook of her husband's arm. 'Come along. It seems they need a little time to themselves.'

It wasn't until Jaimie and Tess were in bed and spooned together that Jaimie got a further opportunity to be alone with his wife. He still couldn't quite believe he was going to be a father. His family was growing by leaps and bounds. In just a year he'd added Tess and Grey, and now there was to be a child. He dropped a kiss on her shoulder.

'Was it a terrible shock?' Tess whispered, as always knowing the exact direction of his thoughts.

He smiled against her silky skin and stroked her arm. She gave a little shiver. 'Not at all. It is the best news I ever had, apart from the day you asked me to be your husband.'

She laughed. 'You always know the right thing to say.'

She rolled over and kissed him until they were both breathless, then snuggled against his shoulder. He took her hand and guided it to where it was needed most. She caressed him.

He groaned. 'Wife, did I tell you I love you?'

She gave a little moan as his hand caressed her breast. 'This morning.'

'Then clearly I have been neglectful. I love you every moment of every day.'

'And I love you—'

He cut off her words with a kiss that deepened to passion.

Not as much as I love you.

The words in his head were his own.

* * * * *

*If you enjoyed this story,
you won't want to miss these stories loosely linked to
RESCUED BY THE EARL'S VOWS:*

*CAPTURED FOR THE CAPTAIN'S PLEASURE
FALLING FOR THE HIGHLAND ROGUE*

*And check out these other great
Regency reads by Ann Lethbridge*

*AN INNOCENT MAID FOR THE DUKE
SECRETS OF THE MARRIAGE BED*

Get 2 Free Books,
Plus 2 Free Gifts—
just for trying the Reader Service!

Get 2 Free Books,
Plus 2 Free Gifts—
just for trying the Reader Service!

HARLEQUIN *Desire*